PUFFIN BOOKS

ARTEMIS FOWL

THE ARCTIC INCIDENT

Eoin Colfer was born and raised in Wexford, a seaside town in the south-east of Ireland. He began writing plays at an early age, forcing his unfortunate classmates to dress up as marauding Vikings when they would have preferred to be outdoors doing some real marauding.

Browbeaten by constant encouragement from his family, Eoin continued to write as an adult. His first novel, *Benny and Omar*, was an instant bestseller in Ireland, and *Artemis Fowl*, his first book featuring the brilliant young anti-hero, was an immediate international bestseller. It was shortlisted for the Whitbread Children's Book of the Year and the Blue Peter Book Award, and was winner of both the WHSmith 'People's Choice' Children's Book of the Year and the Children's Book of the Year at the British Book Awards.

Eoin Colfer

Artemis Fowl

The Arctic Incident

PUFFIN BOOKS

PUFFIN BOOKS

Published by the Penguin Group
Penguin Books Ltd, 80 Strand, London WC2R 0RL, England
Penguin Putnam Inc., 375 Hudson Street, New York, New York 10014, USA
Penguin Books Australia Ltd, 250 Camberwell Road, Camberwell, Victoria 3124, Australia
Penguin Books Canada Ltd, 10 Alcorn Avenue, Toronto, Ontario, Canada M4V 3B2
Penguin Books India (P) Ltd, 11 Community Centre, Panchsheel Park, New Delhi – 110 017, India
Penguin Books (NZ) Ltd, Cnr Rosedale and Airborne Roads, Albany, Auckland, New Zealand
Penguin Books (South Africa) (Pty) Ltd, 24 Sturdee Avenue, Rosebank 2196, South Africa

Penguin Books Ltd, Registered Offices: 80 Strand, London WC2R 0RL, England

www.penguin.com

www.eoincolfer.com

First published in hardback in Puffin Books 2002
Published in paperback in Puffin Books 2003

1

Set in 13.5/16.3pt Perpetua

Printed in England by Clays Ltd, St Ives plc

British Library Cataloguing in Publication Data
A CIP catalogue record for this book is available from the British Library

ISBN 0–141–31213–0

For Betty

COΠTEΠTS

Artemis Fowl: A Psychological Assessment   ix

Prologue   1

Chapter 1:   Family Ties   6

Chapter 2:   Cruisin' for Chix   13

Chapter 3:   Going Underground   40

Chapter 4:   Fowl Is Fair   62

Chapter 5:   Daddy's Girl   72

Chapter 6:   Photo Opportunity   79

Chapter 7:   Joining the Dots   102

Chapter 8:   To Russia with Gloves   115

Chapter 9:   No Safe Haven   143

Chapter 10:   Trouble and Strife   165

Chapter 11:   Mulch Ado About Nothing   185

Chapter 12:   The Boys Are Back   214

Chapter 13:   Into the Breach   229

Chapter 14:   Father's Day   266

An Epilogue or Two   281

Artemis Fowl:

A Psychological Assessment

Extract from *The Teenage Years*

By the age of thirteen, our subject, Artemis Fowl, was showing signs of an intellect greater than that of any human since Wolfgang Amadeus Mozart. Artemis had beaten European chess champion Evan Kashoggi in an on-line tournament, patented over twenty-seven inventions and won the architectural competition to design Dublin's new opera house. He had also written a computer program that diverted millions of dollars from Swiss bank accounts to his own, forged over a dozen Impressionist paintings and cheated the Fairy People out of a substantial amount of gold.

The question is, why? What drove Artemis to get involved in criminal enterprises? The answer lies with his father.

Artemis Fowl Senior was the head of a criminal empire that stretched from Dublin's docklands to the backstreets of Tokyo, but he had ambitions to establish himself as a legitimate businessman. He bought a cargo ship, stocked it with 250,000 cans of cola and set course for Murmansk, in northern Russia, where he had set up a business deal that could have proved profitable for decades to come.

Unfortunately, the Russian Mafiya decided they did not want an Irish tycoon cutting himself a slice of their market, and sank the *Fowl Star* in the Bay of Kola. Artemis Fowl the First was declared missing, presumed dead.

Artemis Junior was now the head of an empire with limited funds. In order to restore the family fortune, he embarked on a criminal career that would earn him over fifteen million pounds in two short years.

This vast fortune was mainly spent financing rescue expeditions to Russia. Artemis refused to believe that his father was dead, even though every passing day made it seem more likely.

Artemis avoided other teenagers and resented being sent to school, preferring to spend his time plotting his next crime.

So even though his involvement with the goblin uprising during his fourteenth year was to be traumatic, terrifying and dangerous, it was probably the best thing that could have happened. At least he spent some time outdoors and got to meet some new people.

It's a pity most of them were trying to kill him.

Report compiled by: Doctor J. Argon, B. Psych, for the LEP Academy files.

PROLOGUE

THE two Russians huddled around a flaming barrel in a futile attempt to ward off the Arctic chill. The Bay of Kola was not a place you wanted to be after September, especially not Murmansk. In Murmansk even the polar bears wore scarves. Nowhere was colder, except perhaps Noril'sk.

The men were Mafiya enforcers and were more used to spending their evenings inside stolen BMWs. The larger of the two, Mikhael Vassikin, checked the fake Rolex beneath the sleeve of his fur coat.

'This thing could freeze up,' he said, tapping the diving bezel. 'What am I going to do with it then?'

'Stop your complaining,' said the one called Kamar. 'It's your fault we're stuck outside in the first place.'

Vassikin paused. 'Pardon me?'

'Our orders were simple: sink the *Fowl Star*. All you had

to do was blow the cargo bay. It was a big enough ship, heaven knows. Blow the cargo bay and down she goes. But no, the great Vassikin hits the stern. Not even a back-up rocket to finish the job. So now we have to search for survivors.'

'She sank, didn't she?'

Kamar shrugged. 'So what? She sank slowly, plenty of time for the passengers to grab on to something. Vassikin, the famous sharpshooter! My grandmother could shoot better.'

Lyubkhin, the Mafiya's man on the docks, approached before the discussion could develop into an all-out brawl.

'How are things?' asked the bear-like Yakut.

Vassikin spat over the quay wall. 'How do you think? Did you find anything?'

'Dead fish and broken crates,' said the Yakut, offering both enforcers a steaming mug. 'Nothing alive. It's been over eight hours now. I have good men searching all the way down to Green Cape.'

Kamar drank deeply, then spat in disgust. 'What is this stuff? Pitch?'

Lyubkhin laughed. 'Hot cola. From the *Fowl Star*. It's coming ashore by the crate-load. Tonight we are truly on the Bay of Kola.'

'Be warned,' said Vassikin, spilling the liquid on to the snow. 'This weather is souring my temper. So no more terrible jokes. It's enough that I have to listen to Kamar.'

'Not for much longer,' muttered his partner. 'One more sweep and we call off the search. Nothing could survive these waters for eight hours.'

Vassikin held out his empty cup. 'Don't you have something stronger? A shot of vodka to ward off the cold? I know you always keep a flask hidden somewhere.'

Lyubkhin reached for his hip pocket, but stopped when the walkie-talkie on his belt began to emit static. Three short bursts.

'Three squawks. That's the signal.'

'The signal for what?'

Lyubkhin hurried down the docks, shouting back over his shoulder. 'Three squawks on the radio. It means that the K9 unit has found someone.'

The survivor was not Russian. That much was obvious from his clothes. Everything, from the designer suit to the leather overcoat, had obviously been purchased in Western Europe, perhaps even America. They were tailored to fit, and made from the highest-quality material.

Though the man's clothes were relatively intact, his body had not fared so well. His bare feet and hands were mottled with frostbite. One leg hung strangely limp below the knee, and his face was a horrific mask of burns.

The search crew had carried him from a ravine three klicks south of the harbour on a makeshift tarpaulin stretcher. The men crowded around their prize, stamping their feet against the cold that invaded their boots. Vassikin elbowed his way through the gathering, kneeling for a closer look.

'He'll lose the leg for sure,' he noted. 'A couple of fingers too. The face doesn't look too good either.'

'Thank you, Doctor Mikhael,' commented Kamar drily. 'Any ID?'

Vassikin conducted a quick thief's search. Wallet and watch.

'Nothing. That's odd. You'd think a rich man like this would have some personal effects, wouldn't you?'

Kamar nodded. 'Yes, I would.' He turned to the circle of men. 'Ten seconds, then there'll be trouble. Keep the currency, everything else I need returned.'

The sailors considered it. The man was not big. But he was Mafiya, the Russian organized-crime syndicate.

A leather wallet sailed over the crowd, skidding into a dip in the tarpaulin. Moments later it was joined by a Cartier chronograph. Gold with diamond studding. Worth five years of an average Russian's wages.

'Wise decision,' said Kamar, scooping up the treasure trove.

'Well?' asked Vassikin. 'Do we keep him?'

Kamar pulled a platinum Visa card from the kidskin wallet, checking the name.

'Oh we keep him,' he replied, activating his mobile

phone. 'We keep him, and put some blankets over him. The way our luck's going, he'll catch pneumonia. And believe me, we don't want anything to happen to this man. He's our ticket to the big time.'

Kamar was getting excited. This was completely out of character for him.

Vassikin clambered to his feet. 'Who are you calling? Who is this guy?'

Kamar picked a number from his speed-dial menu. 'I'm calling Britva. Who do you think I'm calling?'

Vassikin paled. Calling the boss was dangerous. Britva was well known for shooting the bearers of bad news. 'It's good news, right? You're calling with good news?'

Kamar flipped the Visa at his partner. 'Read that.'

Vassikin studied the card for several moments. 'I don't read *Angliskii*. What does it say? What's the name?'

Kamar told him. A slow smile spread across Mikhael's face. 'Make the call,' he said.

CHAPTER 1: FAMILY TIES

 THE loss of her husband had a profound effect on Angeline Fowl. She had retreated to her room, refusing to go outside. She took refuge in her mind, preferring dreams of the past to real life. It is doubtful whether she would have recovered had not her son, Artemis the Second, done a deal with the elf Holly Short: his mother's sanity in return for half the ransom gold he had stolen from the fairy police. His mother fully recovered, Artemis Junior focused his efforts on locating his father, investing large chunks of the family fortune in Russian excursions, local intelligence and Internet-search companies.

Young Artemis had received a double share of Fowl guile. However, with the recovery of his mother, a moral and beautiful lady, it became increasingly difficult for him to realize his ingenious schemes. Schemes that were ever more necessary to fund the search for his father.

Angeline, distraught by her son's obsession and afraid

of the effects of the past two years on his mind, signed up her thirteen-year-old for treatment with the school counsellor.

You have to feel sorry for him. The counsellor, that is ...

St Bartleby's School for Young Gentlemen, County Wicklow, Ireland, present day

Doctor Po leaned back in his padded armchair, eyes flicking across the page in front of him.

'Now, Master Fowl, let's talk, shall we?'

Artemis sighed deeply, smoothing his dark hair back from a wide, pale brow. When would people learn that a mind such as his could not be dissected? He himself had read more psychology textbooks than the counsellor. He had even contributed an article to *The Psychologists' Journal* under the pseudonym Doctor F. Roy Dean Schlippe.

'Certainly, Doctor. Let's talk about your chair. Victorian?'

Po rubbed the leather arm fondly. 'Yes, quite correct. Something of a family heirloom. My grandfather acquired it at auction at Sotheby's. Apparently it once stood in the palace. The Queen's favourite.'

A taut smile stretched Artemis's lips perhaps a

centimetre. 'Really, Doctor. They don't generally allow fakes in the palace.'

Po's grip stretched the worn leather. 'Fake? I assure you, Master Fowl, this is completely authentic.'

Artemis leaned in for a closer examination. 'It's clever, I grant you. But look here.' Po's gaze followed the youth's finger. 'Those furniture tacks. See the criss-cross pattern on the head? Machine tooled. Nineteen twenty at the earliest. Your grandfather was duped. But what matter? A chair is a chair. A possession of no importance, eh, Doctor?'

Po scribbled furiously, burying his dismay. 'Yes, Artemis, very clever. Just as your file says. Playing your little games. Now, shall we get back to you?'

Artemis Fowl the Second straightened the crease in his trousers.

'There is a problem here, Doctor.'

'Really? And what might that be?'

'The problem is that I know the textbook replies to any question you care to ask.'

Doctor Po jotted in his pad for a full minute. 'We do have a problem, Artemis. But that's not it,' he said eventually.

Artemis almost smiled. No doubt the doctor would treat him to another predictable theory. Which disorder would he have today? Multiple personality perhaps, or maybe he'd be a pathological liar?

'The problem is that you don't respect anyone enough to treat them as an equal.'

Artemis was thrown by the statement. This doctor was smarter than the rest. 'That's ridiculous. I hold several people in the highest esteem.'

Po did not glance up from his notebook. 'Really? Who, for example?'

Artemis thought for a moment. 'Albert Einstein. His theories were usually correct. And Archimedes, the Greek mathematician.'

'What about someone that you actually know?'

Artemis thought hard. No one came to mind.

'What? No examples?'

Artemis shrugged. 'You seem to have all the answers, Doctor Po. Why don't you tell me?'

Po opened a window on his laptop. 'Extraordinary. Every time I read this ...'

'My biography, I presume?'

'Yes, it explains a lot.'

'Such as?' asked Artemis, interested in spite of himself.

Doctor Po printed off a page.

'Firstly there's your associate, Butler. A bodyguard, I understand. Hardly a suitable companion for an impressionable boy. Then there's your mother. A wonderful woman in my opinion, but with absolutely no control over your behaviour. Finally, there's your father.

According to this, he wasn't much of a role model even when he was alive.'

The remark stung, but Artemis wasn't about to let the doctor realize how much. 'Your file is mistaken, Doctor,' he said. 'My father is alive. Missing perhaps, but alive.'

Po checked the sheet. 'Really? I was under the impression that he has been missing for almost two years. Why, the courts have declared him legally dead.'

Artemis's voice was devoid of emotion, though his heart was pounding. 'I don't care what the courts say, or the Red Cross. He is alive, and I will find him.'

Po scratched another note.

'But even if your father were to return, what then?' he asked. 'Will you follow in his footsteps? Will you be a criminal like him? Perhaps you already are?'

'My father is no criminal,' Artemis pointed out testily. 'He was moving all our assets into legitimate enterprises. The Murmansk venture was completely above board.'

'You're avoiding the question, Artemis,' said Po.

But Artemis had had enough of this line of questioning. Time to play a little game. 'Why, Doctor?' said Artemis, shocked. 'This is a sensitive area. For all you know, I could be suffering from depression.'

'I suppose you could,' said Po, sensing a breakthrough. 'Is that the case?'

Artemis dropped his face into his hands. 'It's my mother, Doctor.'

'Your mother?' prompted Po, trying to keep the excitement from his voice. Artemis had retired half a dozen counsellors from St Bartleby's already this year. Truth be told, Po was on the point of packing his own bags. But now ...

'My mother, she ...'

Po leaned forward on his fake Victorian chair. 'Your mother, yes?'

'She forces me to endure this ridiculous therapy when the school's so-called counsellors are little better than misguided do-gooders with degrees.'

Po sighed. 'Very well, Artemis. Have it your way, but you are never going to find peace if you continue to run away from your problems.'

Artemis was spared further analysis by the vibration of his mobile phone. It was on a coded secure line. Only one person had the number. The boy retrieved it from his pocket, flipping open the tiny communicator. 'Yes?'

Butler's voice came through the speaker. 'Artemis. It's me.'

'Obviously. I'm in the middle of something here.'

'We've had a message.'

'Yes. From where?'

'I don't know exactly. But it concerns the *Fowl Star*.'

A jolt flew along Artemis's spine. 'Where are you?'

'The main gate.'

'Good man. I'm on my way.'

Doctor Po whipped off his spectacles. 'This session is not over, young man. We made some progress today, even if you won't admit it. Leave now and I will be forced to inform the Dean.'

The warning was lost on Artemis. He was already somewhere else. A familiar electric buzz was crackling over his skin. This was the beginning of something. He could feel it.

CHAPTER 2: CRUISIN' FOR CHIX

WEST BANK, HAVEN CITY, THE LOWER ELEMENTS

 THE traditional image of a leprechaun is one of a small, green-suited imp. Of course, this is the human image. Fairies have their own stereotypes. The People generally imagine officers of the Lower Elements Police Reconnaissance squad to be truculent gnomes or bulked-up elves, recruited straight from their college crunchball squads.

Captain Holly Short fits neither of these descriptions. In fact, she would probably be the last person you would pick as a member of the LEPrecon squad. If you had to guess her occupation, the catlike stance and the sinewy muscles might suggest a gymnast or perhaps a professional potholer. But take a closer look, past the pretty face, into the eyes, and you will see determination so fiery it could light a candle at ten paces, and a streetwise intelligence that made her one of Recon's most respected officers.

Of course, technically, Holly was no longer attached to Recon. Ever since the Artemis Fowl Affair, when she had been captured and held to ransom, her position as Recon's first female officer had been under review. The only reason she wasn't at home watering her ferns right now was that Commander Root had threatened to turn in his own badge if Holly was suspended. Root knew, even if Internal Affairs wasn't convinced, that the kidnapping had not been Holly's fault, and only her quick thinking had prevented loss of life.

But the Council members weren't particularly interested in loss of human life. They were more concerned with loss of fairy gold. And according to them, Holly had cost them a fair chunk from the Recon ransom fund. Holly was quite prepared to fly above ground and wring Artemis Fowl's neck until he returned the gold, but that wasn't the way it worked: the Book, the fairy bible, stated that once a human managed to separate a fairy from his gold, then that gold was his to keep.

So, instead of confiscating her badge, Internal Affairs had insisted Holly handle grunt work — somewhere that she couldn't do any harm. Stakeout was the obvious choice. Holly was farmed out to Customs and Excise, stuck in a Cham pod and suckered to the rock face overlooking a pressure-elevator chute. Dead-end duty.

That said, smuggling was a serious concern for the Lower Elements Police. It wasn't the contraband itself, which was generally harmless junk – designer sunglasses, DVDs, cappuccino machines and such. It was the method of acquiring these items.

The B'wa Kell goblin triad had cornered the smuggling market and was becoming increasingly brazen in its overground excursions. It was even rumoured that the goblins had constructed their own cargo shuttle to make their expeditions more economically viable.

The main problem was that goblins were dim-witted creatures. All it would take was for one of them to forget to shield and goblin photos would be bouncing from satellites to news stations around the world. Then the Lower Elements, the last Mud-Man-free zone on the planet, would be discovered. When that happened, human nature being what it was, pollution, strip-mining and exploitation were sure to follow.

This meant that whichever poor souls were in the Department's bad books got to spend months at a time on surveillance duty, which is why Holly was now anchored to the rock face outside a little-used chute's entrance.

E37 was a pressure elevator that emerged in downtown Paris, France. The European capital was red-flagged as a high-risk area, so visas were rarely approved. LEP business only. No civilian had been in the chute for decades, but it still merited twenty-four seven surveillance — which meant six officers on eight-hour shifts.

Holly was saddled with Chix Verbil for a pod mate. Like most sprites, Chix believed himself God's green-skinned gift to females, and spent more time trying to impress Holly than doing his job.

'Lookin' good tonight, Captain,' was Chix's opening line that particular night. 'You do something with your hair?'

Holly adjusted the screen focus, wondering what you could do with an auburn crew cut.

'Concentrate, Private. We could be up to our necks in a firefight at any second.'

'I doubt it, Captain. This place is quiet as the grave. I love assignments like this. Nice 'n' easy. Just cruisin'.'

Holly surveyed the scene below. Verbil was right. The once thriving suburb had become a ghost town with the chute's closure to the public. Only the occasional foraging troll stumbled past their pod. When trolls began staking out territory in an area, you knew it was deserted.

'It's jus' you an' me, Cap. And the night's still young.'

'Stow it, Verbil. Keep your mind on the job. Or isn't private a low-enough rank for you?'

'Yes, Holly, sorry, I mean, yes, sir.'

Sprites. They were all the same. Give him a pair of wings and he thought he was irresistible.

Holly chewed her lip. They'd wasted enough taxpayers' gold on this stakeout. The brass should just call it a day, but they wouldn't. Surveillance duty was ideal for keeping embarrassing officers out of the public eye.

In spite of this, Holly was determined to do the job to the best of her ability. The Internal Affairs tribunal wasn't going to have any extra ammunition to throw at her if she could help it.

Holly called up their daily pod checklist on the plasma screen. The gauges for the pneumatic clamps were in the green. Plenty of gas to keep their pod hanging there for four long, boring weeks.

Next on the list was thermal imaging. 'Chix, I want you to do a fly-by. We'll run a thermal.'

Verbil grinned. Sprites loved to fly. 'Roger, Captain,' he said, strapping a thermoscan bar to his chest.

Holly opened a hole in the pod and Verbil swooped out, climbing quickly to the shadows. The bar on his chest bathed the area below with heat-sensitive rays. Holly punched up the thermoscan program on her computer. The view screen swam with fuzzy images in various shades of grey. Any living creature would show up, even behind a layer of solid rock. But there was nothing, just a few swear toads and the tail end of a troll shambling off the screen.

Verbil's voice crackled over the speaker. 'Hey, Captain. Should I take 'er in for a closer look?'

That was the trouble with portable scanners. The further away you were, the weaker the rays became.

'OK, Chix. One more sweep. Be careful.'

'Don't worry, Holly. The Chix man will keep himself in one piece for you.'

Holly drew a breath to make a threatening reply, but the retort died in her throat. On the screen. Something was moving.

'Chix. You getting this?'

'Affirmative, Cap. I'm getting it, but I dunno what I'm getting.'

Holly enhanced a section of the screen. Two beings were moving around on the second level. The beings were grey.

'Chix. Hold your position. Continue scanning.'

Grey? How could grey things be moving? Grey was dead. No heat, cold as the grave. Nevertheless ...

'On your guard, Private Verbil. We have possible hostiles.'

Holly opened a channel to Police Plaza. Foaly, the LEP's technical wizard, would undoubtedly have their video feed running in the Operations' booth. 'Foaly. You watching?'

'Yep, Holly,' answered the centaur. 'Just bringing you up on the main screen.'

'What do you make of these shapes? Moving grey? I've never seen anything like it.'

'Me neither.' There followed a brief silence, punctuated by the clicking of a keyboard. 'Two possible explanations. One, equipment malfunction. These could be phantom images from another system. Like interference on a radio.'

'The other explanation?'

'It's so ludicrous that I hardly like to mention it.'

'Yeah, well do me a favour, Foaly, mention it.'

'Well, ridiculous as it sounds, someone may have found a way to beat my system.'

Holly paled. If Foaly was even admitting the possibility, then it was almost definitely true. She cut the centaur off, switching her attention back to Private Verbil. 'Chix! Get out of there. Pull up! Pull up!'

The sprite was far too busy trying to impress his pretty captain to realize the seriousness of his situation. 'Relax, Holly. I'm a sprite. Nobody can hit a sprite.'

That was when a projectile erupted through a chute window, blowing a fist-sized hole in Verbil's wing.

Holly tucked a Neutrino 2000 into its holster, issuing commands through her helmet's com-set. 'Code Fourteen, repeat Code Fourteen. Fairy down. Fairy down. We are under fire. E37. Send warlock medics and back-up.'

Holly dropped through the hatch, rappelling to the tunnel floor. She ducked behind a statue of Frond, the first elfin king. Chix was lying on a mound of rubble across the avenue. It didn't look good. The side of his helmet had been bashed in by the jagged remains of a low wall, rendering his com-system completely useless.

She needed to reach him soon or he was a goner. Sprites only had limited healing powers. They could magic away a wart, but gaping wounds were beyond them.

'I'm patching you through to the commander,' said Foaly's voice in her ear. 'Standby.'

Commander Root's gravelly tones barked across the airwaves. He did not sound in the best of moods. No surprises there.

'Captain Short. I want you to hold your position until back-up gets there.'

'Negative, Commander. Chix is hit. I have to reach him.'

'Holly. Captain Kelp is minutes away. Hold your position. Repeat. Hold your position.'

Behind the helmet's visor, Holly gritted her teeth in frustration. She was one step away from being booted out of the LEP, and now this. To rescue Chix she would have to disobey a direct order.

Root sensed her indecision. 'Holly, listen to me. Whatever they're shooting at you, it punched straight through Verbil's wing. Your LEP vest is no good. So sit tight and wait for Captain Kelp.'

Captain Kelp. Possibly the LEP's most gung-ho officer,

famous for choosing the name Trouble at his graduation ceremony. Still, there was no officer Holly would have preferred to have at her back going through a door.

'Sorry, sir, I can't wait. Chix took a hit in the wing. You know what that means.'

Shooting a sprite in the wing was not like shooting a bird. Wings were a sprite's largest organ and contained seven major arteries. A hole like that would have ruptured at least three.

Commander Root sighed. Over the speakers it sounded like a rush of static.

'OK, Holly. But stay low. I don't want to lose any of my people today.'

Holly drew her Neutrino 2000 from its holster, flicking the setting up to three. She wasn't taking any chances with the snipers. Presuming they were goblins from the B'wa Kell triad, on this setting the first shot would knock them unconscious for eight hours at the very least.

She gathered her legs beneath her and rocketed out from behind the statue. Immediately a hail of gunfire blew chunks from the structure.

Holly raced towards her fallen comrade, projectiles buzzing around her head like supersonic bees. Generally, in a situation of this kind, the last thing you do is move the victim, but with gunfire raining down on them, there was no choice. Holly grabbed the private by his epaulettes, hauling him behind a rusted-out delivery shuttle.

Chix had been out there a long time. He was grinning feebly. 'You came for me, Cap. I knew you would.'

Holly tried to keep the worry from her voice. 'Of course I came, Chix. Never leave a man behind.'

'I knew you couldn't resist me,' he breathed. 'I knew it.' Then he closed his eyes. There was a lot of damage done here. Maybe too much.

Holly concentrated on the wound. Heal, she thought, and the magic welled up inside her like a million pins and needles. It spread through her arms and ran down to her fingers. She placed her hands on Verbil's wound. Blue sparks tingled from her fingers into the hole. The sparks played around the wound, repairing the scorched tissue and replicating spilt blood. The sprite's breathing calmed, and a healthy green tinge started to return to his cheeks.

Holly sighed. Chix would be OK. He probably wouldn't fly any more missions on that wing, but he would live. Holly laid the unconscious sprite on his side, careful not to put pressure on the injured wing. Now for the mysterious grey shapes. Holly upped the setting on her weapon to four and ran without hesitation towards the chute entrance.

On your very first day in the LEP Academy, a big hairy gnome, with a chest the size of a bull troll, pins each cadet to a wall and warns them *never* to run into an unsecured building during a firefight. He says this in a most insistent fashion. He repeats it every day until the maxim is etched on every cadet's brain. Nevertheless, this was exactly what Captain Holly Short of the LEPrecon Unit proceeded to do.

She blasted the terminal's double doors, diving through to the shelter of a check-in desk. Less than four hundred years ago, this building had been a hive of activity, with tourists queuing for above-ground visas. Paris had once been a very popular tourist destination. But inevitably, it seemed, humans had claimed the European capital for themselves. The only place fairies felt safe was in Disneyland, Paris, where no one looked twice at diminutive creatures, even if they were green.

Holly activated a motion-sensor filter in her helmet and scanned the building through the desk's quartz security panel. If anything moved, the helmet's computer would automatically flag it with an orange corona. She looked up, just in time to see two figures loping along a viewing gallery towards the shuttle bay. They were goblins all right, reverting to all fours for extra speed, trailing a hover trolley behind them. They were wearing some kind of reflective foil suits, complete with headgear, obviously to fox the thermal sensors. Very clever. Too clever for goblins.

Holly ran parallel to the goblins, one floor down. All around her, ancient advertising hoardings sagged in their brackets. *TWO-WEEK SOLSTICE TOUR. TWENTY GOLD*

GRAMS. CHILDREN UNDER TEN TRAVEL FREE.

She vaulted the turnstile gate, racing past the security zone and duty-free booths. The goblins were descending now, boots and gloves flapping on a frozen escalator. One lost his headgear in his haste. He was big for a goblin, over a metre. His lidless eyes rolled in panic, and his forked tongue flicked upwards to moisten his pupils.

Captain Short squeezed off a few bursts on the run. One clipped the backside of the nearest goblin. Holly groaned. Nowhere near a nerve centre. But it didn't have to be. There was a disadvantage to these foil suits. They conducted neutrino charges. The charge spread through the suit's material like fiery ripples across a pond. The goblin jumped a good two metres straight up, then tumbled, unconscious, to the foot of the escalator. The hover trolley spun out of control, crashing into a luggage carousel. Hundreds of small cylindrical objects spilled from a shattered crate.

Goblin Number Two fired a dozen rounds Holly's way. He missed, partly because his arms were jittery with nerves. But also because firing from the hip only works in the movies. Holly tried to take a screen shot of his weapon with her helmet camera for the computer to run a match on, but there was too much vibration.

The chase continued down the conduits and into the departure bay itself. Holly was surprised to hear the hum of docking computers. There wasn't supposed to be any power here. LEP Engineering would have dismantled the generators. Why would power be needed here?

She already knew the answer. Power would be needed to operate the shuttle monorail and Mission Control. Her suspicions were confirmed as she entered the hangar. The goblins had built a shuttle!

It was unbelievable. Goblins had barely enough electricity in their brains to power a ten-watt bulb. How could they possibly build a shuttle? Yet there it was, sitting in the dock like a used-craft seller's worst nightmare. There wasn't a bit of it less than a decade old, and the hull was a patchwork of weld spots and rivets.

Holly swallowed her amazement, concentrating on the pursuit. The goblin had paused to grab a set of wings from the cargo hold. She could have taken a shot then, but it was too risky. She wouldn't be surprised if the shuttle's nuclear battery was protected by nothing more than a single layer of lead.

The goblin took advantage of his reprieve to skip down the access tunnel. The monorail ran the length of the scorched rock to the massive chute. This chute was one of many of the natural vents that riddled the Earth's mantle and crust. Magma streams from the planet's molten core blasted up through these chutes towards the surface at irregular intervals. If it wasn't for these pressure releases, the Earth would have shaken itself to fragments aeons ago. The LEP had harnessed this natural power for express surface shots. Recon officers rode the magma flares in titanium eggs in times of emergency. For a more leisurely trip, shuttles avoided the flares, ascending the chutes on hot-air currents to the various terminals around the world.

Holly slowed her pace. There was nowhere for the goblin to go. Not unless he was going to fly into the chute itself, and nobody was that crazy. Anything that got caught up in a magma flare got fried right down to sub-atomic level.

The chute's entrance loomed ahead. Massive and ringed by charred rock.

Holly switched on the helmet's PA. 'That's far enough,' she shouted over the howl of core wind. 'Give it up. You're not going into the chute without science.'

Science was LEP-speak for technical information. In this case, science would be flare-prediction times. Accurate to within a tenth of a second. Generally.

The goblin raised a strange rifle, this time taking careful aim. The firing pin dropped, but whatever this weapon was firing, there wasn't any left.

'That's the problem with non-nuclear weapons, you run out of charge,' quipped Holly, fulfilling the age-old tradition of firefight banter, even though her knees were threatening to fold.

In response, the goblin hefted the rifle in Holly's direction. It was a terrible throw, landing five metres short. But it served its purpose as a distraction. The triad member used the moment to fire up his wings. They were old models – rotary motor and a broken muffler. The roar of the engine filled the tunnel.

There was another roar, behind the wings. A roar that Holly knew well from a thousand logged flight hours in the chutes. There was a flare coming.

Holly's mind raced. If the goblins had somehow managed to hook up the terminal to a power source, then all the safety features would have been activated. Including …

Captain Short whirled, but the blast doors were already closing. The fireproof barriers were automatically triggered by a thermo sensor in the chute. When a flare passed by below, two-metre-thick steel doors shut off the access tunnel from the rest of the terminal. They were trapped in there, with a column of magma on the way. Not that the magma would kill them – there wasn't much overspill from the flares. But the super-heated air would bake them drier than autumn leaves.

The goblin was standing on the tunnel's edge, oblivious to the impending eruption. Holly realized that it wasn't a question of the fugitive being crazy enough to fly into the chute. He was just plain stupid.

With a jaunty wave, the goblin hopped into the chute, rising rapidly from view. Not rapidly enough. A seven-metre-long jet of roiling lava pounced on him like a waiting snake, consuming him completely.

Holly did not waste time grieving. She had problems of her own. LEP jumpsuits had thermal coils to disperse excess heat, but that wouldn't be enough. In seconds, a wall of dry heat would roll in there, and raise the temperature enough to crack the walls.

Holly glanced up. A line of reinforced ancient coolant tanks were still bolted to the tunnel roof. She slid her blaster to maximum power and began sinking charges into the belly of the tanks. This was no time for subtlety.

The tanks buckled and split, belching out rancid air and a few trickles of coolant. Useless. They must have bled out over the centuries, and the goblins had never bothered replacing them. But there was one left, untouched. A black oblong, out of place among the standard green LEP models. Holly positioned herself directly underneath and fired.

Three thousand gallons of coolant-enhanced water crashed on to her head at the very moment a heatwave came billowing in from the chute. It was a curious sensation being burnt and frozen almost simultaneously. Holly felt blisters pop on her shoulders only to be flattened by water pressure. Captain Short was driven to her knees, lungs starving for air. But she couldn't take a breath, not now, and she couldn't raise a hand to switch on her helmet tank.

After an eternity, the roaring stopped and Holly

opened her eyes to a tunnel full of steam. She activated the demister in her visor and got up off her knees. Water slid in sheets from her non-friction suit. She released her helmet seals, taking deep breaths of tunnel air. Still warm, but breathable.

Behind her, the blast doors slid open and Captain Trouble Kelp appeared in the gap, along with an LEP rapid-response team.

'Nice manoeuvre, Captain.'

Holly didn't answer, too absorbed by the weapon abandoned by the recently vaporized goblin. This was the prize pig of rifles, almost half a metre long, with a starlite scope clipped above the barrel.

Holly's first thought had been that somehow the B'wa Kell was manufacturing its own weapons. But now she realized that the truth was far more dangerous. Captain Short pried the rifle from the half-melted rock. She recognized it from her *History of Law Enforcement* in service. An old Softnose laser. Softnoses had been outlawed long ago. But that wasn't the worst of it. Instead of a fairy power source, the gun was powered by a human AAA alkaline battery.

'Trouble,' she called. 'Have a look at this.'

'D'Arvit,' breathed Kelp, reaching immediately for the radio controls on his helmet. 'Get me a priority channel to Commander Root. We have *Class A* contraband. Yes, *Class A*. I need a full team of techies. Get Foaly too. I want this entire quadrant shut down …'

Trouble continued spouting orders, but they faded to a distant buzz in Holly's ears. The B'wa Kell was trading with the Mud People. Humans and goblins working together to reactivate outlawed weapons. And if the weapons were here, how long could it be before the Mud People followed?

Help arrived just after the nick of time. In thirty minutes there were so many halogen spotlights buzzing around E37 that it looked like a GolemWorld movie premiere.

Foaly was down on his knees examining the unconscious goblin by the escalator. The centaur was the main reason that humans hadn't yet discovered the People's underground lairs. A technical genius, who had pioneered every major development from flare prediction to mind-wiping technology, every discovery made him less respectful and more annoying. But rumour had it that he had a soft spot for a certain female Recon officer. Actually, the only female Recon officer.

'Good job, Holly,' he said, rubbing the goblin's reflective suit. 'You just had a firefight with a kebab.'

'That's it, Foaly, draw attention away from the fact that the B'wa Kell foxed your sensors.'

Foaly tried on one of the helmets. 'Not the B'wa Kell. No way. Too dumb. Goblins just don't have the cranial capacity. These are human manufacture.'

Holly snorted. 'And how do you know that? Recognize the stitching?'

'Nope,' replied Foaly, tossing the helmet to Holly.

Holly read the label. 'Made in Germany.'

'I'd guess that this is a fire suit. The material keeps the heat out as well as in. This is serious, Holly. We're not talking a couple of designer shirts and a case of chocolate bars here. Some human is doing some serious smuggling with the B'wa Kell.'

Foaly stepped out of the way to allow the technical crew access to their prisoner. The techies would tag the unconscious goblin with a subcutaneous sleeper. The sleeper contained microcapsules of a sedative agent and a tiny detonator. Once tagged, a criminal could be knocked out by computer if the LEP realized he was involved in an illegal situation.

'You know who's probably behind this, don't you?' said Holly.

Foaly rolled his eyes. 'Oh, let me guess. Captain Short's arch-enemy, Master Artemis Fowl.'

'Well, who else could it be?'

'Take your pick. The People have been in contact with thousands of Mud Men over the years.'

'Is that so?' retorted Holly. 'And how many that haven't been mind-wiped?'

Foaly pretended to think about it, adjusting the foil hat jammed on his head to deflect any brain-probing signals that could be focused his way. 'Three,' he muttered eventually.

'Pardon?'

'Three, OK?'

'Exactly. Fowl and his pet gorillas. Artemis is behind this. Mark my words.'

'You'd just love that to be the case now, wouldn't you? You'd finally have the chance to get your own back. You do remember what happened the last time the LEP went up against Artemis Fowl?'

'I remember. But that was last time.'

Foaly smirked. 'I would remind you that he'll be thirteen now.'

Holly's hand dropped to her buzz baton. 'I don't care how old he is. One zap with this and he'll be sleeping like a baby.'

Foaly nodded towards the entrance. 'I'd save my charges if I were you. You're going to need them.'

Holly followed his gaze. Commander Julius Root was sweeping across the secured zone. The more he saw, the redder his face grew, hence the nickname, Beetroot.

'Commander,' began Holly. 'You need to see this.'

Root's gaze silenced her. 'What were you thinking?'

'Pardon me, sir?'

'Don't give me that. I was in Ops for the whole thing. I was watching the video feed from your helmet.'

'Oh.'

'*Oh* hardly covers it, Captain!' Root's buzz-cut grey hair was quivering with emotion. 'This was supposed to be a surveillance mission. There were several back-up squads sitting on their well-trained behinds only waiting for you to call. But no, Captain Short decides to take on the B'wa Kell on her own.'

'I had a man down, sir. There was no choice.'

'What was Verbil doing out there anyway?'

For the first time, Holly's gaze dropped. 'I sent him out to do a thermal, sir. Just following regulations.'

Root nodded. 'I've talked to the paramedic warlock. Verbil will be OK, but his flying days are over. There'll be a tribunal, of course.'

'Yes, sir. Understood.'

'A formality, I'm sure, but you know the Council.'

Holly knew the Council all too well. She would be the first LEP officer in history to be the subject of two simultaneous investigations.

'So what's this I hear about a Class A?'

All contraband was classed. Class A was code for dangerous human technology. Power sources, for instance.

'This way, sir.'

Holly led them to the rear of the maintenance area, to the shuttle bay itself, where a restricted-access perspex dome had been erected. She pressed through the frosted flaps.

'You see. This is serious.'

Root studied the evidence. In the shuttle's cargo bay were crates of AAA batteries. Holly selected a pack.

'Pencil batteries,' she said. 'A common human power source. Crude, inefficient and an environmental disaster. Twelve crates of them right here. Who knows how many are in the tunnels already.'

Root was unimpressed. 'Forgive me for not quaking in my boots. So a few goblins get to play human video games. So what?'

Foaly had spotted the goblin's Softnose laser. 'Oh no!' he said, checking the weapon.

'Exactly,' agreed Holly.

The commander did not appreciate being left out of the conversation.

'Oh no? I hope you're being melodramatic.'

'No, chief,' replied the centaur, sombre for once. 'This is deadly serious. The B'wa Kell is using human batteries to power the old Softnose lasers. They'd only get about six shots per battery. But you give every goblin a pocketful of power cells, and that's a lot of shots.'

'Softnose lasers? They were outlawed decades ago. Weren't they all recycled?'

Foaly nodded. 'Supposedly. My division supervised the meltdowns. Not that we considered it priority. They were originally powered by a single solar cell, with a life of less than a decade. Obviously somebody managed to sneak a few out of the recycling lock-up.'

'Quite a few by the look of all these batteries. That's the last thing I need, goblins with Softnoses.'

The theory behind the Softnose technique involved placing an inhibitor on the blaster, which allowed the laser to travel at slower speeds so that it actually penetrated the target. Initially developed for mining purposes, they were quickly adapted by some greedy weapons manufacturer.

The Softnoses were just as quickly outlawed, for the obvious reason that these weapons were designed to kill and not incapacitate. Now and then one found its way into the hands of a gang member. But this did not look like small-scale, black-market trading. This looked like somebody was planning something big.

'You know what the worrying thing about this is?' said Foaly.

'No,' said Root, with deceptive calmness. 'Do tell me what the worrying thing is.'

Foaly turned the gun around. 'The way this weapon has been adapted to take a human battery. Very clever. There's no way a goblin figured this out on his own.'

'But why adapt the Softnoses?' asked the commander. 'Why not just use the old solar cells?'

'Those solar cells are very rare. They're worth their weight in gold. Antique dealers use them to power all sorts of old gadgets. And it would be impossible to build a power-cell factory of any kind without my sensors picking up emissions. Much simpler just to steal them from the humans.'

Root lit one of his trademark fungal cigars. 'Tell me that's it. Tell me there's nothing else.'

Holly's gaze flickered to the rear of the hangar. Root caught the glance and pressed past the crates to the makeshift shuttle in the docking bay. The commander climbed into the craft.

'And what the hell is this, Foaly?'

The centaur ran a hand along the ship's hull. 'It's amazing. Unbelievable. They put a shuttle together from junk. I'm surprised this thing gets off the ground.'

The commander bit down hard on his fungus cigar. 'When you're finished admiring the goblins, Foaly, maybe you can explain how the B'wa Kell got a hold of this stuff. I thought all outdated shuttle technology was supposed to be destroyed.'

'That's what I thought. I retired some of this stuff myself. This starboard booster used to be in E1, until Captain Short blew it out last year. I remember signing the destruct order.'

Root spared a second to shoot Holly a withering glance.

'So now we have shuttle parts escaping the recycling smelters as well as Softnose lasers. Find out how this shuttle got here. Take it apart, piece by piece. I want every strand of wire lasered for prints and DNA. Feed all the serial numbers into the mainframe. See if there are any common denominators.'

Foaly nodded. 'Good idea. I'll get someone on it.'

'No, Foaly. You get on it. This is priority. So give your conspiracy theories a rest for a few days and find me the inside fairy who's selling this junk.'

'But, Julius,' protested Foaly. 'That's grunt work.'

Root took a step closer. 'One, don't call me Julius, civilian. And two, I'd say it was more like donkey work.'

Foaly noticed the vein pulsing in the commander's temple. 'Point taken,' he said, removing a handheld computer from his belt. '*I'll* get right on it.'

'You do that. Now, Captain Short, what is our B'wa Kell prisoner saying?'

Holly shrugged. 'Nothing much, still unconscious. He'll be coughing soot for a month when he wakes up. Anyway, you know how the B'wa Kell works. The soldiers aren't told anything. This guy is just a grunt. It's a pity the Book forbids using the *mesmer* on other fairies.'

'Hmm,' said Root, his face glowing as red as a baboon's behind. 'An even greater pity the Atlantis Convention outlawed truth drugs. Otherwise we could pump this convict full of serum until he sang like a drunken Mud Man.' The commander took several deep breaths, calming down before his heart popped. 'Right now, we need to find out where these batteries came from, and if there are any more in the Lower Elements.'

Holly took a breath. 'I have a theory, sir.'

'Don't tell me,' groaned Root. 'Artemis Fowl, right?'

'Who else could it be? I knew he'd be back. I knew it.'

'You know the rules, Holly. He beat us last year. Game over. That's what the Book says.'

'Yes, sir, but that was a different game. New game, new rules. If Fowl is supplying power cells to the B'wa Kell, the least we can do is check it out.'

Root considered it. If Fowl was behind this, things could get very complicated, very fast.

'I don't like the idea of interrogating Fowl on his turf. But we can't bring him down here. The pressure below ground would kill him.'

Holly disagreed. 'Not if we keep him in a secure environment. The city is equalized. So are the shuttles.'

'OK, go,' the commander said at last. 'Bring him in for a little chat. Bring the big one too.'

'Butler?'

'Yes, Butler.' Root paused. 'But remember, we're going to run a few scans, Holly, that's it. I don't want you using this as an opportunity to settle a score.'

'No, sir. Strictly business.'

'Do I have your word on that?'

'Yes, sir. I guarantee it.'

Root ground the cigar butt beneath his heel. 'I don't

want anyone else getting hurt today, not even Artemis Fowl.'

'Understood.'

'Well,' added the commander, 'not unless it's absolutely necessary.'

CHAPTER 3: GOING UNDERGROUND

 BUTLER had been in Artemis Fowl's service since the moment of the boy's birth. He had spent the first night of his charge's life standing guard on the Sisters of Mercy maternity ward. For over a decade, Butler had been teacher, mentor and protector to the young heir. The pair had never been separated for more than a week, until now. It shouldn't bother him, he knew that. A bodyguard should never become emotionally attached to his package. It affects his judgement. But in his private moments, Butler couldn't help thinking of the Fowl heir as the son or younger brother he'd never had.

Butler parked the Bentley Arnage Red Label on the college avenue. If anything, the Eurasian manservant had bulked up since mid-term. With Artemis in boarding school, he was spending a lot more time in the gym. Truth be told, Butler was bored pumping iron, but the college authorities absolutely refused to allow him a bunk in Artemis's room. And when the gardener had discovered the bodyguard's hideout just off the seventeenth green, they had banned him from the college grounds altogether.

Artemis slipped through the college gate, Doctor Po's comments still in his thoughts.

'Problems, sir?' said Butler, noticing his employer's sour expression.

Artemis ducked into the Bentley's wine-leather interior, selecting a still water from the bar. 'Hardly, Butler. Just another quack spouting psychobabble.'

Butler kept his voice level. 'Should I have a word with him?'

'Never mind him now. What news of the *Fowl Star*?'

'We got an e-mail at the manor this morning. It's an MPEG.'

Artemis scowled. He could not access MPEG video files on his mobile phone.

Butler pulled a portable computer from the glove compartment. 'I thought you might be anxious to see the file, so I downloaded it on to this.'

He passed the computer over his shoulder. Artemis activated the compact machine, folding out the flat colour screen. At first he thought the battery was dead, then realized he was looking at a field of snow. White on white, with only the faintest shadows to indicate dips and drumlins.

Artemis felt the uneasiness rolling in his gut. Funny how such an innocent image could be so foreboding.

The camera panned upwards, revealing a dull twilit sky. Then a black hunched object in the distance. A rhythmic crunching issued through the compact speakers as the cameraman advanced through the snow. The object grew clearer. It was a man sitting on, no, *tied to*, a chair. The ice clinked in Artemis's glass. His hands were shaking.

The man was dressed in the rags of a once fine suit. Scars branded the prisoner's face like lightning bolts, and one leg appeared to be missing. It was difficult to tell. Artemis's breath was jumpy now, like a marathon runner's.

There was a sign around the man's neck. Cardboard and twine. On the sign was scrawled in thick black letters: *Zdrazdvuy, syn*. The camera zoomed in on the message for several seconds, then went blank.

'Is that all?'

Butler nodded. 'Just the man and the sign. That's it.'

'*Zdrazdvuy, syn*,' muttered Artemis, his accent flawless. Since his father's disappearance he had been teaching himself the language.

'Should I translate for you?' asked Butler, also a Russian speaker. He had picked it up during a five-year stint with an espionage unit in the late eighties. His accent, however, was not quite so sophisticated as his young employer's.

'No, I know what it means,' replied Artemis. '*Zdrazdvuy, syn*: Hello, son.'

Butler pulled the Bentley on to the dual carriageway. Neither of them spoke for several minutes. Eventually Butler had to ask.

'Do you think it's him, Artemis? Could that man be your father?'

Artemis rewound the MPEG, freezing it on the mysterious man's face. He touched the display, sending rainbow distortions across the screen.

'I think so, Butler. But the picture quality is too poor. I can't be certain.'

Butler understood the emotions battering his young charge. He too had lost someone aboard the *Fowl Star*. His uncle, the Major, had been assigned to Artemis's father on that fateful trip. Unfortunately, the Major's body had turned up in the Tchersky morgue.

Artemis regained his composure. 'I must pursue this, Butler.'

'You know what's coming next, of course?'

'Yes. A ransom demand. This is merely the teaser, to get my attention. I need to cash in some of the People's gold. Contact Lars in Zurich immediately.'

Butler accelerated into the fast lane.

'Master Artemis, I have had some experience in these matters.'

Artemis did not interrupt. Butler's career before his current charge's birth had been varied to say the least.

'The pattern with kidnappers is to eliminate all witnesses. Then they will generally try to eliminate each other to avoid splitting the ransom.'

'Your point being?'

'My point being that paying a ransom in no way guarantees your father's safety. If indeed that man *is* your father. It is quite possible that the kidnappers will take your money and then kill all of us.'

Artemis studied the screen. 'You're right, of course. I will have to devise a plan.'

Butler swallowed. He remembered the last plan. It had almost got them both killed, and could have plunged the planet into a cross-species war. Butler was a man who didn't scare easily, but the spark in Artemis Fowl's eyes was enough to send a shiver crackling down his spine.

Chute Terminal E1: Tara, Ireland

Captain Holly Short had decided to work a double shift and proceed directly to the surface. She paused only for a nutri-bar and energy shake before hopping on the first shuttle to the terminal at Tara.

One of Tara's officials was not making her journey any easier. The head of security was annoyed that Captain Short had not only put all chute traffic on hold to take a priority pod from E1, but had then proceeded to commandeer an entire shuttle for the return journey.

'Why don't you check your system again?' said Holly, through gritted teeth. 'I'm sure the authorization from Police Plaza has arrived by now.'

The truculent gnome consulted his hand-held computer. 'No, ma'am. I ain't got nuthin.'

'Look, Mister ...'

'Commandant Terryl.'

'*Commandant* Terryl. I'm on an important mission here. National security. I need you to keep the arrivals hall completely clear for the next couple of hours.'

Terryl made a great show of almost collapsing. 'The next coupl'a hours! Are you crazy, girly? I got three shuttles comin' in from Atlantis. What'm I s'posed to tell 'em? Tour's off 'cause of some LEP secret shenanigans. This is high season. I can't just shut things down. No way, no how.'

Holly shrugged. 'Fine. You just let all your tourists catch sight of the two humans I'm bringing down here. There'll be a riot. I guarantee it.'

'Two humans?' said the head of security. 'Inside the terminal? Are you nuts?'

Holly was running out of patience, and time. 'Do you see this?' she demanded, pointing to the insignia on her helmet. 'I'm LEP. A captain. No rent-a-cop gnome is going to stand in the way of my orders.'

Terryl drew himself up to his full height, which was about seventy centimetres. 'Yeah, I heard a you. The crazy girly captain. Caused quite a stir up here last year, didn't you? My tax ingots gonna be payin' for that little screw-up for quite some time.'

'Just ask Central, you bureaucratic idiot.'

'Call me what you want, missy. We have our rules here, and without confirmation from below, ain't nuthin I can do to change 'em. 'Specially not fer some gun-totin' girly with an attitude problem.'

'Well get on the blower to Police Plaza then!'

Terryl sniffed. 'The magma flares have just started actin' up. It's hard to get a line. Maybe I'll try again, after my rounds. Just you take yourself a seat in the departure lounge.'

Holly's hand strayed towards her buzz baton.

'You know what you're doing, don't you?'

'What?' croaked the gnome.

'You're obstructing an LEP operation.'

'I ain't obstructin' nuthin ...'

'And, as such, it is in my power to remove said obstruction using any force that I deem necessary.'

'Don't you threaten me, missy.'

Holly drew the baton, twirling it expertly. 'I'm not threatening you. I'm just informing you of police procedure. If you continue to obstruct me, I remove the obstruction, in this case you, and proceed to the next in command.'

Terryl was unconvinced. 'You wouldn't dare.'

Holly grinned. 'I'm the crazy girly captain. Remember?'

The gnome considered it. It was unlikely the officer would buzz him, but then again who knew with female elves?

'OK,' he said, printing off a sheet on the computer. 'This is a twenty-four-hour visa. But if you're not back here in that time, I'll have you taken into custody on your return. Then I'll be the one making the threats.'

Holly snatched the sheet. 'Whatever. Now, remember, make sure Arrivals is clear when I get back.'

IRELAND, EN ROUTE FROM ST BARTLEBY'S TO FOWL MANOR

Artemis was bouncing ideas off Butler. It was a technique he often used when trying to come up with a plan. After all, if anybody was an expert on covert operations, it was his bodyguard.

'We can't trace the MPEG?'

'No, Artemis. I tried. They put a decay virus in with the e-mail. I only just managed to get the film on disk before the original disintegrated.'

'What about the MPEG itself? Could we get a geographical fix from the stars?'

Butler smiled. Young Master Artemis was starting to think like a soldier.

'No luck. I sent a shot to a friend of mine in NASA. He didn't even bother putting it into the computer. Not enough definition.'

Artemis was silent for a minute.

'How fast can we get to Russia?'

Butler drummed his fingers on the steering wheel. 'It depends.'

'Depends on what?'

'On how we go, legal or illegal.'

'Which is quicker?'

Butler laughed. Something you didn't hear very often. 'Illegal is usually faster. Either way is going to be pretty slow. We can't go by air, that's for sure. The Mafiya are going to have foot soldiers at every airstrip.'

'Are we sure it's the Mafiya?'

Butler glanced in the rear-view mirror. 'I'm afraid so. All kidnappings go through the Mafiya. Even if an ordinary criminal managed to abduct your father, he would have to hand him over once the Mafiya had found out about it.'

Artemis nodded. 'That's what I thought. So we will have to travel by sea, and that will take a week at the very least. We could really use some help with transport.

Something the Mafiya won't expect. How's our ID situation?'

'No problem. I thought we'd go native. We'll arouse less suspicion. I have passports and visas.'

'*Da*. What is our cover?'

'What about Stefan Bashkir and his Uncle Constantin?'

'Perfect. The chess prodigy and his chaperone.' They had used this cover many times before on previous search missions. Once, a checkpoint official, himself a chess grandmaster, had doubted their story until Artemis beat him in six moves. The technique had since become known as the Bashkir Manoeuvre.

'How soon can we leave?'

'Almost immediately. Missus Fowl and Juliet are in Nice this week. That gives us eight days. We can mail the school, make up some excuse.'

'I dare say St Bartleby's will be glad to be rid of me for a while.'

'We could go straight to the airport from Fowl Manor. The Lear jet is stocked. At least we can fly as far as Scandinavia and we can try to pick up a boat from there. I just have to pick up a few things at the manor first.'

Artemis could imagine exactly the kind of *things* his manservant wished to pick up. Sharp things and explosive things.

'Good. The sooner the better. We've got to find these

people before they know we're looking. We can monitor e-mail as we go.'

Butler took the exit for Fowl Manor.

'You know, Artemis,' he said, glancing in the mirror. 'We're going up against the Russian Mafiya. I've had dealings with these people before. They don't negotiate. This could get bloody. If we take these gangsters on, people are going to get hurt. Most likely us.'

Artemis nodded absently, watching his own reflection in the window. He needed a plan. Something audacious and brilliant. Something that had never been attempted before. Artemis was not unduly worried on that front. His brain had never let him down.

TARA SHUTTLE PORT

The fairy shuttle port at Tara was an impressive operation. Ten thousand cubic metres of terminal concealed beneath an overgrown hillock in the middle of the McGraney farm.

For centuries, the McGraneys had respected the fairy fort's boundaries and, for centuries, they had enjoyed exceptional good luck. Illnesses mysteriously cleared up overnight. Priceless art treasures unearthed themselves with incredible regularity, and mad cow disease seemed to avoid their herds altogether.

Having solved her visa problem, Holly finally made her way to the security door and slipped through the holographic camouflage. She had managed to secure a set of Koboi DoubleDex for the trip. The rig ran on a satellite-bounced solar battery, and employed a revolutionary wing design. There were two sets, or decks; one fixed for gliding, and a smaller set for manoeuvrability. Holly had been dying to try out the DoubleDex, but only a few rigs had made their way across from Koboi Labs. Foaly was reluctant to let them out because he hadn't designed them. Professional envy. Holly had taken advantage of his absence from the lab to swipe a set from the rack.

She soared fifteen metres above the ground, allowing unfiltered surface air to fill her lungs. Though laden with pollutants, it was still sweeter than the recycled tunnel variety. For several minutes, she enjoyed the experience, before turning her concentration to the mission at hand: how to abduct Artemis Fowl.

Not from his home, Fowl Manor, that was for certain. Legally, she put herself on very shaky ground by entering a dwelling without permission. Even though, technically, Fowl had invited her in by kidnapping her last year. Not many lawyers would take your case on the basis of that defence. Anyway, the manor was a virtual fortress and had already seen off an entire LEPretrieval team. Why should she fare any better?

There was also the complication that Artemis could very well be expecting her, especially if he *was* trading with the B'wa Kell. The idea of walking into a trap did not appeal to Holly. She had already been imprisoned once in Fowl Manor. Doubtless her cell was still furnished.

Holly activated the computer navigation package, calling up Fowl Manor on her helmet visor. A soft crimson light began to blip beside the 3D plan of the house. The building had been red-flagged by the LEP. Holly groaned. Now she would be treated to a video warning, just in case there was one Recon officer under the world who had not heard of Artemis Fowl.

Corporal Lili Frond's face appeared on the screen. Of course they chose Lili for this assignment. The bimbo face of the LEP. Sexism was alive and well and living in Police Plaza. It was rumoured that Frond's LEP scores had been bumped up because of her descendancy from the elfin king.

'You have selected Fowl Manor,' said Frond's image, fluttering her eyelids. 'This is a red-flagged building. Unauthorized access is strictly forbidden. Do not even attempt a fly-over. Artemis Fowl is considered an active threat to the People.'

A picture of Fowl appeared beside Frond, a digitally enhanced scowl on his face.

'His accomplice, known only as Butler, is not to be approached under any circumstances. He is generally armed and always dangerous.'

Butler's massive head appeared beside the two other images. Armed and dangerous hardly did him justice. He was the only human in history to have taken on a troll and won.

Holly sent the co-ordinates to the flight computer and let the wings do the steering for her. The countryside sped by below. Even since her last visit, the Mud People infestation seemed to have taken a stronger hold. There was barely an acre of land without dozens of their dwellings digging into its soil, and barely a mile of river without one of their factories pouring its poison into the waters.

The sun finally dipped below the horizon and Holly raised the filters on her visor. Time was on her side now. She had the entire night to come up with a plan. Holly found that she missed Foaly's sarcastic comments in her ear. Annoying as the centaur's observations were, they generally proved accurate and had saved her hide on more than one occasion. She tried to establish a link, but the flares were still high and there was no reception. Nothing but static.

Fowl Manor loomed in the distance, completely dominating the surrounding landscape. Holly scanned the building with her thermal bar and found nothing but insect and small rodent life forms. Spiders and mice. Nobody home. That suited her fine. She landed on the head of a particularly gruesome stone gargoyle, and settled in to wait.

Fowl Manor, Dublin, Ireland

The original Fowl castle had been built by Lord Hugh Fowl in the fifteenth century, overlooking low-lying country on all sides. A tactic borrowed from the Normans: never let your enemies sneak up on you. Over the centuries, the castle had been extensively remodelled until it became a manor, but the attention to security remained. The manor was surrounded by metre-thick walls, and wired with a state-of-the-art security system.

Butler pulled off the road, opening the estate gates with a remote. He glanced back at his employer's pensive face. Sometimes he thought that, in spite of all his contacts, informants and employees, Artemis Fowl was the loneliest boy he'd ever met.

'We could bring a couple of those fairy blasters,' he said.

Butler had relieved LEPretrieval One of their weaponry during the previous year's siege.

Artemis nodded. 'Good idea, but remove the nuclear batteries and put the blasters in a bag with some old games and books. We can pretend they're toys if we're captured.'

'Yes, sir. Good thinking.'

The Bentley Red Label crunched up the driveway, activating the ground's security lights. There were several lamps on in the main house. These were on randomly alternating timers.

Butler undid his seat belt, stepping lithely from the Bentley.

'You need anything special, Artemis?'

Artemis nodded. 'Grab some caviar from the kitchen. You wouldn't believe the muck they feed us in Bartleby's for ten thousand a term.'

Butler smiled again. A teenager asking for caviar. He'd never get used to it.

The smile withered on his lips halfway to the recently remodelled entrance. A shiver passed across his heart. He knew that feeling well. His mother used to say that someone had just walked over his grave. A sixth sense. Gut instinct. There was peril somewhere. Invisible, but here nevertheless.

Holly spotted the headlights raking the sky from over a mile away. Optix were no good from this vantage point. Even when the automobile's windscreen came into view, the glass was tinted and the shadows beyond were deep. She felt her heart rate increase at the sight of Fowl's car.

The Bentley wound along the avenue, flickering between the rows of willow and horse chestnut. Holly ducked instinctively, though she was completely shielded from human eyes. You couldn't be certain with Artemis

Fowl's manservant. Last year Artemis had cannibalized a fairy helmet, constructing an eyepiece that allowed Butler to spot and neutralize an entire crack squad of LEPretrieval commandos. It was hardly likely that he was wearing the lens at the moment but, as Trouble Kelp and his boys had learned, it didn't pay to underestimate Artemis or his manservant.

Holly set the Neutrino to slightly above the recommended stun setting. A couple of Butler's brain cells might get fried, but she wasn't about to lose any sleep over it.

The car swung into the driveway, crunching across the gravel. Butler climbed out. Holly felt her back teeth grinding. Once upon a time, she had saved his life, healing him after a mortal encounter with a troll. She wasn't sure if she'd do it again.

Holding her breath, LEPrecon Captain Holly Short set the DoubleDex to slow descent. She dropped soundlessly, skimming past the storeys, and aimed her weapon at Butler's chest. Now there was a target a sun-blinded dwarf couldn't miss.

The human couldn't have detected her presence. Not possible. Yet something made him pause. He stopped and sniffed the air. The Mud Man was like a dog. No, not a dog, a wolf. A wolf with a big handgun.

Holly focused her helmet lens on the weapon, sending a photo to her computer database. Moments later, a hi-res rotating 3D image of the gun appeared in the corner of her visor.

'Sig Sauer,' said a recorded byte of Foaly's voice. 'Nine millimetre. Thirteen in the magazine. Big bullets. One of these hits you and it could blow your head off; something even the magic can't fix. Other than that you should be all right, presuming you remembered to wear the regulation above-ground micro-fibre jumpsuit recently patented by me. Then again, being a Recon jock, you probably didn't.'

Holly scowled. Foaly was all the more annoying when he was right. She had jumped on the first available shuttle without even bothering to change into an above-ground suit.

Holly's eyes were level with Butler's now, yet she was still hovering over a metre from the ground. She released the visor seals, wincing at the pneumatic hiss.

Butler heard the escaping gas, swinging the Sig Sauer towards the source.

'Fairy,' he said. 'I know you're there. Unshield or I start shooting.'

This was not exactly the tactical advantage Holly had in mind. Her visor was up, and the manservant's finger was creaking on his pistol's hair trigger. She took a deep breath and shut down her shield.

'Hello, Butler,' she said evenly.

Butler cocked the Sig Sauer. 'Hello, Captain. Come down slowly, and don't try any of your ...'

'*Put your gun away,*' said Holly, her voice layered with the hypnotic *mesmer.*

Butler fought it, the gun barrel shaking erratically.

'*Put it down, Butler. Don't make me fry your brain.*'

A vein pulsed in Butler's eyelid.

Unusual, thought Holly. I've never seen that before.

'*Don't fight me, Mud Man. Give in to it.*'

Butler opened his mouth to speak. To warn Artemis. She pushed harder, the magic cascading around the human's head.

'*I said put it down!*'

A bead of sweat ran down the bodyguard's cheek.

'*PUT IT DOWN!*'

And Butler did, gradually and grudgingly.

Holly smiled. '*Good, Mud Man. Now, back to the car and act as though nothing's wrong.*'

The manservant's legs obeyed, ignoring the signals from his own brain.

Holly buzzed up her shield. She was going to enjoy this.

Artemis was composing an e-mail on his laptop.

Dear Principal Guiney ... it read ...

Because of your counsellor's tactless interrogation of my little Arty, I have taken him out of school for a course of therapy sessions with real professionals in the Mont Gaspard Clinic in

59

Switzerland. I am considering legal action. Do not attempt to contact me as that would only serve to irritate me further and, when irritated, I generally call my attorneys.

Sincerely,

Angeline Fowl

Artemis sent the message, allowing himself the luxury of a small grin. It would have been nice to watch Principal Guiney's expression when he read the electronic letter. Unfortunately, the button camera he'd planted in the headmaster's office could only be accessed within a mile radius.

Butler opened the driver's door and, after a moment, slipped into the seat.

Artemis folded his phone into its wallet. 'Captain Short, I presume. Why don't you stop vibrating and settle into the visible spectrum?'

Holly speckled into view. There was a gleaming gun in her hand. Guess where it was pointed.

'Really, Holly, is that necessary?'

Holly snorted. 'Well, let's see. Kidnapping, actual bodily harm, extortion, conspiracy to commit murder. I'd say it's necessary.'

'Please, Captain Short,' said Artemis, with a smile, 'I was young and selfish. Believe it or not, I do harbour some doubts over that particular venture.'

'Not enough doubts to return the gold?'

'No,' admitted Artemis. 'Not quite.'

'How did you know I was here?'

Artemis steepled his fingers. 'There were several clues. One, Butler did not conduct his usual bomb check under the car. Two, he returned without the items he went to fetch. Three, the door was left open for several seconds, something no good security man would permit. And four, I detected a slight haze as you entered the vehicle. Elementary really.'

Holly scowled. 'Observant little Mud Boy, aren't you?'

'I try. Now, Captain Short, if you would be so kind as to tell me why you are here.'

'As if you don't know.'

Artemis thought for a moment. 'Interesting. I would guess that something has happened. Obviously something that I am being held responsible for.' He raised an eyebrow fractionally. An intense expression of emotion for Artemis Fowl. 'There are humans trading with the People.'

'Very impressive,' said Holly. 'Or it would be if we didn't both know that you're behind it. And if we can't get the truth out of you, I'm sure your computer files will prove most revealing.'

Artemis closed the laptop's lid. 'Captain. I realize there is no love lost between us, but I don't have time for this now. It is imperative that you give me a few days to sort out my affairs.'

'No can do, Fowl. There are a few people below ground who would like a word.'

Artemis shrugged. 'I suppose after what I did, I can't really expect any consideration.'

'That's right. You can't.'

'Well then,' sighed Artemis. 'I don't suppose I have a choice.'

Holly smiled. 'That's right, Fowl, you don't.'

'Shall we go?' Artemis's tone was meek, but his brain was sparking off ideas. Maybe co-operating with the fairies wasn't such a bad idea. They had certain abilities after all.

'Why not?' Holly turned to Butler. '*Drive south. Stay on the back roads.*'

'Tara, I presume. I often wondered where exactly the entrance to E1 was.'

'Keep wondering, Mud Boy,' muttered Holly. '*Now, sleep.* All this deduction is wearing me out.'

CHAPTER 4: FOWL IS FAIR

 ARTEMIS woke in the LEP interrogation room. He could have been in any police interview room in the world. Same uncomfortable furniture, same old routine.

Root jumped right in. 'OK, Fowl, start talking.'

Artemis took a moment to get his bearings. Holly and Root were facing him across a low plastic-topped table. A high-watt bulb shone directly into his face.

'Really, Commander. Is this it? I expected more.'

'Oh there's more. Just not for criminals like you.'

Artemis noted that his hands were shackled to the chair.

'You're not still upset about last year, are you? After all, I won. That is supposed to be that, according to your own Book.'

Root leaned forward until the tip of his cigar was centimetres from Artemis's nose. 'This is an entirely different case, Mud Boy. So don't give me the innocent act.'

Artemis was unperturbed. 'Which one are you? Good Cop or Bad Cop?'

Root laughed heartily, the tip of his cigar drawing patterns in the air. 'Good Cop, Bad Cop! Hate to tell you this, Dorothy, but you ain't in Kansas any more.' The commander loved quoting *The Wizard of Oz*. Three of his cousins were in the movie.

A figure emerged from the shadows. It had a tail, four legs, two arms and was holding what looked like a pair of common kitchen plungers.

'OK, Mud Boy,' said the figure. 'Just relax and this might not hurt too much.'

Foaly attached the suction cups to Artemis's eyes and the boy immediately fell unconscious.

'The sedative is in the rubber seals,' explained the centaur. 'Gets in through the pores. They never see it coming. Tell me I'm not the cleverest individual in the universe.'

'Oh, I don't know,' said Root innocently. 'That pixie Koboi is one pretty sharp female.'

Foaly stamped a hoof angrily. 'Koboi? Koboi? Those wings of hers are ridiculous. If you ask me, we're using far too much Koboi technology these days. It's not good to let one company have all the LEP's business.'

64

'Unless it's yours, of course.'

'I'm serious, Julius. I know Opal Koboi from my days at university. She's not stable. There are Koboi chips in all the new Neutrinos. If those labs go under, all we'd have left are the DNA cannons in Police Plaza and a few cases of electric stun guns.'

Root snorted. 'Koboi just upgraded every gun and vehicle in the force. Three times the power, half the heat emission. Better than the last statistics from your lab, Foaly.'

Foaly threaded a set of fibre-optic cables back to the computer.

'Yes, well, maybe if the Council would give me a decent budget ...'

'Quit your moaning, Foaly. I saw the budget for this machine. It better do more than unblock the drains.'

Foaly flicked his tail, highly offended.

'This is a Retimager, I'm considering going private with this baby.'

'And it does *what* exactly?'

Foaly activated a plasma screen on the holding-cell wall.

'You see these dark circles? These are the human's retinas. Every image leaves a tiny etching, like a photo negative. We can feed whatever pictures we want into the computer and search for matches.'

Root didn't exactly fall to his knees in awe. 'Isn't that handy.'

'Well, yes, it is actually. Observe.'

Foaly called up an image of a goblin, cross-referencing it with the Retimager's database.

'For every matching point we get a hit. About two hundred hits is normal. General shape of the head, features and so on. Anything significantly above that and he's seen that goblin before.'

One eighty-six flashed up on the screen.

'Negative on the goblin. Let's try a Softnose.'

Again, the count was under two hundred.

'Another negative. Sorry, Captain, but Master Fowl here is innocent. He's never even seen a goblin, much less traded with the B'wa Kell.'

'They could have mind-wiped him.'

Foaly removed the seals from Artemis's eyes. 'That's the beauty of this baby. Mind-wipes don't work. The Retimager operates on actual physical evidence. You'd have to scrub the retinas.'

'Anything on the human's computer?'

'Plenty,' replied Foaly. 'But nothing incriminating. Not a single mention of goblins or batteries.'

Root scratched his square jaw. 'What about the big one? He could have been the go-between.'

'Did him already with the Retimager. Nothing. Face it, the LEP have pulled in the wrong Mud Men. Wipe 'em and send 'em home.'

Holly nodded. The commander didn't.

'Wait a minute. I'm thinking.'

'About what?' asked Holly. 'The sooner we get Artemis Fowl's nose out of our business, the better.'

'Maybe not. Since they're already here ...'

Holly's jaw dropped. 'Commander. You don't know Fowl like I do. Give him half a chance and he'll be a bigger problem than the goblins.'

'Maybe he could help us with our Mud Man problem.'

'I have to object, Commander. These humans are not to be trusted.'

Root's face would have glowed in the dark.

'Do you think I like this, Captain? Do you think I relish the idea of crawling to this Mud Boy? I do not. I would rather swallow live stink worms than ask Artemis Fowl for help. But someone is powering the B'wa Kell's arms, and I need to find out who. So get with the programme, Holly. There's more at stake here than your little vendetta.'

Holly bit her tongue. She couldn't oppose the commander, not after all he'd done for her, but asking Artemis Fowl for help was the wrong course of action whatever the situation. She didn't doubt for a minute that the human would have a solution to their problem, but at what cost?

Root drew a deep breath. 'OK, Foaly, bring him round. And fit him with a translator. Speaking Mud Man gives me a headache.'

*

Artemis massaged the puffy skin beneath his eyes.

'Sedative in the seals?' he said, glancing at Foaly. 'Micro-needles?'

The centaur was impressed. 'You're pretty sharp for a Mud Boy.'

Artemis touched the crescent-shaped nodule fixed above his ear.

'Translator?'

Foaly nodded at the commander. 'Speaking in tongues gives some people a headache.'

Artemis straightened his school tie. 'I see. Now, how can I be of service?'

'What makes you think we need help from you, human?' growled Root around the butt of his cigar.

The boy smirked. 'I have a feeling, Commander, that if you did not need something from me, I would be regaining consciousness in my own bed, with absolutely no memory of our encounter.'

Foaly hid his grin behind a hairy hand.

'You're lucky you're not waking up in a cell,' said Holly.

'Still bitter, Captain Short? Can't we wipe the slate clean?'

Holly's glare was all the answer he needed.

Artemis sighed. 'Very well. I shall guess. There are humans trading with the Lower Elements. And you need Butler to track these merchants down. Close enough?'

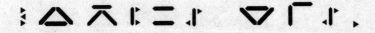

The fairies were silent for a moment. Hearing it from Fowl suddenly brought the reality home to them.

'Close enough,' admitted Root. 'OK, Foaly, bring Mud Boy up to speed.'

The consultant loaded a file from the LEP central server. A series of *Network News* clips flashed up on the plasma screen. The reporter was a middle-aged elf with a quiff the size of a Honolulu roller.

'Downtown Haven,' crooned the reporter. 'Another contraband seizure by the LEP. Hollywood laser disks with an estimated street value of five hundred gold grams. The B'wa Kell goblin triad is suspected.'

'It gets worse,' said Root grimly.

Artemis smiled. 'There's worse?'

The reporter appeared again. This time flames billowed from the windows of a warehouse behind him. His quiff looked a bit crispy.

'Tonight the B'wa Kell has staked its claim to the East Bank by torching a warehouse used by Koboi Laboratories. Apparently the *pixie with the golden touch* refused to pay the triad's protection fee.'

The flames were replaced by another news bite, this time featuring an angry mob.

'Controversy today outside Police Plaza as the public protest at the LEP's failure to deal with the goblin problem. Many ancient houses have been put out of business by the B'wa Kell's racketeering. Most heavily targeted has been Koboi Laboratories, which has suffered six counts of sabotage in the past month alone.'

Foaly froze the image. The public did not look happy.

'The thing you have to understand, Fowl, is that goblins are dumb. I'm not insulting them. It's scientifically proven. Brains no bigger than rats.'

Artemis nodded. 'So who's organizing them?'

Root ground out his cigar. 'We don't know. But it's getting worse. The B'wa Kell has graduated from petty crime to an all-out war on the police. Last night we intercepted a delivery of batteries from the surface. These batteries are being used to power outlawed Softnose laser weapons.'

'And Captain Short thought that I might be the Mud Man on the other end of the deal.'

'Can you blame me?' muttered Holly.

Artemis ignored the comment. 'How do you know the goblins aren't just ripping off wholesalers? After all, batteries are rarely under guard.'

Foaly chuckled. 'No, I don't think you understand just how stupid goblins are. Let me give you an example. One of the B'wa Kell generals, and this is their top fairy, was caught trying to pass off forged credit slips by signing his own name. No, whoever is behind this would need a human contact to make sure the deals weren't fouled up.'

'So you'd like me to find out who this human contact

is,' said Artemis. 'And more importantly, how much he knows.'

As he spoke, Artemis's mind was racing. He could work this entire situation to his advantage. The People's powers would be valuable aces to hold in a negotiation with mobsters. The seeds of a plan began to sprout in his brain.

Root nodded reluctantly. 'That's it. I can't risk putting LEPrecon agents above ground. Who knows what technology the goblins have traded. I could be walking my men into a trap. As humans, you could both blend in.'

'Butler blend in?' said Artemis, smiling. 'I doubt it.'

'At least he doesn't have four legs and a tail,' observed Foaly.

'Point taken. And there is no doubt that if any man alive can track down your rogue trader, it's Butler. But …'

Here we go, thought Holly. Artemis Fowl does nothing for nothing.

'But?' prompted Root.

'But if you want my help, I will require something in return.'

'What exactly?' said Root warily.

'I need transport to Russia,' replied Artemis. 'The Arctic Circle to be precise. And I need help with a rescue attempt.'

Root frowned. 'Northern Russia is not good for us. We can't shield there because of the radiation.'

'Those are my conditions,' said Artemis. 'The man I intend to rescue is my father. For all I know, it's already too late. So I really don't have time to negotiate.'

The Mud Boy sounded sincere. Even Holly's heart softened for a moment. But you never knew with Artemis Fowl – this could all be part of yet another scheme. Root made an executive decision.

'Deal,' he said, holding out his hand.

They shook. Fairy and human. A historic moment.

'Good,' said Root. 'Now, Foaly, wake the big one and give that goblin shuttle a quick systems check.'

'What about me?' asked Holly. 'Back on stakeout duty?'

If Root had not been a commander, he probably would have cackled. 'Oh no, Captain. You're the best shuttle pilot we have. You're going to Paris.'

CHAPTER 5: **DADDY'S GIRL**

 KOBOI Laboratories was carved from the rock of Haven's East Bank. It stood eight storeys high, surrounded by half a mile of granite on five sides, with access from the front only. Management had beefed up their security, and who could blame them? After all, the B'wa Kell had specifically targeted Koboi for arson attacks. The Council had gone so far as to grant the company special weapons permits – if Koboi went under, the entire Haven City defence network went under with it.

Any B'wa Kell goblins attempting to storm Koboi Laboratories would have been met with DNA-coded stun cannons, which scanned an intruder before blasting him.

There were no blind spots in the building, no place to hide. The system was foolproof.

But the goblins didn't have to worry about that. The Laboratories' defences were actually designed to keep out any LEP officers who might come snooping around at the wrong moment. It was Opal Koboi herself who was funding the goblin triad. The attacks on Koboi were actually a smokescreen to divert suspicions away from her own personal dealings: the tiny pixie was the mastermind behind the battery operation and the increased B'wa Kell activity. Well, one of the masterminds. But why would an individual of almost limitless wealth possibly wish to associate with a goblin tunnel gang?

Since the day of her birth, nothing much had ever been expected of Opal Koboi. Born to a family of old-money pixies on Principality Hill, her parents would have been quite content had young Opal done nothing more than attend private school, complete some wishy-washy Arts degree and marry a suitable vice-president.

In fact, as far as her father, Ferall Koboi, was concerned, a dream daughter would have been moderately intelligent, quite pretty and, of course, complacent. But Opal did not display the personality traits Ferall would have wished for. By the age of ten months she was already walking unaided, by a year and a half she had a vocabulary of over five hundred words.

Before her second birthday she had dismantled her first hard drive.

Opal grew to be precocious, headstrong and beautiful. A dangerous combination. Ferall lost count of the times he sat his daughter down, advising her to leave business to the male pixies. Eventually Opal refused to see him at all. Her blatant hostility was worrying.

Ferall was right to be worried. Opal's first action in college was to ditch her History of Art degree in favour of the male-dominated Brotherhood of Engineers Masters. No sooner was the scroll in her hand than Opal set up shop in direct opposition to her father. Patents quickly followed. An engine muffler that doubled as an energy streamliner, a 3D entertainment system and, of course, her speciality, the DoubleDex wing series.

Once Opal had destroyed her father's business, she proceeded to buy shares in it at rock-bottom prices, and then incorporated her businesses under the banner of Koboi Laboratories. Within five years, Koboi Laboratories held more defence contracts than any other company. Within ten years, Opal Koboi had personally registered more patents than any fairy alive. Except the centaur Foaly.

But it wasn't enough. Opal Koboi yearned for the kind of power that hadn't been held by any single fairy since the days of the monarchy. Luckily, she knew someone who might be able to assist her with that particular ambition. A disillusioned officer in the LEP, and a classmate from her college days. A certain Briar Cudgeon ...

Briar had good reason to despise the LEP; after all, they had allowed his public humiliation at the hands of Julius Root to go unpunished. Not only that, but he had been stripped of his commander's acorns after his disastrous involvement in the Artemis Fowl Affair ...

It had been a simple matter for Opal to slip a truth pill into Cudgeon's drink in one of Haven's swankier eateries. To her glee, she found that the delightfully twisted Cudgeon was already formulating a plan to topple the LEP. Quite an ingenious plan as it happened. All he needed was a partner. One with large reserves of gold and a secure facility at her disposal. Opal was happy to supply both.

Opal was curled, catlike, in her hoverchair, eavesdropping on the goings-on in Police Plaza when Cudgeon entered the facility. She had installed mole cameras in the LEP network when her engineers were upgrading their system. The units operated on precisely the same frequency as Police Plaza's own surveillance cameras, plus they drew power from the heat leaking from the LEP's fibre optics. Completely undetectable.

'Well?' demanded Cudgeon, with customary bluntness.

Koboi didn't bother to turn around. It had to be Briar. Only he had the necessary access chip to the inner sanctum, implanted in his knuckle.

'We lost the last shipment of power cells. A routine LEP stakeout. Bad luck.'

'D'Arvit!' swore Cudgeon. 'Still, no matter. We have enough stored. And to the LEP, they are simply batteries after all.'

Opal took a breath. 'The goblins were armed ...'

'Don't tell me.'

'With Softnoses.'

Cudgeon pounded a worktop. 'Those idiots! I warned them not to use those weapons. Now Julius will know something is afoot.'

'He may know,' said Opal placatingly. 'But he is powerless to stop us. By the time they figure it out, it will already be too late.'

Cudgeon did not smile. He hadn't in over a year. Instead his scowl grew more pronounced.

'Good. My time is at hand ... Perhaps we should have simply manufactured the batteries ourselves,' he mused.

'No. Just to build a factory would have set us back two years, and there's no guarantee that Foaly wouldn't have discovered it. We had no choice.'

Koboi swivelled to face her partner. 'You look terrible. Have you been using that ointment I gave you?'

Cudgeon rubbed his head tenderly. It was bubbled with

horrific lumps. 'It doesn't work. There's cortisone in it. I'm allergic.'

Cudgeon's condition was unusual, perhaps unique. The previous year he had been sedated by Commander Root during the Fowl Manor siege. Unfortunately, the tranquillizer had reacted badly with some banned mind-accelerating substances the former acting-commander had been experimenting with. Cudgeon was left with a forehead like melted tar, plus a droopy eye. Ugly and demoted, not a great combination.

'You should get those boils lanced. I can barely stand the sight of you.'

Sometimes Opal Koboi forgot who she was talking to. Briar Cudgeon was not the usual corporate lackey. He calmly drew a customized Redboy blaster, firing two bursts into the hoverchair's arm. The contraption whirled across the stippled rubber tiles, coming to rest leaving Opal sprawled across a bank of hard drives.

The disgraced LEP elf caught Opal by the pointed chin. 'You better get used to looking at me, my dear Opal. Because soon this face will be on every view screen under this planet, *and* on top of it.'

The tiny pixie curled her fingers into a fist. She was unaccustomed to insubordination, not to mention actual violence. But at moments like this she could see the madness in Cudgeon's eyes. The drugs had cost him more than his magic and looks, they had cost him his mind.

And suddenly he was himself again, graciously helping her up as though nothing had happened.

'Now, my dear, progress report. The B'wa Kell is eager for blood.'

Opal smoothed the front of her catsuit. 'Captain Short is escorting the human, Artemis Fowl, to E37.'

'Fowl is here?' exclaimed Cudgeon. 'Of course! I should have guessed that he would be suspected. This is perfect! Our human slave will take care of him – Carrère has been mesmerized. I still have *that* power.'

Koboi applied a layer of blood-red lipstick. 'There could be trouble if Carrère is captured.'

'Don't worry,' Cudgeon assured her. 'Monsieur Carrère has been mesmerized so many times that his mind is blanker than a wiped disk. He couldn't tell any tales, even if he wanted to. Then, once he has done our dirty work for us, the French police will lock him up in a nice padded cell.'

Opal giggled. For someone who never smiled, Cudgeon had a delicious sense of humour.

CHAPTER 6: **PHOTO OPPORTUNITY**

 THE unlikely allies took the goblin shuttle up E37. Holly was none too pleased. First of all, she was being ordered to work with public-enemy number one, Artemis Fowl. And secondly, the goblin shuttle was held together by spit and prayers.

Holly hooked a com rig over one pointy ear. 'Hey, Foaly? You there?'

'Right here, Captain.'

'Remind me again why I'm flying this old slammer.'

LEPrecon pilots referred to suspect shuttles as *slammers* because of their alarming tendency to slam into the chute walls.

'The reason you're flying that old slammer, Captain, is that the goblins built this shuttle inside the port, and all three of the original access ramps were removed years ago. It would take days to get a new rig in there. So, I'm afraid we're stuck with the goblin ship.'

Holly strapped herself into the pilot's wraparound seat. The thruster toggles almost seemed to jump into her hands. For a split second, Captain Short's natural good humour returned. She was an ace pilot, top of her class in the Academy. On her final assessment, Wing Commander Vinyáya had written that *Cadet Short could fly a shuttle pod through the gap in your teeth*. It was a compliment with a sting in the tail. On her first try-out in a pod, Holly had lost control, crash-landing the craft two metres from Vinyáya's nose.

So, for five seconds, Holly was happy. Then she remembered who her passengers were.

'I wonder, could you tell me,' said Artemis, settling into the co-pilot's chair, 'how close the Russian terminal is to Murmansk?'

'Civilians behind the yellow line,' growled Holly, ignoring the enquiry.

Artemis pressed on. 'This is important to me. I am trying to plan a rescue.'

Holly grinned tightly. 'There's so much irony here, I could write a poem. The kidnapper looking for help with a kidnapping.'

Artemis rubbed his temples. 'Holly, I am a criminal. It's what I do best. When I abducted you, I was thinking only of the ransom. You were never supposed to be in any danger.'

'Oh really?' said Holly. 'Apart from bio-bombs and trolls.'

'True,' admitted Artemis. 'Sometimes plans don't translate smoothly from paper to real life.' He paused, cleaning some non-existent dirt from his manicured nails. 'I have matured, Captain. This is my father. I need all the information I can gather before facing the Mafiya.'

Holly relented. It wasn't easy growing up without a father. She knew. Her own father had passed away when she was barely sixty. More than twenty years ago now.

'OK, Mud Boy, listen up. I'm only saying this once.'

Artemis sat up. Butler stooped as he entered the cockpit. He could smell a war story.

'Over the past two centuries, with the advances in human technology, the LEP have been forced to shut down over sixty terminals. We pulled out of northern Russia in the sixties. The entire Kola peninsula is a nuclear disaster. The People have no tolerance to radiation, we never built up a resistance. In truth, there wasn't much to close down. Just a Grade Three terminal and a couple of cloaking projectors. The People aren't very fond of the Arctic. A bit frosty. Everybody was glad to be leaving. So, to answer your question: there's one unmanned terminal, with little or no above-ground facilities, located about twenty klicks north of Murmansk –'

Foaly's voice blurted from the intercom, interrupting what was dangerously close to a civil conversation. 'OK, Captain. You've got a clear run to the subway. There's still a bit of waffle from the last flare, so go easy.'

Holly pulled down her mouth mike. 'Roger that, Foaly. Have the rad suits ready when I get back. We're on a tight schedule.'

Foaly chuckled. 'Take it easy on the thrusters, Holly. Technically, this is Artemis's first time in the chutes, seeing as he and Butler were mesmerized on the way down. We wouldn't want him getting a fright.'

Holly gunned the throttle quite a bit more than was absolutely necessary. 'No,' she growled. 'We wouldn't want him getting a fright.'

Artemis decided to strap on his restraining harness. A good idea, as it turned out.

Captain Short gunned the makeshift shuttle down the magnetized approach rail. The fins shook, sending twin waves of sparks cascading past the portholes. Holly adjusted the internal gyroscopes, otherwise there'd be Mud People vomiting all over the cockpit.

Holly's thumbs hovered over the turbo buttons. 'OK. Well, let's see what this bucket can do.'

'Don't go trying for any records, Holly,' said Foaly over the speakers. 'That ship is not built for speed. I've seen more aerodynamic dwarfs.'

Holly grunted. After all, what was the point in flying

slowly? None whatsoever. And if you happened to terrify a few Mud Men along the way, well, that was just an added bonus.

The service tunnel opened on to the main chute. Artemis gasped. It was an awe-inspiring sight. You could drop Mount Everest down this chute and it wouldn't even hit the sides. A deep red glow pulsed from the Earth's core like the fires of hell, and the constant crack of contracting rock smacked the hull like physical blows.

Holly fired up all four flight engines, tumbling the shuttle into the abyss. Her worries evaporated like the eddies of mist swirling around the cockpit. It was a fly-boy thing. The lower you went without pulling out of the dive, the tougher you were. Even the fiery demise of Retrieval Officer Bom Arbles couldn't stop the LEP pilots core diving. Holly held the current record. Five hundred metres from the Earth's core before dipping the flaps. That had cost her two weeks' suspension, plus a hefty fine.

Not today though. No records in a slammer. With the g-force rippling the skin on her cheeks, Holly dragged the joysticks back, pulling the nose out of vertical. It gave her no small satisfaction to hear both humans sigh with relief.

'OK, Foaly, we're on the up 'n' up. What's the situation above ground?'

She could hear Foaly tapping a keyboard. 'Sorry, Holly. I can't get a lock on any of our surface equipment. Too much radiation from the last flare. You're on your own.'

Holly eyed the two pale humans in the cockpit.

On my own, she thought. I wish.

PARIS, FRANCE

So, if Artemis wasn't the human helping Cudgeon in his quest to arm the B'wa Kell, who was? Some tyrannical dictator? Perhaps a disgruntled general with access to an unlimited supply of power cells? Well, no. Not exactly.

Luc Carrère was responsible for selling batteries to the B'wa Kell. Not that you'd know it to look at him. In fact, he didn't even know it himself. Luc was a small-time French private eye, who was well known for his inefficiency. In PI circles, it was said that Luc couldn't trace a golf ball in a barrel of mozzarella.

Cudgeon decided to use Luc for three reasons. One, Foaly's files showed that Carrère had a reputation as a wheeler-dealer. In spite of his ineptness as an investigator, Luc had a knack for laying his hand on whatever it was the client wanted to buy. Two, the man was greedy and had never been able to resist the lure of easy money. And three, Luc was stupid. And as every little fairy knows, weak minds are easier to mesmerize.

The fact that he had located Carrère in Foaly's database was nearly enough to make Cudgeon smile. Of course,

Briar would have preferred not to have any human link in the chain. But a chain comprised completely of goblin links is one dumb chain.

Establishing contact with any Mud Man was not something Cudgeon took lightly. Deranged as he was, Briar was well aware of what would happen if the humans got wind of a new market below ground. They would swarm to the Earth's core like an army of red-backed flesh-eating ants. Cudgeon was not ready to meet the humans head on. Not yet. Not until he had the might of the LEP behind him.

So instead, Cudgeon sent Luc Carrère a little package. First class, shielded goblin mail …

Luc Carrère had shuffled into his office apartment one July evening to find a small parcel lying on his desk. The package was nothing more than a FedEx delivery. Or something that looked very much like a FedEx delivery.

Luc slit the tape. Inside the box, cushioned on a nest of hundred-euro bills, was a small flat device of some kind. Like a portable CD player, but made from a strange black metal that seemed to absorb light. Luc would have shouted to reception and instructed his secretary to hold all calls. If he had had a reception. If he had had a secretary. Instead the PI began stuffing cash down his grease-stained shirt as though the notes would disappear.

Suddenly, the device popped open, clam-like, revealing

a micro-screen and speakers. A shadowy face appeared on the display. Though Luc could see nothing but a pair of red-rimmed eyes, that was enough to set goose bumps popping across his back.

Funny though, because when the face began to speak, Luc's worries slid away like an old snakeskin. How could he have been worried? This person was obviously a friend. What a lovely voice. Like a choir of angels, all on its own.

'*Luc Carrère?*'

Luc nearly cried. Poetry.

'*Oui.* It's me.'

'*Bonsoir. Do you see the money, Luc? It's all yours.*' Sixty miles below ground, Cudgeon almost smiled. This was easier than expected. He had been worried that the dribble of power left in his brain wouldn't be sufficient to mesmerize the human. But this particular Mud Man seemed to have the will-power of a hungry hog faced with a trough of turnips.

Luc held two wads of cash in his fists. 'This money. It's mine? What do I have to do?'

'*Nothing. The money is yours. Do whatever you want.*'

Now Luc Carrère knew that there was no such thing as free cash, but that voice … That voice was truth in a micro-speaker.

'*But there's more. A lot more.*'

Luc stopped what he was doing, which was kissing a hundred-euro bill. 'More? How much more?'

The eyes seemed to glow crimson. '*As much as you want, Luc. But to get it, I need you to do me a favour.*'

Luc was hooked. 'Sure. What kind of favour?'

The voice emanating from the speaker was as clear as spring water. '*It's simple, not even illegal. I need batteries, Luc. Thousands of batteries. Maybe millions. Do you think you can get them for me?*'

Luc thought about it for about two seconds. The banknotes were tickling his chin. As a matter of fact, he had a contact on the river who regularly shipped boatloads of hardware to the Middle East, including batteries. Luc was confident that some of those shipments could be diverted.

'Batteries. *Oui*, *certainment*, I could do that.'

And so it went on for several months. Luc Carrère hit his contact for every battery he could lay his hands on. It was a sweet deal. Luc would crate the cells up in his apartment and in the morning they would be gone. In their place would sit a fresh pile of bills. Of course, the euros were fake, run off on an old Koboi printer, but Luc couldn't tell the difference. Nobody outside the Treasury could.

Occasionally, the voice on the screen would make a special request. Some fire suits, for example. But hey, Luc was a player now. Nothing was more than a phone call away. In six months, Luc Carrère went from a one-room studio to a fancy loft apartment in St Germain. So naturally, the Sûreté and Interpol were building separate cases against him. But Luc wasn't to know that. All he knew was that for the first time in his corrupt life, he was riding the gravy train.

One morning there was another parcel on his new marble-topped desk. Bigger this time. Bulkier. But Luc wasn't worried. It was probably more money.

Luc popped the top to reveal an aluminium case and a second communicator. The eyes were waiting for him.

'*Bonjour, Luc. Ça va?*'

'*Bien,*' replied Luc, mesmerized from the first syllable.

'*I have a special assignment for you today. Do this right and you will never have to worry about money again. Your tool is in the case.*'

'What is it?' asked the PI nervously. The instrument looked like a weapon and, even though Luc was mesmerized, Cudgeon did not have enough magic to completely suppress the Parisian's nature. The PI may have been devious, but he was no killer.

'*It's a special camera, Luc, that's all. If you pull that thing that looks like a trigger, it takes a picture,*' said Cudgeon.

'Oh,' said Luc Carrère blearily.

'*Some friends of mine are coming to visit you. And I want you to take their picture. It's just a game we play.*'

'How will I know your friends?' asked Luc. 'A lot of people visit me.'

'*They will ask about the batteries. If they ask about the*

batteries, then you take their picture.'

'Sure. Great.' And it was great. Because the voice would never make him do anything wrong. The voice was his friend.

E37 SHUTTLE PORT

Holly steered the slammer through the chute's final section. A proximity sensor in the shuttle's nose set off the landing lights.

'Hmm,' muttered Holly.

Artemis squinted through the quartz windscreen. 'A problem?'

'No. It's just that those lights shouldn't be working. There hasn't been a power source in the terminal since the last century.'

'Our goblin friends, I presume.'

Holly frowned. 'Doubtful. It takes half a dozen goblins to turn on a glow cube. Wiring a shuttle port takes real know-how. Elfin know-how.'

'The plot thickens,' said Artemis. If he'd had a beard, he would have stroked it. 'I smell a traitor. Now, who would have access to all this technology and a motive for selling it?'

Holly pointed the shuttle's cone towards the landing nodes. 'We'll find out soon enough. You just get me a live trader, and my *mesmer* will soon have him spilling his guts.'

The shuttle docked with a pneumatic hiss as the bay's rubber collar formed an airtight seal around the outer hull.

Butler was out of his chair before the seat-belt light winked off, ready for action.

'Just don't kill anyone,' warned Holly. 'That's not how the LEP likes to operate. Anyway, dead Mud Men don't rat on their partners.'

She brought up a schematic on the wall-screen. It depicted Paris's old city. 'OK,' she said, pointing to a bridge across the Seine. 'We're here. Under this bridge, sixty metres from Notre-Dame. The cathedral, not the football team. The dock is disguised as a bridge support. Stand in the doorway until I give you a green light. We have to be careful here. The last thing we need is some Parisian seeing you emerging from a brick wall.'

'You're not accompanying us?' asked Artemis.

'Orders,' said Holly, scowling. 'Apparently this could be a trap. Who knows what hardware is pointed at the terminal door? Lucky for you, you're expendable. Irish tourists on holiday, you'll fit right in.'

'Lucky us. What leads do we have?'

Holly slid a disk into the console. 'Foaly stuck his Retimager on the goblin prisoner. Apparently he has seen this human.'

The captain brought up a mugshot on the screen. 'Foaly got a match on his Interpol files. Luc Carrère. Disbarred attorney, does a bit of PI work.'

She printed off a card. 'Here's his address. He just moved to a swanky new apartment. It could be nothing, but at least we have somewhere to start. I need you to immobilize him, and show him this.' Holly handed the bodyguard what looked like a diver's watch.

'What is it?' asked the manservant.

'Just a com screen. You put it in front of Carrère's face and I can mesmerize the truth out of him from down here. It also contains one of Foaly's doodahs: a personal shield. The Safetynet. A prototype, you'll be delighted to know. You have the honour of testing it. Touch the screen, and the micro-reactor generates a two-metre diameter sphere of tri-phased light. No good for solids, but laser bursts or concussion shocks are OK.'

'Hmm,' said Butler doubtfully. 'We don't get a lot of laser bursts above ground.'

'Hey, don't use it. Do I care?'

Butler studied the tiny instrument. 'One-metre radius? What about the bits that are sticking out.'

Holly thumped the manservant playfully in the stomach. 'My advice to you, big man, is curl up in a ball.'

'I'll try to remember that,' said Butler, cinching the strap around his wrist. 'You two try not to kill each other while I'm gone.'

Artemis was surprised. It didn't happen very often. 'While *you're* gone? Surely you don't expect me to stay behind?'

Butler tapped his forehead. 'Don't worry, you'll see everything on the iris-cam.'

Artemis fumed for several moments, before settling back down into the co-pilot's seat. 'I know. I would only slow you down, and that, in turn, would slow down the search for my father.'

'Of course, if you insist …'

'No. This is no time for childishness.'

Butler smiled gently. Childishness was one thing Master Artemis was hardly likely to be accused of.

'How long do I have?'

Holly shrugged. 'As long as it takes. Obviously the sooner the better for everybody's sake.' She glanced at Artemis. 'Especially his father's.'

In spite of everything, Butler felt good. This was life at its most basic. The hunt. Not exactly Stone Age, not with a large semi-automatic weapon under his arm. But the principle was the same: the survival of the fittest. And there was no doubt in Butler's mind that he was the fittest.

He followed Holly's directions to a service ladder, scaling it quickly to the doorway above. He waited beside the metal door until the light above changed from red to green, and the camouflaged entrance slid noiselessly back. The bodyguard emerged cautiously. While it was likely that the bridge was deserted, he could hardly explain himself away as a homeless person, dressed as he was in a dark designer suit.

Butler felt a breeze play across the shaven dome of his crown. The morning air felt good, even after a few hours below ground. He could easily imagine how fairies must feel, forced out of their native environment by humans. From what Butler had seen, if the People ever decided to reclaim what was theirs, the battle wouldn't last long. But luckily for mankind, fairies were a peace-loving people, and not prepared to go to war over real estate.

The coast was clear. Butler stepped casually on to the riverside walkway, proceeding west towards the St Germain district.

A riverboat swept past on his right, ferrying a hundred tourists around the city. Butler automatically covered his face with a massive hand. Just in case some of those tourists had cameras pointed in his direction.

The bodyguard mounted a set of stone steps to the road above. Behind him the pointed spire of Notre-Dame rose into the sky, and to his left the Eiffel Tower's famous profile punctured the clouds. Butler strode confidently across the main road, nodding at several French ladies who stopped to stare. He was familiar with this area of Paris, having spent a month recuperating here after a

particularly dangerous assignment for the French Secret
Service.

Butler strolled along Rue Jacob. Even at this hour, cars
and lorries jammed the narrow street. Drivers leaned on
their horns, hanging from car windows, Gallic tempers
running wild. Mopeds dodged between bumpers, and
several pretty girls strolled past. Butler smiled. Paris. He
had forgotten.

Carrère's apartment was on Rue Bonaparte, opposite
the church. Apartments in St Germain cost more per
month than most Parisians made in a year. Butler ordered a
coffee and croissant at the Bonaparte cafe, settling himself
at an outside table. According to his calculations, it gave
him the perfect view of Monsieur Carrère's balcony.

Butler didn't have long to wait. In less than an hour, the
chunky Parisian appeared on the balcony, leaning on the
ornate railing for several minutes. He very obligingly
presented front and side views of himself.

Holly's voice sounded in Butler's ear. 'That's our boy. Is
he alone?'

'I can't tell,' muttered the bodyguard into his hand. The
flesh-tone mike glued to his throat would pick up any
vibrations and translate them for Holly.

'Just a sec.'

Butler heard a keyboard being tapped, and suddenly
the iris-cam in his eye sparked. The vision in one eye
jumped into a completely different spectrum.

'Heat-sensitive,' Holly informed him. 'Hot equals red. Cold equals blue. Not a very powerful system, but the lens should penetrate an outer wall.'

Butler cast a fresh eye over the apartment. There were three red objects in the room. One was Carrère's heart, which pulsed crimson in the centre of his pink body. The second appeared to be a kettle or possibly a coffee pot, and the third was a TV.

'OK. All clear, I'm going in.'

'Affirmative. Watch your step. This is a bit too convenient.'

'Agreed.'

Butler crossed the cobbled street to the four-storey apartment building. There was an intercom security system, but this structure was nineteenth century, and a solid shoulder at the right point popped the bolt right out of its housing.

'I'm in.'

There was noise on the stairs above. Someone coming this way. Butler wasn't unduly concerned. Nevertheless he slid a palm inside his jacket, fingers resting on his handgun's grip. It was unlikely he would need it. Even the most boisterous young bucks generally gave Butler a wide berth. Something to do with his merciless eyes. Being over two metres tall didn't hurt either.

A group of teenagers rounded the corner.

'*Excusez-moi*,' said Butler, gallantly stepping aside.

The girls giggled. The boys glared. One, a mono-eyebrowed rugby type, even thought about passing comment. Then Butler winked at him. It was a peculiar wink, somehow simultaneously cheerful and terrifying. No comments were passed.

Butler ascended to the fourth floor without incident. Carrère's apartment was on the gable end. Two walls of windows. Very expensive.

The bodyguard was considering his breaking and entering options when he noticed the door was open. Open doors generally meant one of two things: one, nobody was left alive to close it, or two, he was expected. Neither of these options appealed to him particularly.

Butler entered cautiously. The apartment walls were lined with open crates. Battery packs and fire suits poked through the Styrofoam packing. The floor was littered with thick wads of currency.

'Are you a friend?' It was Carrère. He was slumped in an oversized armchair, a weapon of some kind nestling in his lap.

Butler approached slowly. An important rule of combat is that every opponent is taken seriously.

'Take it easy.'

The Parisian raised the weapon. The grip was made for smaller fingers. A child, or a fairy. 'I asked if you were a friend.'

Butler cocked his own pistol. 'No need to shoot.'

'Stand still,' ordered Carrère. 'I'm not going to shoot you, just take your photo maybe. The voice told me.'

Holly's voice sounded in Butler's earpiece. 'Get closer. I need to see the eyes.'

Butler holstered his weapon, taking a step forward. 'You see, no one has to get hurt here.'

'I'm going to enhance the image,' said Holly. 'This may sting a bit.'

The tiny camera in his eye buzzed, and suddenly Butler's vision was magnified by four – which would have been just fine had the magnification not been accompanied by a sharp jolt of pain. Butler blinked back a stream of tears from his eye.

Below, in the goblin shuttle, Holly studied Luc's pupils. 'He's been mesmerized,' she pronounced. 'Several times. You see how the iris has actually become jagged. You mesmerize a human too much and they can go blind.'

Artemis studied the image. 'Is it safe to mesmerize him again?'

Holly shrugged. 'Doesn't matter. He's already under a spell. This particular individual is just following orders. His brain doesn't know a thing about it.'

Artemis grabbed the mike stand. 'Butler! Get out of there. Right now.'

In the apartment, Butler stood his ground. Any sudden movement might be his last.

'Butler,' said Holly. 'Listen carefully. That gun pointed

at you is a wide-bore low-frequency blaster. We call it a Bouncer. It was developed for tunnel skirmishes. If he pulls that trigger, a wide arc laser is going to ricochet off the walls until it hits something.'

'I see,' muttered Butler.

'What did you say?' asked Carrère.

'Nothing. I just don't like having my photo taken.'

A spark of Luc's greedy personality surfaced. 'I like that watch on your wrist. It looks expensive. Is it a Rolex?'

'You don't want this,' said Butler, very reluctant to part with the com screen. 'It's cheap. A piece of trash.'

'Just give me the watch.'

Butler peeled back the strap of the instrument on his wrist. 'If I give you this watch, maybe you can tell me about all these batteries.'

'It is you! Say cheese,' squealed Carrère, forcing his pudgy thumb into the undersized trigger guard and pumping for all he was worth.

For Butler, time seemed to slow to a crawl. It was almost as though he were inside his personal time-stop. His soldier's brain absorbed all the facts and analysed his options. Carrère's finger was too far gone. In a moment, a wide-bore laser burst would be speeding his way, and would continue to bounce around the room until they were both dead. His gun was of no use in a situation like this. All he had was the Safetynet, but a two-metre sphere was not going to be enough. Not for two good-sized humans.

So, in the fraction of a second left to him, Butler formulated a new strategy. If the sphere could stop concussive waves coming towards him, perhaps it could stop them coming out of the blaster. Butler touched the screen of the Safetynet, and hurled the device in Carrère's direction.

Not a nanosecond too soon, a spherical shield blossomed, enveloping the expanding beam from Carrère's blaster: 360 degrees of protection. It was a sight to see, a fireworks display in a bubble. The shield hovered in the air, shafts of light ricocheting against the sphere's curved planes.

Carrère was hypnotized by the sight, and Butler took advantage of the distraction to disarm him.

'Start the engines,' grunted the bodyguard into his throat mike. 'The Sûreté are going to be all over this place in minutes. Foaly's Safetynet didn't stop the noise.'

'Roger that. What about Monsieur Carrère?'

Butler dumped the dazed Parisian flat on the carpet. 'Luc and I are going to have a little chat.'

For the first time Carrère seemed to be aware of his surroundings.

'Who are you?' he mumbled. 'What's happening?'

Butler ripped open the man's shirt, placing his palm flat on the PI's heart. Time for a little trick he'd learned from Madame Ko, his Japanese sensei. 'Don't worry,

Monsieur Carrère. I'm a doctor. There's been an accident, but you're perfectly fine.'

'An accident? I don't remember any accident.'

'Trauma. It's quite normal. I'm just going to check your vitals.'

Butler placed a thumb on Luc's neck, locating the artery. 'I'm going to ask you a few questions, to check for concussion.'

Luc didn't argue. Then again, who'd argue with a two-metre-plus Eurasian with muscles like a Michelangelo statue?

'Is your name Luc Carrère?'

'Yes.'

Butler noted the pulse rate. One from the heartbeat, and a second reference on the carotid artery. Steady, in spite of the accident.

'Are you a private eye?'

'I prefer the title investigator.'

No increase in pulse rate. The man was telling the truth.

'Have you ever sold batteries to a mystery buyer?'

'No, I have not,' protested Luc. 'What kind of doctor are you?'

The man's pulse sky-rocketed. He was lying.

'Answer the questions, Monsieur Carrère,' said Butler sternly. 'Just one more. Have you ever had dealings with goblins?'

Relief flooded through Luc. The police did not ask questions about fairies. 'What are you? Crazy? Goblins? I don't know what you're talking about.'

Butler closed his eyes, concentrating on the pounding beneath his thumb and palm. Luc's pulse had settled. He was telling the truth. He had never had any direct dealings with the goblins. Obviously the B'wa Kell wasn't *that* stupid.

Butler stood up, pocketing the Bouncer. He could hear the sirens on the street below.

'Hey, Doctor,' protested Luc. 'You can't just leave me like this.'

Butler eyed him coldly. 'I would take you with me, but the police will want to know why your apartment is full of what I suspect are counterfeit bills.'

Luc could only watch with his mouth open as the giant figure disappeared into the corridor. He knew he should run, but Luc Carrère hadn't run more than fifty metres since gym class in the nineteen seventies, and anyway, his legs had suddenly turned to jelly. The thought of a long stretch in prison can do that to a person.

CHAPTER 7: JOINING THE DOTS

 ROOT pointed the finger of authority at Holly.

'Congratulations, Captain. You managed to lose some LEP technology.'

Holly was ready for that one. 'Not strictly my fault, sir. The human was mesmerized and you ordered me not to leave the shuttle. I had no control over the situation.'

'Ten out of ten,' commented Foaly. 'Good answer. Anyway the Safetynet has a self-destruct, like everything I send into the field.'

'Quiet, civilian,' snapped the commander.

But there was no venom in the LEP officer's rebuke. He was relieved; they all were. The human threat had been contained, and without the loss of a single life.

They were gathered in a conference room reserved for

civilian committees. Generally debriefings of this importance would be held in the Operations' Centre, but the LEP was not ready to show Artemis Fowl the nerve centre of its defences just yet.

Root jabbed an intercom button on the desk.

'Trouble, are you out there?'

'Yessir.'

'OK. Now listen, I want you to stand down the alert. Send the teams into the deep tunnels, see if we can't root out a few goblin gangs. There are still plenty of loose ends: who's organizing the B'wa Kell for one, and for what reason?'

Artemis knew he shouldn't say anything. The sooner his side of the bargain was completed, the sooner he could be in the Arctic. But the entire Paris scenario seemed suspicious.

'Does anyone else think this is too neat? It's just what you all wanted to happen. Not to mention the fact that there could be more mesmerized humans up there.'

Root did not appreciate being lectured by a Mud Boy. Especially this particular Mud Boy.

'Look, Fowl, you've done what we asked. The Paris connection has been broken off. There won't be any more illegal shipments coming down that chute, I assure you. In fact, we have doubled security on all chutes, whether they're operational or not. The important thing is that whoever is trading with the humans hasn't told them about the People. There will, of course, be a major investigation, but that's an internal problem. So don't you worry your juvenile head about it. Concentrate on growing some bristles.'

Foaly interrupted before Artemis could respond. 'About Russia,' he said, hurriedly placing his torso between Artemis and the commander. 'I've got a lead.'

'You traced the e-mail?' said Artemis, his attention switching immediately to the centaur.

'Exactly,' confirmed Foaly, launching into lecture mode.

'But it's been spiked. Untraceable.'

Foaly chuckled openly. 'Spiked? Don't make me laugh. You Mud Men and your communications systems. You're still using wires, for heaven's sake. If it's been sent, I can trace it.'

'So, where did you trace it to?'

'Every computer has a signature, as individual as a fingerprint,' continued Foaly. 'Networks too. They leave micro-traces, depending on the age of the wiring. Everything is molecular, and if you pack gigabytes of data into a little cable, some of that cable is going to wear off.'

Butler was growing impatient. 'Listen, Foaly. Time is of the essence. Mister Fowl's life could hang in the balance. So get to the point before I start breaking things.'

The centaur's first impulse was to laugh. Surely the human was joking? Then he remembered what Butler had done to Trouble Kelp's Retrieval squad, and decided to proceed directly to the point.

'Very well, Mud Man. Keep your hair on.'

Well, almost directly to the point.

'I put the MPEG through my filters. Uranium residue points to northern Russia.'

'Now there's a shock.'

'I'm not finished,' said Foaly. 'Watch and learn.'

The centaur brought up a satellite photo of the Arctic Circle on the wall-screen. With every keystroke, the highlighted area shrank.

'Uranium means Severomorsk. Or somewhere within fifty miles. The copper wiring is from an old network. Early twentieth century, patched up over the years. The only match is Murmansk. As easy as joining the dots.'

Artemis sat forward in his chair.

'There are two hundred and eighty-four thousand landlines on that network.' Foaly had to stop for a laugh. '*Landlines*. Barbarians.'

Butler cracked his knuckles loudly.

'Ah, so two hundred and eighty-four thousand landlines. I wrote a program to search for hits on our MPEG. Two possible matches. One, the Hall of Justice.'

'Not likely. The other?'

'The other line is registered to a Mikhael Vassikin on Lenin Prospekt.'

Artemis felt his stomach churn. 'And what do we know about Mikhael Vassikin?'

Foaly wiggled his fingers like a concert pianist. 'I ran a search on my own intelligence files archives. I like to keep tabs on Mud People's so-called intelligence agencies. Quite a few mentions of you by the way, Butler.'

The manservant tried to look innocent, but his facial muscles couldn't quite pull it off.

'Mikhael Vassikin is ex-KGB, now working for the Mafiya. The official term is *khuligany*. An enforcer. Not high level, but not street trash either. Vassikin's boss is a Murmansker known as Britva. The group's main source of income is the kidnapping of European businessmen. In the past five years they have abducted six Germans and a Swede.'

'How many were recovered alive?' asked Artemis, his voice a whisper.

Foaly consulted his statistics. 'None,' he said. 'And in two cases, the negotiators went missing. Eight million dollars in lost ransom.'

Butler struggled from a tiny fairy chair. 'Right, enough talk. I think it's time Mister Vassikin was introduced to my friend, Mister Fist.'

Melodramatic, thought Artemis. But I couldn't have put it better myself.

'Yes, old friend. Soon enough. But I have no wish to add you to the list of lost negotiators. These men are smart. So we must be smarter. We have advantages that none of our predecessors had. We know who the kidnapper is, we know where he lives and, most importantly, we have fairy magic.' Artemis glanced at Commander Root. 'We do have fairy magic, don't we?'

'You have this fairy at any rate,' replied the commander. 'I won't force any of my people to go to Russia. But I could use some back-up.' He glanced at Holly. 'What do you think?'

'Of course I'm coming,' said Holly. 'I'm the best shuttle pilot you have.'

KOBOI LABORATORIES

There was a firing range in the Koboi Labs' basement. Opal had it constructed to her exact specifications. It incorporated her 3D projection system, was completely soundproof and was mounted on gyroscopes. You could drop an elephant from twenty metres in there and no seismograph under the world would detect so much as a shudder.

The purpose of the firing range was to give the B'wa Kell somewhere to practise with their Softnose lasers before the operation began in earnest. But it was Briar Cudgeon who had logged more hours on the simulators than anyone else. He seemed to spend every spare minute fighting virtual battles with his nemesis, Commander Julius Root.

When Opal found him, he was pumping shells from his prized Softnose Redboy into a 3D holoscreen running one of Root's old training films. It was pathetic really; a fact she didn't bother mentioning.

Cudgeon twisted out his earplugs. 'So. Who died?'

Opal handed him a video pad. 'This just came in on the spy cameras. Carrère proved as inept as usual. Everyone survived but, as you predicted, Root has called off the alert. And now the commander has agreed to personally escort the humans to northern Russia, inside the Arctic Circle.'

'I know where northern Russia is,' Cudgeon snapped. He paused, stroking his bubbled forehead thoughtfully for several moments. 'This could turn out to our advantage. Now we have the perfect opportunity to eliminate the commander. With Julius out of the way, the LEP will be like a headless stink worm. Especially with their surface communications down. Their communications *are* down I take it?'

'Of course,' replied Opal. 'The jammer is linked into the chute sensors. All interference with surface transmitters will be blamed on the magma flares.'

'Perfect,' said Cudgeon, his mouth twitching in what could almost be described as glee. 'I want you to disable all LEP weaponry now. No need to give Julius any advantages.'

When Koboi Laboratories had upgraded LEP weapons and transport, a tiny dot of solder had been included in each device. The solder was actually a mercury/glycerine solution that would detonate when a signal of the appropriate frequency was broadcast from the Koboi communications dish. LEP blasters would be useless, while the B'wa Kell would be armed to the teeth with Softnose lasers.

'Consider it done,' said Opal. 'Are you certain Root won't be returning? He could upset our entire plan.'

Cudgeon polished the Redboy on the leg of his uniform. 'Don't fret, my dear. Julius won't be coming back. Now that I know where he's going, I'll arrange for a little welcome party. I'm certain our scaly friends will be only too eager to oblige.'

The funny thing was that Briar Cudgeon didn't even *like* goblins. In fact, he detested them. They made his skin crawl with their reptilian ways. Their gas-burner breath, their lidless eyes and their constantly darting forked tongues.

But they did supply a certain something that Cudgeon needed: dumb muscle.

For centuries, the B'wa Kell triad had skulked around Haven's borders, vandalizing what they couldn't steal and fleecing any tourists stupid enough to stray off the beaten path. But they were never really any threat to society. Whenever they got too cheeky, Commander Root would send a team into the tunnels to flush out the culprits.

One evening, a disguised Briar Cudgeon strolled into The Second Skin, a notorious B'wa Kell hang-out, plonked an attaché case of gold ingots on the bar and said, 'I want to talk to the triad.'

Cudgeon was searched and blindfolded by several of the club's bouncers. When the tape came off his face, he was in a damp warehouse, walls lined with creeping moss. Three elderly goblins were seated across the table from him. He recognized them from their mugshots. Scalene, Sputa and Phlebum. The triad old guard.

The gift of gold, and the promise of more, were enough to pique their curiosity. His first utterance was carefully planned.

'Ah, Generals, I am honoured you greet me in person.'

The goblins puffed out their wrinkled old chests proudly. Generals?

The rest of Cudgeon's patter was equally smooth. He could 'help' organize the B'wa Kell, streamline it and, most importantly, arm it. Then, when the time was right, they would rise up and overthrow the Council and their lackeys, the LEP. Cudgeon promised that his first act as Governor General would be to free all the goblin prisoners in Howler's Peak. It didn't hurt that he subtly laced his speech with hints of the hypnotic *mesmer*.

It was an offer the goblins could not refuse. Gold, weapons, freedom for their brothers and, of course, a chance to crush the hated LEP. It never occurred to the B'wa Kell that Cudgeon could betray them just as easily as he had the LEP. They were as dumb as stink worms and twice as short-sighted.

Cudgeon met with General Scalene in a secret chamber beneath the Koboi Labs. He was in a foul mood following Luc's failure to put a scratch on any of his enemies. But there was always Plan B ... The B'wa Kell was always eager to kill someone. It didn't really matter who.

The goblin was excited, thirsty for blood. He panted blue flames like a broken heater. 'When do we go to war, Cudgeon? Tell us when?'

The elf kept his distance. He dreamed of the day when these stupid creatures would no longer be necessary.

'Soon, General Scalene. Very soon. But first I need a favour. It concerns Commander Root.'

The goblin's yellow eyes narrowed. 'Root? The hated one. Can we kill him? Can we crack his skull and fry his brains?'

Cudgeon smiled magnanimously. 'Certainly, General. All of these things. Once Root is dead, the city will fall easily.'

The goblin was bobbing now, jiggling with excitement. 'Where is he? Where is Root?'

'I don't know,' Cudgeon admitted. 'But I know where he will be in six hours.'

'Where? Tell me, elf!'

Cudgeon heaved a large case on to the table. It contained four pairs of Koboi DoubleDex. 'Chute 93. Take these, send your best hit squad. And tell them to wrap up warm.'

CHUTE E93

Julius Root always travelled in style. In this instance, he had commandeered the Atlantean ambassador's shuttle. All leather and gold. Seats softer than a gnome's behind, and drag buffers that negated all but the most serious jolts. Needless to say, the Atlantean ambassador hadn't been all that thrilled about handing over the starter chip. But it was difficult to refuse the commander when his fingers were drumming a tattoo on the tri-barrelled blaster strapped to his hip. So now the humans and their two elfin chaperones were climbing E93 in some considerable comfort.

Artemis helped himself to a still water from the chiller cabinet. 'This tastes unusual,' he commented. 'Not unpleasant, but different.'

'Clean is the word you're searching for,' said Holly. 'You wouldn't believe how many filters we have to put it through to purge the Mud People from it.'

'No bickering, Captain Short,' warned Root. 'We're on the same side now. I want a smooth mission. Now suit up, all of you. We won't last five minutes out there without protection.'

Holly cracked open an overhead locker. 'Fowl, front and centre.'

Artemis complied, a bemused smile twitching at his lips.

Holly pulled several cubic packages from the locker. 'What are you, about a six?'

Artemis shrugged. He wasn't familiar with the People's system of measurement.

'What? Artemis Fowl doesn't know? I thought you were the world's expert on the People. It was you who stole our Book last year, wasn't it?'

Artemis unwrapped the package. It was a suit of some ultra-light rubber polymer.

'Anti-radiation,' explained Holly. 'Your cells will thank me in fifty years, if you're still around.'

Artemis pulled the suit over his clothes. It shrank to fit like a second skin. 'Clever material.'

'Memory latex. Moulds itself to your shape, within reason. One use only unfortunately. Wear it and recycle it.'

Butler clinked over. He was carrying so much fairy weaponry that Foaly had supplied him with a Moonbelt. The belt reduced the effective weight of its attachments to one fifth of the Earth norm.

'What about me?' asked Butler, nodding at the rad suits.

Holly frowned. 'We don't have anything that big. Latex can only go so far.'

'Forget it. I've been in Russia before. It didn't kill me.'

'Not yet it hasn't. Give it time.'

Butler shrugged. 'What choice do I have?'

Holly smiled, and there was a nasty twist to it. 'Oh, I didn't say there wasn't a choice.'

She reached into the locker, pulling out a large pump 'n' spray can. And, for some reason, that little can scared Butler more than a bunker full of missiles.

'Now, hold still,' she said, aiming a gramophone-type nozzle at the bodyguard. 'This may stink worse than a hermit dwarf, but at least your skin won't glow in the dark.'

CHAPTER 8: TO RUSSIA WITH GLOVES

 MIKHAEL Vassikin was growing impatient. For over two years now he'd been on babysitting duty. At Britva's request. Not that it had actually been a request. The term *request* implied that you had a choice in the matter. You did not argue with Britva. You did not even protest quietly. The *Menidzher,* or manager, was from the old school where his word was law.

Britva's instructions had been simple: feed him, wash him and, if he doesn't come out of the coma in another year, kill him and dump the body in the Kola.

Two weeks before the deadline, the Irishman had bolted upright in his bed. He awoke screaming a name. That name was Angeline. Kamar got such a shock, he'd dropped the bottle of wine he'd been opening. The bottle smashed, piercing his Ferruci loafers and cracking a big toenail. Toenails grow back, but Ferruci loafers were hard to come by in the Arctic Circle. Mikhael had been forced to sit on his partner to stop him killing the hostage.

So now they were playing the waiting game. Kidnapping was an established business and there were rules. First you sent the teaser note, or in this case the e-mail. Wait a few days to give the pigeon a chance to put some funds together, then hit him with the ransom demand.

They were locked in Mikhael's apartment on Lenin Prospekt, waiting for the call from Britva. They didn't even dare to go out for air. Not that there was much to see. Murmansk was one of those Russian cities that had been poured directly from a concrete mould. The only time Lenin Prospekt looked good was when it was buried in snow.

Kamar emerged from the bedroom. His sharp features were stretched in disbelief. 'He wants caviar, can you believe it? I give him a nice bowl of stroganina and he wants caviar, the ungrateful *Irlanskii*.'

Mikhael rolled his eyes. 'I liked him better asleep.'

Kamar nodded, spitting into the fireplace. 'The sheets are too rough, he says. He's lucky I don't wrap him in a sack and roll him into the bay —'

The phone rang, interrupting his empty threats.

'This is it, my friend,' Vassikin said, clapping Kamar on the shoulder. 'We are on our way.'

Vassikin picked up the phone. 'Yes?'

'It's me,' said a voice, made tinny by old wiring.

'Mister Brit —'

'Shut up, idiot! Never use my name!'

Mikhael swallowed. The *Menidzher* didn't like to be connected to his various businesses. That meant no paperwork and no mention of his name if it could be recorded. It was his custom to make calls while driving around the city so that his location could not be triangulated.

'I'm sorry, boss.'

'You should be,' continued the Mafiya kingpin. 'Now listen, and don't talk. You have nothing to contribute.'

Vassikin covered the handset. 'Everything's fine,' he whispered, giving Kamar the thumbs up. 'We're doing a great job.'

'The Fowls are a clever outfit,' continued Britva. 'And I have no doubt they are concentrating on tracing the last e-mail.'

'But I spiked the last —'

'What did I tell you?'

'You said not to talk, Mister Brit … sir.'

'That's right. So send the ransom message and then move Fowl to the drop point.'

Mikhael paled. 'The drop point?'

'Yes, the drop point. No one will be looking for you there, I guarantee it.'

⁞Ϝ△ΙΓϟ⁞

'But –'

'Again with the talking! Get yourself a spine, man. It's only for a couple of days. So, you might lose a year off your life. It won't kill you.'

Vassikin's brain churned, searching for an excuse. Nothing came.

'OK, boss. Whatever you say.'

'That's right. Now listen to me. This is your big chance. Do this right and you move up a couple of steps in the organization.'

Vassikin grinned. A life of champagne and expensive cars beckoned.

'If this man really is young Fowl's father, the boy will pay up. When you get the money, dump them both in the Kola. I don't want any survivors to start a vendetta. Call me if there's any trouble.'

'OK, boss.'

'Oh, and one more thing.'

'Yes?'

'Don't call me.'

The line went dead. Vassikin was left staring at the handset as though it were a handful of plague virus.

'Well?' asked Kamar.

'We are to send the second message.'

A broad grin split Kamar's face. 'Excellent. At last this thing is nearly over.'

'Then we are to move the package to the drop zone.'

The broad grin disappeared like a fox down a hole. 'What? Now?'

'Yes. Now.'

Kamar paced the tiny living room. 'That is crazy. Completely insane. Fowl cannot be here for a couple of days at the earliest. There's no need for us to spend two days breathing in that poison. What is the reasoning?'

Mikhael extended the phone. 'You tell him. I'm sure the *Menidzher* will appreciate being told he is a madman.'

Kamar sank on to the threadbare sofa, dropping his head into his hands. 'Will this thing never end?'

His partner fired up their ancient sixteen-megabyte hard drive. 'I don't know for certain,' he said, sending the pre-prepared message. 'But I do know what will happen if we don't do what Britva says.'

Kamar sighed. 'I think I'll go shout at the prisoner for a while.'

'Will that help?'

'It won't,' admitted Kamar. 'But it will make me feel better.'

E93, ARCTIC SHUTTLE PORT

The Arctic Station had never been high on the fairy tourist list. Sure, icebergs and polar bears were pretty, but nothing was worth saturating your lungs with irradiated air for.

Holly docked the shuttle in the only serviceable bay. The terminal itself resembled nothing more than a deserted warehouse. Static conveyer belts snaked along the floor and low-level heating pipes rattled with insect life.

Holly handed out human overcoats and gloves from an ancient locker.

'Wrap up, Mud Boys. It's cold outside.'

Artemis did not need to be told. The terminal's solar batteries had long since shut down, and the ice's grip had cracked the walls like a nut in a vice.

Holly tossed Butler his coat from a distance. 'You know something, Butler? You stink!' she said, laughing.

The manservant growled. 'You and your radiation gel. I think my skin's changed colour.'

'Don't worry about it. Fifty years and it'll wash right off.'

Butler buttoned a Cossack greatcoat up to his neck. 'I don't know why you're getting all wrapped up. You've got the fancy suits.'

'The coats are camouflage,' explained Holly, smearing rad gel on her face and neck. 'If we shield, the vibration makes the suits useless. Might as well dip your bones in a reactor core. So for tonight only, we're all humans.'

Artemis frowned. If the fairies couldn't shield, it would make rescuing his father all the more difficult. His evolving plan would have to be adjusted.

'Less of the chat,' growled Root, pulling a bearskin hat

over his pointed ears. 'We move out in five. I want everybody armed and dangerous. Even you, Fowl, if your little wrists can support a weapon.'

Artemis selected a fairy handgun from the shuttle's arsenal. He jacked the battery into its slot, flicking the setting up to three.

'Don't worry about me, Commander. I've been practising. We have quite a stash of LEP weaponry at the manor.'

Root's complexion cranked up one more notch. 'Well, there's a big difference between stunning a cardboard cut-out and a real person.'

Artemis gave his vampire smile. 'If everything proceeds according to plan, there will be no need for weapons. The first stage is simplicity itself: we set up a surveillance post near Vassikin's apartment. When the opportunity arises, Butler will snatch our Russian friend and the five of us can have a little chat. I'm sure that he will tell us everything we need to know under the influence of your *mesmer*. Then, it will be a simple matter to stun any guards and rescue my father.'

Root pulled a heavy scarf over his mouth. 'And what if things don't go according to plan?'

Artemis's eyes were cold and determined. 'Then, Commander, we will have to improvise.'

Holly felt a shiver rattle around her stomach. And it had nothing to do with the climate.

*

The terminal was buried twenty metres below an ice pack. They took the courtesy elevator to the surface, and the party emerged into the Arctic night looking for all the world like an adult and three children. Albeit three children with inhuman weaponry clanking under every loose fold of cloth.

Holly checked the GPS locator on her wrist. 'We're in the Rosta district, Commander. Twenty klicks north of Murmansk.'

'What's Foaly got on the weather? I don't want to be caught in the middle of a blizzard miles from our destination.'

'No luck. I can't get a line. Magma flares must still be up.'

'D'Arvit!' swore Root. 'Well, I suppose we'll have to take our chances on foot. Butler, you're the expert here, you take point. Captain Short, bring up the rear. Feel free to boot any human backside if it lags behind.'

Holly winked at Artemis. 'No need to tell me twice, sir.'

'I'll bet there isn't,' grunted Root, with only the barest hint of a smile playing about his lips.

The motley band trudged south-east by moonlight until they reached the railway line. Walking along the sleepers was the one place they could be safe from drifts and suck holes. Progress was slow. A northerly wind snaked through every pore in their clothing, and the cold attacked any exposed skin like a million electric darts.

There was little conversation. The Arctic had that effect on people, even if three of them were wearing coil-heated suits.

Holly broke the silence. Something had been nagging at her for a while. 'Tell me something, Fowl,' she said from behind him. 'Your father. Is he like you?'

Artemis's step faltered for an instant. 'That's a strange question. Why do you ask?'

'Well, you're no friend to the People. What if the man we're trying to rescue is the man who will destroy us?'

There was a long silence, broken only by the chattering of teeth. Holly saw Artemis's chin drop on to his chest.

'You have no cause to be alarmed, Captain. My father, though some of his ventures were undoubtedly illegal, was ... is ... a noble man. The idea of harming another creature would be repugnant to him.'

Holly tugged her boot from twenty centimetres of snow. 'So, what happened to you?'

Artemis's breath came over his shoulder in icy sheets. 'I ... I made a mistake.'

Holly squinted at the back of the human's head. Was this actual sincerity from Artemis Fowl? It was hard to believe. Even more surprising was the fact that she didn't know how to react. Whether to extend the hand of forgiveness, or the boot of retribution. Eventually, she decided to reserve judgement. For the moment.

They passed into a ravine, worn smooth by the whistling wind. Butler didn't like it. His soldier's sense was beating a tattoo on the inside of his skull. He raised a clenched fist.

Root double-timed until he caught up.

'Trouble?'

Butler squinted into the snow field, searching for footprints. 'Maybe. Nice spot for a surprise attack.'

'Maybe. If anyone knew we were coming.'

'Is that possible? Could someone know?'

Root snorted, breath forming clouds in the air before him. 'Impossible. The chute is totally isolated, and LEP security is the tightest on the planet.'

And that was when the goblin hit squad soared over the ridge.

Butler grabbed Artemis by the collar, unceremoniously flinging him into a drift. His other hand was already drawing his weapon.

'Keep your head down, Artemis. Time for me to earn my salary.'

Artemis would have responded testily had his head not been under a metre of snow.

There were four goblins flying in loose formation, dark against the starlit sky. They quickly rose to three hundred metres, making no attempt to conceal their presence. They neither attacked nor fled, simply hovered overhead.

'Goblins,' grunted Root, pulling a Farshoot neutrino rifle into his shoulder. 'Too stupid to live. All they had to do was pick us off.'

Butler picked a spot, spreading his legs for steadiness. 'Do we wait until we see the whites of their eyes, Commander?'

'Goblin eyes don't have whites,' responded Root. 'But even so, holster your weapon. Captain Short and I will stun them. No need for anyone to die.'

Butler slid the Sig Sauer into its pouch beneath his arm. It was next to useless at that range anyway. It would be interesting to see how Holly and Root handled themselves in a firefight. After all, Artemis's life was pretty much in their hands. Not to mention his own.

Butler glanced sideways. Holly and the commander were pumping the triggers of various weapons. Without any result. Their weapons were as dead as mice in a snake pit.

'I don't understand it,' muttered Root. 'I checked these myself.'

Artemis, naturally, was first to figure it out. He shook the snow from his hair.

'Sabotage,' he proclaimed, tossing aside the useless fairy handgun. 'There is no other alternative. This is why the B'wa Kell needs Softnose weapons, because it has somehow disabled fairy lasers.'

But the commander was not listening, and neither was Butler. This was no time for clever deductions; this was a time for action. They were sitting ducks out here, dark against the pale Arctic glow. This theory was confirmed when several Softnose laser bursts bored hissing holes in the snow at their feet.

Holly activated her helmet Optix, zooming in on the enemy.

'It looks like one of them has a Softnose laser, sir. Something with a long barrel.'

'We need cover. Fast!'

Butler nodded. 'Look. An overhang. Under the ridge.'

The manservant grabbed his charge by the collar, hoisting him aloft as easily as a child would lift a kitten. They struggled through the snow to the shelter of the overhang. Maybe a million years ago the ice had melted sufficiently for a layer to slump slightly, then freeze up again. The resulting wrinkle had somehow lasted through the ages and could now possibly save their lives.

They dived underneath the lip, wriggling backwards against a wall of ice. The frozen canopy was easily thick enough to withstand gunfire from any conventional weapon.

Butler shielded Artemis with his body, risking an upward glance.

'Too far. I can't make them out. Holly?'

Captain Short poked her head from under the frozen ledge and her Optix zoomed into focus.

'Well, what are they up to?'

Holly waited a beat, until the figures sharpened.

'Funny thing,' she commented. 'They're all firing now, but …'

'But what, Captain?'

Holly tapped her helmet to make sure the lenses were working. 'Maybe I'm getting some Optix distortion, sir, but it looks like they're missing on purpose, shooting way over our heads.'

Butler felt the blood pounding in his brain. 'It's a trap!' he roared, reaching behind him to grab Artemis. 'Everybody out! Everybody out!'

And that was when the goblin charges sent fifty tonnes of rock, ice and snow tumbling to the ground.

They nearly made it. Of course, *nearly* never won a bucket of squid at gnommish roulette. If it hadn't been for Butler, not one of the group would have survived. Something happened to him. An inexplicable surge of strength, not unlike the energy bursts that allow mothers to lift fallen trees off their children. The manservant grabbed Artemis and Holly, spinning them forward like stones across a pond. It wasn't a very dignified way to travel, but it certainly beat having your bones pulverized by falling ice.

For the second time in so many minutes, Artemis

landed nose first in a snowdrift. Behind him, Butler and Root were scrabbling from beneath the ledge, boots slipping on the icy surface. The air was rent by avalanche thunder, and the pack ice beneath them heaved and split. Thick chunks of rock and ice speared the cave's opening like bars. Butler and Root were trapped.

Holly was on her feet, racing towards her commander. But what could she do? Throw herself back underneath the ledge?

'Stay back, Captain,' said Root into his helmet mike. 'That's an order!'

'Commander,' Holly breathed. 'You're alive.'

'Somehow,' came the reply. 'Butler is unconscious and we're pinned down. The ledge is on the point of collapsing. The only thing holding it up is the debris. If we brush that aside to get out …'

They were alive then at least. Trapped, but alive. A plan, they needed a plan.

Holly found herself strangely calm. This was one of the qualities that made her such an excellent field agent. In times of excessive stress, Captain Short had the ability to target a course of action. Often the only viable course. In the combat simulator for her captain's exam, Holly had defeated insurmountable virtual enemies by blasting the projector. Technically, she had defeated all her enemies, so the panel had to pass her.

Holly spoke into her helmet mike. 'Commander, undo

Butler's Moonbelt and strap yourselves on. I'm going to haul you both out of there.'

'Roger, Holly. Do you need a piton?'

'If you can get one out to me.'

'Standby.'

A piton dart jetted through a gap in the icy bars, landing a metre from Holly's boots. The dart trailed a length of fine-grade cord.

Holly snapped the piton into the cord receptacle on her own belt, making sure there were no kinks in the line. Meanwhile, Artemis had dragged himself from the drift.

'This plan is patently ridiculous,' he said, brushing the snow from his sleeves. 'You cannot hope to drag their combined weight with sufficient velocity to break the icicles and avoid being crushed.'

'I'm not going to drag them,' snapped Holly.

'Well then, who is?'

Captain Short pointed down the track. There was a green train winding its way towards them.

'That is,' she said.

There were three goblins left. Their names were D'Nall, Aymon and Nyle. Three rookies vying for the recently vacated lieutenant's spot. Lieutenant Poll had handed in his resignation when he'd strayed too close to the avalanche and been swatted by a five-hundred-kilo pane of transparent ice.

᛬ ⵊⵊⵊ ⵏ ⵊⵊⵊ ⵏ ⵏⵊⵏ ▽ ⋀ ᛬

They hovered at three hundred metres, well out of range. Of course, they weren't out of fairy-weapon range, but LEP weapons weren't operational at the moment. Koboi Laboratories' upgrades had seen to that.

'That was some hole in Lieutenant Poll,' whistled Aymon. 'I could see right through 'im. An' I don't mean that like he was a bad liar.'

Goblins didn't get too attached to each other. Considering the amount of backstabbing, backbiting and general vindictiveness that went on in the B'wa Kell, it didn't pay to make any special friends.

'What you think?' asked D'Nall, the handsome one, relatively speaking. 'Maybe one of you guys should take a spin down there.'

Aymon snorted. 'Sure thing. We go down and get sparked by the big one. Just how dumb do you think we are?'

'The big one is out of the picture. I sparked him myself. Sweet shot.'

'My shot set off the avalanche,' objected Nyle, the baby of the gang. 'You're always claimin' my kills.'

'What kills? The only thing you ever killed was a stink worm. And that was an accident.'

'Rubbish,' sulked Nyle. 'I meant to kill that worm. He was buggin' me.'

Aymon swooped between the two. 'All right. Keep

your scales on, the pair of you. All we gotta do is throw a few rounds into the survivors from up here.'

'Nice plan, genius,' sneered D'Nall. 'Except it won't work.'

'And why not?'

D'Nall pointed below with a manicured nail. 'Because they're boarding that train.'

Four green carriages were winding in from the north, dragged along by an ancient diesel engine. A maelstrom of snow flurries coiled in its wake.

Salvation, thought Holly. Or perhaps not. For some reason, the mere sight of the clanking locomotive set her stomach bubbling with acid. Still, she was in no position to be choosy.

'It's the Mayak Chemical train,' said Artemis.

Holly glanced over her shoulder. Artemis seemed even paler than usual. 'The what?'

'Environmentalists worldwide call it the Green Machine, something of an irony. It transports spent uranium and plutonium assemblies to the Mayak Chemical Combine for recycling. One driver locked up in the engine. No guards. Fully loaded, this thing is hotter than a nuclear submarine.'

'And you know about this because ...'

Artemis shrugged. 'I like to keep track of these things. After all, radiation is the world's problem.'

Holly could feel it now. Uranium tendrils eating through the rad gel on her cheeks. That train was poison. But it was her only chance of getting the commander out alive.

'This just keeps getting better and better,' Holly muttered.

The train was closer. Obviously. Motoring along at about ten klicks an hour. No problem for Holly on her own, but with two men down and one next-to-useless Mud Boy, it was going to take quite a feat to get on board that locomotive.

Holly spared a second to check on the goblins. They were holding steady at three hundred metres. Goblins were no good at improvisation. This train was unexpected; it would take them at least a minute to work out a new strategy. The big hole in their fallen comrade might give them further pause for thought.

Holly could feel the radiation emanating from the carriages, burning through the tiniest gap in the radiation gel, prickling her eyeballs. It was only a matter of time before her magic ran out. After that, she was living on borrowed time.

No time to think about it now. Her priority was the commander. She had to get him out of there alive. If the B'wa Kell was brazen enough to mount an operation against the LEP, there was obviously something pretty big going on below ground. Whatever it was, Julius Root would be needed to spearhead the counterattack. She turned towards Artemis.

'OK, Mud Boy. We've got one shot at this. Grab on to whatever you can.'

Artemis couldn't hide an apprehensive shiver.

'Don't be afraid, Artemis. You can make it.'

Artemis bristled. 'It's cold, fairy. Humans shiver in the cold.'

'That's the spirit,' said the LEP captain, and she began to run. The piton wire played out behind her like a harpoon cable. Though it had the approximate grade of fishing line, the cable could easily suspend two struggling elephants. Artemis raced after her as fast as his loafered feet could manage.

They ran parallel to the tracks, feet crunching through the snow. Behind them the train grew closer, pushing a buffer of air before it.

Artemis struggled to keep up. This was not for him. Running and sweating. Combat, for heaven's sake. He was no soldier. He was a planner. A mastermind. The hurly-burly of actual conflict was best left to Butler and people like him. But his manservant wasn't there to take care of the physical tasks this time. And he never would be again if they didn't manage to board this train.

Artemis's breath came short, crystallizing in front of his face, blurring his vision. The train had drawn level now, steel wheels spewing ice and sparks into the air.

'Second carriage,' panted Holly. 'There's a runner. Mind your footing.'

Runner? Artemis glanced behind. The second carriage was coming up fast. But the noise was blurring his vision. Was that possible? It was terrific. Unbearable. There, below the steel doors. A narrow board. Wide enough to stand on. Barely.

Holly alighted easily, flattening herself against the carriage wall. She made it look so effortless. A simple skip and she was safe from the grab of those pulverizing wheels.

'Come on, Fowl,' shouted Holly. 'Jump.'

Artemis tried, he really did. But the toe of his loafer snagged on a sleeper. He stumbled forward, pin-wheeling for balance. A painful death came rushing up to meet him.

'Two left feet,' muttered Holly, grabbing her least favourite Mud Boy by the collar. Momentum swung Artemis forward, slamming him into the door like something out of a cartoon.

The piton cord was slapping against the carriage. Only seconds left before Holly departed from the train as quickly as she'd arrived. The LEP captain searched for a strongpoint to anchor herself. Root and Butler's weight may have been reduced by the Moonbelt, but the jerk when it came, would be more than sufficient to drag her from the locomotive. And if that happened, it was all over.

Holly hooked one arm through a rung on the carriage's

external ladder. She noticed magical sparks playing over a rip in her suit. They were counteracting the radiation damage. How much longer could her magic last under these conditions? Constant healing really took it out of a girl. She needed to complete the power-restoring Ritual. And the sooner the better.

Holly was about to unclip the cable and attach it to one of the rungs when it snapped taut, pulling Holly's legs from beneath her. She held on to the rung grimly, fingernails digging into her own skin. On reflection, this plan needed a bit of work. Time seemed to stretch, elastic as the cord and, for a moment, Holly thought her elbow would pop right out of its socket. Then the ice gave and Root and Butler were twanged out of their icy tomb like a bolt from a crossbow.

Seconds later, they slapped against the side of the train, their reduced weight keeping them aloft, for now. But it was only a matter of time before what little gravity they had pushed them under the steel wheels.

Artemis latched on to the rung beside her. 'What can I do?'

She nodded at a shoulder pocket. 'In there. A small vial. Take it out.'

Artemis ripped open the Velcro flap, pulling out a tiny spray bottle. 'OK. Got it.'

'Good. It's up to you now, Fowl. Up and over.'

Artemis's mouth dropped open. 'Up and …?'

'Yes. It's our only hope. We have to get this door open to reel in Butler and the commander. There's a bend in the track two klicks away. If this train slows down even one revolution, they're gone.'

Artemis nodded. 'The vial?'

'Acid. For the lock. The mechanism's on the inside. Cover your face and squeeze. Give it the whole tube. Don't get any on you.'

It was a long conversation under the circumstances. Especially since every second was vital. Artemis did not waste another one on goodbyes.

He dragged himself to the next rung, keeping the length of his body pressed close to the carriage. The wind was whipping along the length of the train, tiny motes of ice in every gust. They stung like bees. Nevertheless, Artemis pulled off his gloves with chattering teeth. Better frostbite than being crushed beneath the wheels.

Upwards. One rung at a time, until his head poked above the carriage. Every shred of shelter was now gone. The air pounded his forehead, forcing itself down his throat. Artemis squinted through the blizzard, along the carriage's roof. There! In the centre. A skylight. Across a desert of steel, blasted smooth as glass by the elements. Not a handhold within five metres. The strength of a rhino would be of no use here, Artemis decided. At last an opportunity to use his brain. Kinetics and momentum. Simple enough, in theory.

Keeping to the front rim of the carriage, Artemis inched on to the roof. The wind wormed beneath his legs, raising them five centimetres from the deck, threatening to float him off the train.

Artemis curled his fingers around the rim. These were not gripping fingers. Artemis hadn't gripped anything bigger than his mobile phone in several months. If you wanted someone to type *Paradise Lost* in under twenty minutes, then Artemis was your man. But as for hanging on to carriage roofs in a blizzard. Dead loss. Which, fortunately, was all part of the plan.

A millisecond before his finger joints parted company, Artemis let go. The slipstream shot him straight through the skylight's metal housing.

Perfect, he would have grunted, had there been a cubic centimetre of air in his lungs. But even if he had said it, the wind would have snatched away any words before his own ears heard them. He had moments now before the wind dug its fingers beneath his torso, flipping him on to the icy steppes. Cannon fodder for the goblins.

Artemis fumbled the acid vial from his pocket, snapping the top between his teeth. A fleck of the acid flew past his eye. No time to worry about that now. No time for anything.

The skylight was secured by a thick padlock. Artemis dribbled two drops into the keyhole. All he could spare. It would have to be enough.

The effect was immediate. The acid ate through the metal like lava through ice. Fairy technology. Best under the world.

The padlock pinged open, exposing the hatch to the wind's power. It flipped upwards and Artemis tumbled through on to a pallet of barrels. Not exactly the picture of a gallant rescuer.

The train's motion shook him from the cargo. Artemis landed face up, gazing at the triple-triangled symbol for radiation stamped on the side of each container. At least the barrels were sealed, though rust seemed to have taken hold on quite a few.

Artemis rolled across the slatted floor, clambering to his knees alongside the door. Was Captain Short still anchored there, or was he alone now? For the first time in his life. Truly alone.

'Fowl! Open the door, you pasty-faced Mud Weasel!'

Ah well. Not alone then.

Covering his face with a forearm, Artemis drenched the carriage's triple bolt with fairy acid. The steel lock melted instantly, dripping to the floor like a stream of mercury. Artemis dragged the sliding door back.

Holly was hanging on grimly, her face steaming where radiation was eating through the gel.

Artemis grabbed her waistband. 'On three?'

Holly nodded. No more energy for speech.

Artemis flexed his digits. Fingers, don't fail me now. If

he ever got out of this, he would buy one of those ridiculous home gymnasiums advertised on the shopping channels.

'One.'

The bend was coming. He could see it out of the corner of his eye. The train would slow down or derail itself.

'Two.'

Captain Short's strength was almost spent. The wind rippled her frame like a windsock.

'Three!'

Artemis pulled with all the strength in his thin arms. Holly closed her eyes and let go, unable to believe she was trusting her life to this Mud Boy.

Artemis knew a little something about physics. He timed his count to take advantage of swing, momentum and the train's own forward motion. But nature always throws something into the mix that can't be anticipated. In this case the *something* was a slight gap between two sections of the track. Not enough to derail a locomotive, but certainly enough to cause a bump.

This bump sent the carriage door crashing into its frame like a five-tonne guillotine. But it looked like Holly had made it. Artemis couldn't really tell because she had crashed into him, sending them both careering into the wooden siding. She seemed to be intact, from what he could see. At least her head was still attached to her neck, which was good. But she did seem to be unconscious. Probably trauma.

Artemis knew that he was going to pass out too. He could tell by the darkness eating at the corners of his vision, like some malignant computer virus. He slipped sideways, landing on Holly's chest.

This had more severe repercussions than you might think. Because Holly was unconscious, her magic was on autopilot. And unsupervised magic flows like electricity. Artemis's face made contact with the fairy's left hand, diverting the flow of blue sparks. And while this was good for him, it was most definitely bad for her. Because although Artemis didn't know it, Holly needed every spark of magic she could muster – not all of her had made it inside the train.

Commander Root had just activated his piton cord winch when he received a most unexpected poke in the eye.

The goblin D'Nall removed a small rectangular mirror from his tunic and checked his scales were smooth.

'These Koboi wings are great. You think we'll be allowed to keep 'em?'

Aymon scowled. Not that you'd notice. Goblin lizard ancestry meant that facial movement was pretty limited. 'Quiet, you hot-blooded fool!'

Hot-blooded. That was a pretty serious insult for one of the B'wa Kell.

D'Nall bristled. 'Be careful, friend, or I'll tear that forked tongue right out of your head.'

'We won't have a tongue between us if those elves escape!' retorted Aymon.

It was true. The generals did not take disappointment well.

'So what do we do? I got the looks in this outfit. That must make you the brains.'

'We shoot at the train,' interjected Nyle. 'Simple.'

D'Nall adjusted his Koboi DoubleDex, hovering across to the squad's junior member.

'Idiot,' he snapped, administering a swift slap to the head. 'That thing is radioactive, can't you smell it? One stray burst and we'll all be ash floating on the breeze.'

'Good point,' admitted Nyle. 'You're not as stupid as you look.'

'Thank you.'

'Welcome.'

Aymon throttled down, descending to a hundred and fifty metres. It was so tempting. One tightly focused burst to take out the elf clinging to the carriage, another to dispatch the human on the roof. But he couldn't risk it. One degree off target and he'd sucked his last stink-worm spaghetti.

'OK,' he announced into his helmet mike. 'Here's the

plan. With all the radiation in that carriage, chances are the targets will be dead in minutes. We follow the train for a while just to make sure. Then we go back and tell the general we saw the bodies.'

D'Nall buzzed down beside him. 'And do we see the bodies?'

Aymon groaned. 'Of course not, you fool! Do you want your eyeballs to dry up and fall out?'

'Duh.'

'Exactly. So are we clear?'

'Crystal,' said Nyle, drawing his Softnose Redboy handgun. He shot his comrades from behind. Close range, point blank. They never had a chance. He followed their bodies to Earth on full magnification. The snow would cover them in minutes. Nobody would be stumbling over those particular corpses until the polar caps melted.

Nyle holstered his weapon, punching in the co-ordinates for the shuttle terminal on his flight computer. If you studied his reptilian face carefully, it was just possible to make out a grin. There was a new lieutenant in town.

CHAPTER 9: NO SAFE HAVEN

 FOALY was sitting in front of the LEP mainframe waiting for the results of his latest search. Extensive laser brushing of the goblin shuttle had revealed one complete and one partial thumbprint. The complete print was his own. Easily explicable as Foaly personally inspected all retired shuttle parts. The partial print could well belong to their traitor. Not enough to identify the fairy who'd been running LEP technology to the B'wa Kell, but certainly enough to eliminate the innocent. Cross-reference the remaining names with everybody who had shuttle-part access, and the list got considerably shorter. Foaly switched his tail contentedly. Genius. No point in being humble about it.

At the moment, the computer was crunching through

personnel files with the partial print. All Foaly could do was twiddle his thumbs and wait for contact with the surface team. The magma flares were still up. Very unusual. Unusual and coincidental.

Foaly's suspicious train of thought was interrupted by a familiar voice.

'Search complete,' said the computer, in Foaly's own tones. A little vanity. 'Three hundred and forty-six eliminated. Forty possibles remaining.'

Forty. Not bad. They could easily be interviewed. An opportunity to use the Retimager once again. But there was another way to narrow the field.

'Computer. Cross-reference possibles with Level Three clearance personnel.' Level Three clearance would include everybody with access to the recycling smelters.

'Referencing.'

Of course, the computer would only accept commands from fairies whose voice patterns it was programmed to recognize. And as a further security precaution, Foaly had coded his personal log and other important files in a computer language he'd based on the ancient tongue of the centaurs: Centaurian.

All centaurs were a touch paranoid, and with good reason, since there were less than a hundred left. The humans had managed to kill off their cousins, the unicorns, altogether. There were probably six centaurs under the Earth who could read the language, and only one who could decipher the computer dialect.

Centaurian was possibly the oldest form of writing, dating back over ten millennia to when humans first began hunting fairies. The opening paragraph of *The Scrolls of Capalla,* the only surviving illuminated Centaurian manuscript, read:

ᚠᚨᛁᚱᛃᛖᚱᚲᚨ ᛁᛁᚱᛖᚾᚱᚲᚨᛁ ᚱᛁᛁᚹᚨᚱᚨᛁᚨᛁ
ᚹᚨᛁᚨᚱ ᚾ ᚱᛁᚱᚢᛁᛁᚨᚨᛁᛁᚱᚨᛁᛁᚨᚨᚹᚨᛁᚨᛁ.
ᛁᚹᛁᚾᚨᛁᚠᚨᛁᚱᛃᛁᛁᛁ ᛁᚤᚹᛁᛁᛁᚠᚹᛁᚨᛁ
ᚨᚨᚨᛁᛁᚨᛁᛁᚨᛁᚹᛁᛁᛁᛁᚨᛁᚨ ᚾ ᚱᛁᛁᚱᚹᛁᚨᚨ.

> Fairy creatures, heed this warning,
> On Earth, the human era is dawning.
> So hide, fairy, lest you be found,
> And make a home beneath the ground.

Centaurs were known for their intellect, not their poetry. Still, Foaly felt the words were as relevant today as they had been all those centuries ago.

Cudgeon knocked on the booth's security glass. Now, technically, Cudgeon shouldn't be allowed in Ops, but Foaly buzzed him through. He could never resist having a crack at the ex-commander. Cudgeon had been demoted to lieutenant following a disastrous attempt to replace Root as Recon head honcho. If it hadn't been for his family's considerable political clout, he would have been booted off the force altogether. All in all, he might have been better off in some other line of work. At least he wouldn't have had to suffer Foaly's constant teasing.

'I have some e-forms for you to initial,' said the lieutenant, avoiding eye-contact.

'No problem, *Commander,*' chuckled the centaur. 'How's the plotting going? Any revolutions planned for this afternoon?'

'Just sign the forms please,' said Cudgeon holding out a digi-pen. His hand was shaking.

Amazing, thought Foaly. This broken-down shell of an elf was once on the LEP fast track.

'No, but seriously, Cudgeon. You're doing a bang-up job on the form-signing thing.'

Cudgeon's eyes narrowed in suspicion. 'Thank you, sir.'

A grin tugged at the corner of Foaly's mouth. 'You're welcome. No need to get a swelled head.'

Cudgeon's hand flew to his misshapen forehead. Still a touch of the old vanity left.

'Oops. Sore subject. Sorry about that.'

There was a spark in the corner of Cudgeon's eye. A spark that should have warned Foaly. But he was distracted by a beep from the computer.

'List complete.'

'Excuse me for a moment, *Commander*. Important business. Computer stuff, you wouldn't understand it.'

Foaly turned to the plasma screen. The lieutenant

would just have to wait for his signature. It was probably just an order for shuttle parts anyway.

The penny dropped. A big penny with a clang louder than a dwarf's underpants hitting a wall. Shuttle parts. An inside job. Someone with a grudge to settle. A line of sweat filled each groove on Foaly's forehead. It was so obvious.

He looked at the plasma screen for confirmation of what he already knew. There were only two names. The first, Bom Arbles, could be eliminated immediately. The Retrieval officer had been killed in a core-diving accident. The second name pulsed gently. Lieutenant Briar Cudgeon. Demoted to recycling crew around the time Holly retired that starboard booster. It all made sense.

Foaly knew that if he didn't acknowledge the message in ten seconds, the computer would read the name aloud. He casually punched the delete button.

'You know, Briar,' he croaked. 'All those jibes about your head problem. It's all in fun. My way of being sympathetic. Actually, I have some ointment ...'

Something cold and metallic pressed against the back of the centaur's head. Foaly had seen too many rock 'em sock 'em movies not to know what it was.

'Save your ointment, donkey boy,' said Cudgeon's voice in his ear. 'I have a feeling you'll be developing some head problems of your own.'

THE MAYAK CHEMICAL TRAIN, NORTHERN RUSSIA

The first thing Artemis felt was a rhythmical knocking, jarring along the length of his spine. I'm at the spa in Blackrock, he thought. Irina is massaging my back. Just what my system needs, especially after all that horseplay on the train ... The train!

Obviously they were still aboard the Mayak train. The jerking motion was actually the carriage jolting over the track joins. Artemis forced his eyes open, expecting gargantuan doses of stiffness and pain. But instead he realized he felt fine. More than fine. Great in fact. It must be magic. Holly must have healed his various cuts and bruises while he was unconscious.

Nobody else was feeling quite so chipper. Especially Captain Short, who was still unconscious. Root was draping a large coat over his fallen officer.

'Oh, you're awake, are you?' he said, without so much as a glance at Artemis. 'I don't know how you can sleep at all after what you've just done.'

'Done? But I saved you ... at least, I helped.'

'You helped all right, Fowl. You helped yourself to the last of Holly's magic while she was unconscious.'

Artemis groaned. It must have happened when they fell. Somehow her magic had been diverted. 'I see what must have happened. It was an ...'

Root raised a warning finger. 'Don't say it. The great

Artemis Fowl doesn't do anything by accident.'

Artemis fought against the train's motion, climbing to his knees. 'It can't be anything serious. Just exhaustion, surely?'

And suddenly Root's face was a centimetre from his own, his complexion rosy enough to generate heat. 'Nothing serious!' spluttered the commander, barely able to get the words out in his rage. 'Nothing serious! She lost her trigger finger! The door cut it clean off. Her career is over. And because of you, Holly barely had enough magic to stop the bleeding. She's drained of power now. Empty.'

'She lost a finger?' echoed Artemis numbly.

'Not lost exactly,' said the commander, waving the severed digit. 'It poked me in the eye on the way past.' His eye was already beginning to blacken.

'If we go back now, surely your surgeons can graft it on?'

Root shook his head. '*If* we could go back now. I have a feeling that the situation below ground is a lot different from when we left. If the goblins sent a hit team to get us, you can bet something big is going on below ground.'

Artemis was shocked. Holly had saved all their lives, and this was how he had repaid her. While it was true that he was not directly to blame for the injury, it had been inflicted while trying to save his father. There was a debt to be paid here.

'How long?' he snapped.

'What?'

'How long ago did it happen?'

'I don't know. A minute.'

'Then there's still time.'

The commander sat up. 'Time for what?'

'We can still save the finger.'

Root rubbed a welt of fresh scar tissue on his shoulder, a reminder of his trip along the side of the train. 'With what? I barely have enough power left for the *mesmer*.'

Artemis closed his eyes. Concentrating. 'What about the Ritual? There must be a way.'

All the People's magic came from the Earth. In order to top up their powers, they had to periodically complete the Ritual.

'How can we complete the Ritual here?'

Artemis racked his brain. He had committed large sections of the Fairy Book to memory in preparation for the previous year's kidnapping operation.

'From the earth thine power flows,
Given through courtesy, so thanks are owed.
Pluck thou the magick seed,
Where full moon, ancient oak and twisted water meet.
And bury it far from where it was found,
So return your gift into the ground.'

Artemis scrambled across the flooring and began

patting down Holly's jumpsuit.

Root's heart nearly shut down then and there. 'In heaven's name, Mud Boy, what are you doing?'

Artemis didn't even look up. 'Last year, Holly escaped because she had an acorn.'

Through some miracle, the commander managed to restrain himself. 'Five seconds, Fowl. Talk fast.'

'An officer like Holly wouldn't forget something like that. I'd be willing to bet …'

Root sighed. 'It's a good idea, Mud Boy. But the acorns have to be freshly picked. If it hadn't been for the time-stop, that seed mightn't have worked. You've got a couple of days, tops. I know Foaly and Holly put together some proposal for a sealed acorn unit, but the Council rejected it. Heresy apparently.'

It was a long speech for the commander. He wasn't used to explaining himself. But a part of him was hoping. Maybe, just maybe. Holly had never been averse to bending a few rules.

Artemis unzipped Captain Short's tunic. There were two tiny items on the gold chain around her neck. Her copy of the Book, the fairy bible. Artemis knew that it would combust if he tried to touch it without Holly's permission. But there was another item. A small plexiglass sphere filled with earth.

'That's against regulations,' said Root, not sounding too upset.

Holly stirred, half-emerging from her stupor. 'Hey, Commander. What happened to your eye?'

Artemis ignored her, cracking the tiny sphere against the carriage floor. Earth and a small acorn tumbled into his palm. 'Now all we need to do is bury it.'

The commander slung Holly over his shoulder. Artemis tried not to look at the space where her index finger used to be.

'Then it's time to get off this train.'

Artemis glanced at the Arctic landscape whipping past outside the carriage. Getting off the train wasn't as easy as the commander made it sound.

Butler dropped nimbly through the overhead hatch, where he'd been keeping an eye on the goblin hit squad.

'Nice to see you're so limber,' commented Artemis drily.

The manservant smiled. 'Good to see you too, Artemis.'

'Well? What did you see up there?' said Root, interrupting the reunion.

Butler placed a hand on his young master's shoulders. They could talk later. 'The goblins are gone. Funny thing. Two of them dropped low for reconnaissance, then the other one shot them in the back.'

Root nodded. 'Power play. Goblins are their own worst enemies. But right now, we've got to get off this train.'

'There's another bend coming up in about half a klick,' said Butler. 'That's our best chance.'

'So, how do we disembark?' asked Artemis.

Butler grinned. 'Disembark is a pretty gentle term for what I have in mind.'

Artemis groaned. More running and jumping.

OPERATIONS' BOOTH

Foaly's brain was bubbling like a sea slug in a deep-fat fryer. He still had options, providing Cudgeon didn't actually shoot him. One shot and it was all over. Centaurs didn't have magic. Not a drop. They got by on brains alone. That and their ability to trample their enemies underfoot. But Foaly had a feeling that Briar wouldn't plug him just yet. Too busy gloating.

'Hey, Foaly,' said the lieutenant. 'Why don't you go for the intercom? See what happens.'

Foaly could guess what would happen. 'Don't worry, Briar. No sudden moves.'

Cudgeon laughed, and he sounded genuinely happy. 'Briar? First name terms now, is it? You must realize how much trouble you're in.'

Foaly was starting to realize just that. Beyond the tinted glass, LEP techs were beavering away trying to track down the mole, oblivious to the drama being played out not two metres away. He could see and hear them, but it was one-way surveillance.

The centaur had only himself to blame. He had insisted that the Operations' booth be constructed to his own paranoid standards. A titanium cube with blast-proof windows. The entire room was wireless, not even a fibre-optic cable to connect Operations to the outside world.

Totally impregnable. Unless, of course, you opened the door to throw a few insults at an old enemy. Foaly groaned. His mother had always said that his smart mouth would get him into trouble. But all was not lost. He still had a few tricks up his sleeve. A plasma floor, for instance.

'So what's this all about, Cudgeon?' asked the centaur, raising his hooves just off the tiles. 'And please don't say world domination.'

Cudgeon continued to smile. This was his moment.

'Not immediately. The Lower Elements will suffice for now.'

'But why?'

Cudgeon's eyes were tinged with madness. 'Why? You have the gall to ask me why? I was the the Council's golden boy! In fifty years I would have been chairman! And then along comes the Artemis Fowl Affair. In one short day all my hopes are dashed. I end up deformed and demoted! And it was all because of you, Foaly. You and Root! So the only way to get my life back on track is to discredit both of you. You will be blamed for the goblin attacks, and Julius will be dead and dishonoured. And as an added bonus, I even get Artemis Fowl. It's as close to perfect as I could have hoped.'

Foaly snorted. 'Do you really think you can defeat the LEP with a handful of Softnose weapons?'

'Defeat the LEP? Why would I want to do that? I am the hero of the LEP. Or rather I will be. You will be the villain of this piece.'

'We'll see about that, baboon face,' said Foaly, activating a switch, sending an infra-red signal to a receiver in the floor. In five-tenths of a second, a secret membrane of plasma would warm up. Half a second later, a neutrino charge would spread across the plasma gel like wildfire, hopping anyone connected to the floor off at least three walls. In theory.

Cudgeon giggled delightedly. 'Don't tell me. Your plasma tiles aren't working.'

Foaly was flummoxed. Momentarily. Then he lowered his hooves gingerly and pressed another button. This one engaged a voice-activated laser. Basically, the next person to talk got plugged. The centaur held his breath.

'No plasma tiles,' continued Cudgeon. 'And no voice-activated laser. You really are slipping, Foaly. Not that I'm surprised. I always knew you'd be exposed for the donkey you are.'

The lieutenant settled into a swivel chair, propping his

feet on the computer bank. 'So have you figured it out yet?'

Foaly thought. Who could it be? Who could beat him at his own game? Not Cudgeon, that was for sure. A techno fool if ever there was one. No, there was only one person with the ability to crack the Centaurian code and deactivate the booth's safety measures.

'Opal Koboi,' he breathed.

Cudgeon patted Foaly's head. 'That's right. Opal planted a few spy cams during the upgrading work. Once you were kind enough to translate a few documents for the camera, it was a simple matter to crack your code and do a little reprogramming. And the funny thing is, the Council footed the bill. She even charged for the spy cameras. Even now, the B'wa Kell is preparing to launch its attack on the city. LEP weapons and communications are down, and the best thing is that you, my horsy friend, will be held responsible. After all, you have locked yourself in the Operations' booth in the middle of a crisis.'

'Nobody will believe it!' protested Foaly.

'Oh yes they will, especially when you disengage the LEP security, including the DNA cannons.'

'Which I won't be doing anytime soon.'

Cudgeon twirled a matt-black remote between his fingers. 'I'm afraid it's not up to you any more. Opal took your little operation apart and wired the whole lot into this little beauty.'

Foaly swallowed. 'You mean …?'

'That's right,' said Cudgeon. 'Nothing works unless I press the button.'

He pressed the button. And even if Foaly had had the reactions of a sprite, he would never have had time to draw up all his hooves before the plasma shock blasted him right out of his specially modified swivel chair.

ARCTIC CIRCLE

Butler instructed everyone to attach themselves to the Moonbelt, one per link. Floating slightly in the buffeting wind, the group manoeuvred itself to the carriage doorway like a drunken crab.

It's simple physics, Artemis told himself. Reduced gravity will prevent us being dashed against the Arctic ice. In spite of all his logic, when Root launched the group into the night, Artemis couldn't hold back a single gasp. Later, when he replayed the incident in his mind's eye, Artemis would edit out the breath.

The slipstream spun them beyond the railway sleepers, into a drift. Butler turned off the anti-gravity belt a second before impact, otherwise they could have bounced away, like men on the moon.

Root was first to detach, scooping handfuls of snow

158

from the surface until his fingers reached the compacted ice below.

'It's no use,' he said. 'I can't break through the ice.'

He heard a click behind his shoulder.

'Stand back,' advised Butler, taking aim with his handgun.

Root obliged, shielding his eyes with a forearm. Ice slivers could blind you just as efficiently as six-inch nails. Butler put a full clip into a narrow spread, blasting a shallow hollow in the frozen surface. Instant sleet drenched the already sodden group.

Root was checking the results before the smoke cleared. He brought Butler up to speed – they had seconds left before Holly's time ran out. They needed to complete the Ritual. After a certain time it mightn't be wise to attempt a graft. Even if they could.

The commander jumped into the dip, sweeping aside layers of loose ice. There was a disk of brown among the white.

'Yes!' he crowed. 'Earth!'

Butler lowered Holly's twitching form into the hole. She seemed like a doll in his powerful hands. Tiny and limp. Root curled Holly's fingers around the illegal acorn, thrusting her left hand deep into the shattered soil. He pulled a roll of tape from his belt, crudely securing the finger to roughly its original position.

The elf and two humans gathered around and waited.

'It mightn't take,' muttered Root nervously. 'This sealed acorn thing is new. Never been tested. Foaly and his ideas. But they usually work. They usually do.'

Artemis laid a hand on his shoulder. It was all he could think to do. Giving comfort was not one of his strong points.

Five seconds. Ten. Nothing.

Then ...

'Look!' cried Artemis. 'A spark.'

A solitary blue spark travelled lazily along the length of Holly's arm, winding along the veins. It crossed her chest, climbed her pointed chin and sank into the flesh right between the eyes.

'Stand back,' advised Root. 'I saw a two-minute healing in Tulsa one night. Damn near destroyed an entire shuttle port. I've never even heard of a four-minuter.'

They back-pedalled to the lip of the crater and not a moment too soon. More sparks erupted from the Earth, targeting Holly's hand as the area most in need of assistance. They sank into her finger joint like plasma torpedoes, melting the plastic tape.

Holly shot upright, arms swinging like a puppet. Her legs began to jerk, kicking invisible enemies. Then the vocal cords, a high-pitched keening that cracked the thinner sheets of ice.

'Is this normal?' whispered Artemis, as though Holly could hear.

'I think so,' answered the commander. 'The brain is running a systems check. It's not like fixing cuts and bruises, if you know what I mean.'

Every pore in Holly's body started to steam, venting trace radiation. She thrashed and kicked, sinking back down into a pool of slush. Not a pretty sight. The water evaporated, shrouding the LEP captain in mist. Only her left hand was visible, fingers a desperate blur.

Holly suddenly stopped moving. Her hand froze, then dropped through the mist. The Arctic night rushed in to reclaim the silence.

They inched closer, leaning into the fog. Artemis wanted to see, but he was afraid to look.

Butler took a breath, batting aside sheets of mist. All was quiet below. Holly's frame lay still as the grave.

Artemis peered at the shape in the hole. 'I think she's awake ...'

He was cut short by Holly's sudden return to consciousness. She bolted upright, icicles coating her eyelashes and auburn hair. Her chest ballooned as she swallowed huge gulps of air.

Artemis grabbed her shoulders, for once abandoning his shell of icy composure. 'Holly. Holly, speak to me. Your finger. Is it OK?'

Holly wiggled her fingers, then curled them into a fist. 'I think so,' she said, and whacked Artemis right between the eyes. The surprised boy landed in a snowdrift for the fourth time that day.

Holly winked at an amazed Butler. 'Now, we're even,' she said.

Commander Root didn't have many treasured memories. But in future days, when things were at their grimmest, he would conjure up this moment and have a quiet chuckle.

Operations' booth

Foaly woke up sore, which was unusual for him. He couldn't even remember the last time he'd experienced actual pain. His feelings had been hurt a few times by Julius's barbed comments, but actual physical discomfort was not something he cared to endure when he could avoid it.

The centaur was lying on the Operations' Security-booth floor, tangled in the remains of his office chair.

'Cudgeon,' he growled, and what followed was about two minutes' worth of unprintable obscenity.

When he had finally vented his anger, the centaur's brain kicked in, and he hauled himself up from the plasma tiles. His rump was singed. He was going to have a couple of bald spots on his hind quarters. Very unattractive in a centaur. It was the first thing a prospective mate looked for in a nightclub. Not that Foaly had ever been much of a dancer. Four left hooves.

The booth was sealed. Tighter than a gnome's wallet, as the saying went. Foaly typed in his exit code. 'Foaly. Doors.'

The computer remained silent.

He tried verbal. 'Foaly. One two one override. Doors.'

Not a peep. He was trapped. A prisoner of his own security devices. Even the windows were set to blackout, blocking his view of the Operations' room. Completely locked out, and locked in. Nothing worked.

Well, that wasn't completely accurate. *Everything* worked, but his precious computers wouldn't respond to his touch. And Foaly was only too well aware that there was no way out of the booth without access to the mainframe.

Foaly plucked the tin foil hat from his head, crunching it into a ball.

'A lot of good you did me!' he said, tossing it into the waste recycler. The recycler would analyse the chemical make-up of the item, then divert it to the appropriate tank.

A plasma monitor crackled into life on the wall. Opal Koboi's magnified face appeared, plastered with the widest grin the centaur had ever seen.

'Hello, Foaly. Long time no see.'

Foaly returned the grin, but his wasn't quite as wide. 'Opal. How nice to see you. How are the folks?' Everyone knew how Opal had bankrupted her father. It was a legend in the corporate world.

'Very well, thanks. Cumulus House is a lovely asylum.'

Foaly decided he would try sincerity. It was a tool he didn't use very often. But he would give it a go.

'Opal. Think about what you're doing. Cudgeon is insane, for pity's sake. Once he has what he wants, he will dispose of you in a heartbeat!'

The pixie shook a perfectly manicured finger. 'No, Foaly, you're wrong. Briar needs me. He really does. He'd be nothing without me and my gold.'

The centaur looked deep into Opal's eyes. The pixie actually believed what she was saying. How could someone so brilliant be so deluded?

'I know what this is all about, Opal.'

'Oh, you do?'

'Yes. You're still sore because I won the science medal back in university.'

For a second, Koboi's composure slipped, and her features didn't seem quite so perfect.

'That medal was mine, you stupid centaur. My wing design was far superior to your ridiculous iris-cam. You won because you were a male. And that's the only reason.'

Foaly grinned, satisfied. Even with the odds so hugely against him, he hadn't lost the ability to be the most annoying creature under the world when he wanted to be.

'So what do you want, Opal? Or did you just call to chat about our schooldays?'

Opal took a long drink from a crystal glass. 'I just

called, Foaly, to let you know I'm watching, so don't try anything. I also wanted to show you something from the security cameras downtown. This is live footage by the way, and Briar is with the Council right now, blaming you for it. Happy viewing.'

Opal's face disappeared to be replaced by a high-angle view of downtown Haven. A tourist district, outside Spud's Spud Emporium. Generally, this area would be thronged with Atlantean couples taking photos of each other in front of the fountain. But not today, because today the square was a battleground. The B'wa Kell was waging open war with the LEP and, by the looks of things, it was a one-sided battle. The goblins were firing their Softnose weapons, but the police were not shooting back. They just huddled behind whatever shelter they could find. Completely helpless.

Foaly's jaw dropped. This was disastrous. And he was being blamed for everything. Of course, the thing about scapegoats was that they could not be left alive to protest their innocence. He had to get a message to Holly, and fast, or they were all dead fairies.

CHAPTER 10: **TROUBLE AND STRIFE**

Downtown Haven

 SPUD'S Spud Emporium was not a place you wanted to be on the best of days. The fries were greasy, the meat was mysterious and the milkshakes had gristly lumps. Nevertheless, the Emporium did a roaring trade, especially during the solstice.

At this precise moment, Captain Trouble Kelp would almost have preferred to be inside the fast-food joint, choking down a rubbery burger, than outside it dodging lasers. Almost.

With Root out of the picture, field command fell to Captain Kelp. Usually this was a responsibility he would have relished. But then again, *usually* he would have had the benefit of transport and weapons. Thankfully they still had communications.

Trouble and his patrol had been rousting B'wa Kell hot spots when they were bushwhacked by a hundred members of the reptilian triad. The goblins had positioned themselves on the rooftops, catching the LEP squad in a deadly crossfire from Softnose lasers and fireballs. Pretty complex thinking for the B'wa Kell. The average goblin found simultaneous scratching and spitting a challenge. They had to be getting their orders from someone.

Trouble and one of his junior corporals were pinned down behind a photo booth, while the remaining officers had managed to take cover in Spud's Emporium.

For the moment, they were keeping the goblins at bay with tasers and buzz batons. The tasers had a range of ten metres, and the buzz batons were only good for close quarters. Both ran on electric batteries and would run out eventually. After that they were down to rocks and bare fists. They didn't even have the advantage of shielding as the B'wa Kell was equipped with LEP combat helmets. Older models certainly, but still fitted with anti-shield filters.

A fireball arced over the booth, melting through the asphalt at their feet. The goblins were wising up. Relatively speaking. Instead of trying to blast through the booth, they were lobbing missiles over it. Time was short now.

Trouble tapped his mike. 'Kelp to base. Anything on weapons?'

'Not a thing, Cap,' came the reply. 'Plenty of officers

with nuthin to shoot 'cept their fingers. We're charging up the old 'lectric guns, but that's gonna take eight hours minimum. There are a coupla body-armour suits over in Recon. I'm having 'em double-timed over to you right now. Five minutes. Tops.'

'D'Arvit!' swore the captain. They were going to have to move. Any second now this booth would fall apart and they would be sitting ducks for goblin fire. Beside him the corporal was quivering in terror.

'For heaven's sake,' snapped Trouble. 'Pull yourself together.'

'You shut up, Trub,' retorted his brother, Grub, through wobbly lips. 'You were supposed to look out for me. Mummy said.'

Trouble waved a threatening finger. 'It's *Captain Kelp* while we're on duty, Corporal. And for your information, I *am* looking out for you.'

'Oh, this is looking out for me, is it?' whined Grub, pouting.

Trouble didn't know who annoyed him more, his kid brother or the goblins.

'OK, Grub. This booth isn't going to last much longer. We've got to make a break for the Emporium. Understand?'

Grub's wobbling lip suddenly stiffened considerably. 'No chance. I'm not moving. You can't make me. I don't mind if I stay here for the rest of my life.'

Trouble raised his visor. 'Listen to me. Listen. The rest of your life is going to be about thirty seconds. We have to go.'

'But the goblins, Trub.'

Captain Kelp grabbed his brother by the shoulders. 'Don't you worry about the goblins. You worry about my foot connecting with your behind if you slow down.'

Grub winced. He'd had that experience before. 'We're going to be all right, aren't we, brother?'

Trouble winked. 'Of course we are. I'm the captain, aren't I?'

His little brother nodded, lip losing its stiffness.

'Good. Now you point your nose at the door and go when I say. Got it?'

More nodding. Grub's chin was bobbing faster than a woodpecker's beak.

'Right, Corporal. Standby. On my command ...'

Another fireball. Closer this time. Rising black smoke from Trouble's rubber soles. The captain poked his nose around the wall. A laser burst almost gave him a third nostril. A steel sandwich board spun around the corner, dancing with the force of a dozen charges. *Foto Finish* the sign said. Or *Fot Finish* to be precise. The 'o' had been blasted out of it. Not laserproof then. But it would have to do.

Trouble snared the revolving board, draping it over his shoulders. Armour, of sorts. The LEP suits were lined with micro-filaments that would dissipate neutrino blasts or even sonic bursts, but Softnoses hadn't been used below ground for decades, so the suits hadn't been designed to withstand them. A burst would tear through the LEP uniform like so much rice paper.

He poked his brother in the back. 'Ready?'

Grub may have nodded, or it may have been that his entire body was shaking.

Trouble gathered his legs beneath him, adjusting the sandwich board across his chest and back. It would withstand a couple of rounds. After that, his own body would be providing cover for Grub.

Another fireball. Directly between them and the Emporium. In a moment, the flame would sink a hole in the tarmac. They had to go now. Through the fire.

'Seal your helmet!'

'Why?'

'Just seal it, Corporal.'

Grub did. You could argue with a brother, but not a commanding officer.

Trouble placed a hand on Grub's back and pushed. Hard. 'Go, go, go!'

They went, straight through the white heart of the flame. Trouble heard the filaments in his suit pop as they tried to cope with the heat. Boiling tar sucked at his boots, melting the rubber soles.

Then they were through, stumbling towards the

double doors. Trouble scrubbed the soot from his visor.
His men were waiting, huddled behind riot shields. Two
paramedic warlocks had their gloves off, ready to lay on
hands.

Ten metres to go.

On they ran.

The goblins found range. A hail of charges sang through
the air around them, pulverizing what was left of the
Emporium's shop front. Trouble's crown lurched forward
as a slug flattened itself against his helmet. More charges.
Lower down. A tight grouping between his shoulder
blades. The sandwich board held.

The impact lifted the captain like a kite, slapping him
into his brother, and carrying them both through the
decimated double doors. They were instantly hauled
behind a wall of riot shields.

'Grub,' gasped Captain Kelp, through the pain and
noise and soot. 'Is he OK?'

'Fine,' answered the senior warlock paramedic, rolling
Trouble on to his stomach. 'Your back on the other hand,
is going to have some lovely bruises in the morning.'

Captain Kelp waved the warlock away. 'Any word from
the commander?'

The warlock shook his head. 'Nothing. Root is missing
in action and Cudgeon has been reinstated as commander.
Even worse, now they're saying Foaly is behind this whole
thing.'

Trouble paled, and it wasn't from the pain in his back. 'Foaly! It can't be true.'

Trouble ground his teeth in frustration. Foaly and the commander. He had no choice, he would have to do it. The one thing he had nightmares about.

Captain Kelp struggled up on to one elbow. The air above their heads was alive with the buzz of Softnose bursts. It was only a matter of time before they were completely overrun. It had to be done.

Trouble took a breath. 'OK, people. Listen up. Retreat to Police Plaza.'

The troops froze. Even Grub caught himself in mid-sob. Retreat?

'You heard me!' snarled Trouble. 'Retreat. We can't hold the streets without arms. Now move it out.'

The LEP shuffled to the service entrance, unaccustomed to losing. Call it retreat, call it a tactical manoeuvre. It was still running away. And who would have thought that order would ever come out of Trouble Kelp's mouth?

Arctic shuttle port

Artemis and his fellow travellers took shelter in the shuttle port. Holly made the journey slung over Butler's shoulder. She protested loudly for several minutes until the commander ordered her to shut up.

'You've just had major magical surgery,' he pointed out. 'So just stay quiet and do your exercises.' It was vital that Holly manipulate her finger constantly for the next hour or so to ensure the right tendons got reconnected. It was very important she move her index finger the way she intended to use it later, especially as she would be firing a weapon.

They huddled around a glow cube in the deserted departure lounge.

'Any water?' asked Holly. 'I feel dehydrated after that healing.'

Root winked, something that didn't happen very often. 'Here's a little trick I learned in the field.' He popped a flat-nosed shell from a clip in his belt. It seemed to be made from perspex and filled with clear liquid.

'You won't get much of a drink from that,' commented Butler.

'More than you'd think. This is a Hydrosion shell: a miniature fire extinguisher. The water is compressed into a tiny space. You fire it into the heart of a fire and the impact reverses the compressor. Half a litre of water is blasted at the flames. More effective than a hundred litres poured. We call them Fizzers.'

'Very good,' said Artemis drily. 'If you could use your weapons.'

'Don't need 'em,' said Root, drawing a large knife. 'Manual works just as well.'

He pointed the shell's flat tip at the mouth of a canteen and popped the lid. A fizzing spray jetted into the container.

'There you are, Captain. Never let it be said I don't look after my officers.'

'Clever,' admitted Artemis.

'And the best thing is,' said the commander, pocketing the empty Fizzer. 'These things are completely reusable. All I have to do is stick it in a pile of snow and the compressor will do the rest, so I won't even have Foaly on my case for wasting equipment.'

Holly took a long drink and soon the colour surged back to her cheeks.

'So we were ambushed by a B'wa Kell hit team,' she mused. 'What does that mean?'

'It means you have a leak,' said Artemis, holding his hands close to the cube's warmth. 'It was my impression that this mission was top secret. Not even your Council was informed. The only person who isn't here is that centaur.'

Holly jumped to her feet. 'Foaly? It can't be.'

Artemis raised his palms. 'Logic. That's all it is.'

'This is all very well,' interrupted the commander, 'but it's conjecture. We need to assess our situation. What have we got, and what do we know for sure?'

Butler nodded. The commander was a being after his own heart. A soldier.

Root answered his own question. 'We've still got the shuttle, provided it's not wired. There's a locker full of provisions. Atlantean food mostly, so get used to fish and squid.'

'And what do we know?'

Artemis took over. 'We know that the goblins have a source in the LEP. We also know if they tried to take out the LEP's head, Commander Root, then they must be after the body. Their best chance of success would be to mount both operations simultaneously.'

Holly chewed her lip. 'So that means …'

'That means there is probably some kind of revolution going on below ground.'

'The B'wa Kell against the LEP?' scoffed Holly. 'No problem.'

'Generally, that may be true,' agreed Artemis. 'But if your weapons are out …'

'Then so are theirs,' completed Root, 'in theory.'

Artemis moved closer to the glow cube. 'Worst-case scenario: Haven has been taken by the B'wa Kell, and the Council members are either dead or imprisoned. Quite honestly, things look grim.'

Neither fairy responded. Grim hardly did the situation justice. Disastrous was closer to the mark.

Even Artemis was slightly disheartened. None of this was helping his father.

'I suggest we rest here for a while, pack some

provisions, and then proceed towards Murmansk as soon as we get some cloud cover. Butler can search this man Vassikin's apartment. Perhaps we will be lucky and my father will be there. I realize that we are at a slight disadvantage without weapons, but we still have surprise on our side.'

No one spoke for several moments. It was an uneasy silence. Everybody knew what should be said, but nobody wanted to say it.

'Artemis,' said Butler eventually, laying a hand on the boy's shoulder. 'We're in no shape to go up against the Mafiya. We don't have any firepower, and our colleagues need to get below ground, so we don't have any magic. If we go in there now, we're not coming out. Any of us.'

Artemis stared deep into the heart of the glow cube. 'But my father is so close, Butler. I can't give up now.'

In spite of herself, Holly was touched by his unwillingness to give up, against all the odds. She was certain that, for once, Artemis wasn't trying to manipulate anybody. He was simply a boy who missed his father. Maybe her defences were down, but she felt sorry for him.

'We're not giving up, Artemis,' she said softly. 'We're regrouping. There's a difference. We'll be back. Remember, it's always darkest before the dawn.'

Artemis looked at her. 'What dawn? We're in the Arctic, remember.'

Operations' booth

Foaly was furious with himself. After all the security encryptions he'd built into his systems, Opal Koboi had simply strolled in here and hijacked the entire network. And what's more, the LEP had paid her for the job.

The centaur had to admire her nerve. It was a brilliantly simple plan. Apply for the upgrade contract, submit the lowest estimate. Get the LEP to give you an access-all-areas chip and then piggyback spy cams on the local systems. She had even billed the LEP for the surveillance equipment.

Foaly pushed a few buttons experimentally. No response. Not that he'd expected any. Doubtless, Opal Koboi had everything wired, down to the last fibre optic. Perhaps she was watching him at this very moment. He could just imagine her. Coiled up on a Koboi Hoverboy™ giggling at the plasma screen. His greatest rival, gloating over his destruction.

Foaly growled. She may have caught him off guard once, but it wouldn't happen again. He would not go to pieces for Opal Koboi's entertainment ... Then again, maybe he would.

The centaur cradled his head between his hands, the picture of a beaten fairy, and began to heave theatrical sobs. He peeped out between his fingers ... Now, if I were a button camera, where would I hide? Somewhere the sweeper wouldn't check. Foaly glanced at the bug sweeper, a small, complex-looking mass of cables and chips attached to the roof. The only place the sweeper didn't check was inside the sweeper itself ...

So now he knew Opal's vantage point, for all the good it did him. If the camera was piggybacking inside the sweeper, there would be a small blindspot directly below the unit's titanium casing, but the pixie could still see everything of importance. He was still locked out of the computer and locked in the Operations' booth.

He began to scan the booth. What had come in since the last batch of Koboi upgrades? There must be some untainted equipment ...

But there was nothing except junk. A roll of fibre-optic cable. A few conductor clips and a few tools. Nothing useful. Then something winked at him from beneath a workstation. A green light.

Foaly's heart jumped ten beats per minute. He knew instantly what it was. Artemis Fowl's laptop computer. Complete with modem and e-mail capability. He willed himself to maintain calm. Opal Koboi couldn't possibly have bugged it. The device had only come in hours ago. He hadn't even got around to dismantling it yet.

The centaur clopped across to his toolbox and, in a fit of frustration, dumped the contents on to the plasma tiles. He was not so frustrated that he forgot to snag some cable and snips. The next step in his faked breakdown was to flop on to the worktop, sobbing uncontrollably. Naturally he had to flop over the precise spot where Holly had left the laptop. With a casual kick, Foaly slid the computer into the space where the sweeper's blindspot should be. He then threw himself on to the floor, kicking his legs in a furious tantrum. From the button camera, Opal shouldn't be able to see more than his thrashing legs.

So far so good. Foaly popped the laptop's lid, quickly shutting off the speakers. Humans would insist on their machines beeping at the most inopportune moments. He allowed one hand to drag across the keyboard and moments later he was in the e-mail program.

Now for the problem. Wireless Internet access is one thing, but access from the centre of the Earth is quite another. Cradling his head in the crook of one arm, Foaly jimmied one end of a fibre-optic cable into a scope uplink port. The scopes were shrouded trackers concealed on American communications satellites. Now he had an aerial. Let's hope Mud Boy was switched on.

Koboi Laboratories

Opal Koboi had never had so much fun. The underworld was literally her plaything. She stretched on her Koboi Hoverboy like a contented cat, eyes devouring the chaos on the plasma monitors. The LEP had no chance. It was only a matter of time before the B'wa Kell gained access to Police Plaza, then the city was theirs. Next came Atlantis, then the human world.

Opal floated between screens, soaking up every detail. In the city, goblins flowed from every centimetre of darkness, armed and thirsty for blood. Softnose slugs ripped chunks from historical edifices. Ordinary fairies barricaded themselves in their houses, praying that the marauding gangs would pass them by. Businesses were looted and torched. Not too much torching, she hoped. Opal Koboi had no desire to be queen of a war zone.

A com screen opened on the main display. It was Cudgeon on their secure line. And he actually seemed happy. The cold happiness of revenge.

'Briar,' squealed Opal. 'This is wonderful. I wish you were here to see it.'

'Soon. I must remain with my troops. After all, because I was the one who unearthed Foaly's treachery, the Council has reinstated me as commander. How is our prisoner?'

Opal glanced at the Foaly screen. 'Disappointing, frankly. I expected some plotting. An escape attempt, at least. But all he does is mope about and throw the odd tantrum.'

Cudgeon's smile widened. 'Suicidal, I expect. In fact, I'm certain of it.' Then the recently promoted commander was all business again. 'What of the LEP? Any unexpected brainwaves?'

'No. Exactly as you predicted. They are cowering in Police Plaza like tortoises in their shells. Shall I shut off local communications?'

Cudgeon shook his head. 'No. They broadcast their every move on their so-called secure channels. Keep them open. Just in case.'

Opal Koboi hovered closer to the screen. 'Tell me again, Briar. Tell me about the future.'

For a moment, annoyance flashed across Cudgeon's face. But today, of all days, his good humour could not be suppressed for long.

'The Council has been told that Foaly has orchestrated the sabotage from his locked Operations' booth. But you shall miraculously override the centaur's program and return control of Police Plaza's DNA cannons to the LEP. Those ridiculous goblins shall be overrun. I shall be the hero of the resistance, and you shall be my princess. Every military contract for the next five hundred years shall belong to Koboi Laboratories.'

Opal's breath caught in her throat. 'And then?'

'And then, together we will rid the Earth of these tiresome Mud People. That, my dear, is the future.'

181

Arctic shuttle terminal

Artemis's phone rang. Something even he hadn't anticipated. He stripped off a glove with his teeth, tearing the mobile phone from its Velcro strip.

'Text message,' he said, navigating through the mobile phone's menu. 'No one has this number except Butler.'

Holly folded her arms. 'Obviously someone has.'

Artemis ignored her tone. 'It must be Foaly. He's been monitoring my wireless communications for months. Either he's using my computer, or he's found a way to unify our platforms.'

'I see,' said Butler and Root together. Two big lies.

Holly was unimpressed by all the jargon. 'So what does it say?'

Artemis tapped the tiny screen. 'See for yourself.'

Captain Short took the mobile phone, scrolling through the message and reading it aloud. Her face grew longer with each line …

CMNDR ROOT. TRBLE BELOW. HAVN OVERRN BY GOBLNS. PLICE PLAZA SRROUNDED. CUDGEON + OPL KBOI BHND PLOT. NO WPONS OR CMMUNICATIONS. DNA CNONS CNTRLLED BY KBOI. I M TRPPED IN OP BTH. CNCL THNKS IM 2 BLM. IF ALIVE PLSE HLP. IF NOT, WRNG NMBR.

Holly swallowed, her throat suddenly dry. 'This is not good.'

The commander jumped to his feet, grabbing the mobile phone to read the message for himself.

'No,' he declared moments later. 'It certainly isn't. Cudgeon! All the time it was Cudgeon. Why didn't I see it? Can we get a message to Foaly?'

Artemis considered it. 'No. There's no network here. I'm surprised we could even receive.'

'Couldn't you rig it somehow?'

'Certainly. Just give me six months, some specialized equipment and three kilometres of steel girder.'

Holly snorted. 'Some criminal mastermind you turned out to be.'

Butler placed a gentle hand on her shoulder. 'Shh,' he whispered. 'Artemis is thinking.'

Artemis stared deep into the glow cube's liquid-plasma heart. 'We have two options,' he began, after a moment. Nobody interrupted, not even Holly. After all, it had been Artemis Fowl who had devised a way to escape the time field.

'We could get some human aid. No doubt some of Butler's more dubious acquaintances could be persuaded to help, for a fee, of course.'

Root shook his head. 'No good.'

'They could be mind-wiped afterwards.'

'Sometimes wipes don't take. The last thing we need is

mercenaries with residual memories. Option Two?'

'We break into Koboi Laboratories and return weapons control to the LEP.'

The commander guffawed. 'Break into Koboi Laboratories? Are you serious? That entire compound is built on bedrock. There are no windows, totally blast-resistant walls and DNA stun cannons. Any unauthorized personnel that come within a hundred metres get blasted right between the pointy ears.'

Butler whistled. 'Seems like a whole lot of hardware for an engineering company.'

'I know,' sighed Root. 'Koboi Labs had special permits. I signed them myself.'

Butler considered it for several moments. 'Can't be done,' he pronounced eventually. 'Not without the blueprints.'

'D'Arvit,' swore the commander. 'I never thought I'd say this, but there's only one fairy for a job like this ...'

Holly nodded. 'Mulch Diggums.'

'Diggums?'

'A dwarf. Career criminal. The only fairy ever to break into Koboi Laboratories and live. Unfortunately, we lost him last year. Tunnelling out of your manor as it happens.'

'I remember him,' said Butler. 'Nearly took my head off. A slippery character.'

Root laughed softly. 'Eight times I nabbed old Mulch. The last one was for the Koboi Labs job. As I recall, Mulch and his cousin set up as building contractors. A way to get plans for secure facilities. They got the Koboi contract. Mulch left himself a back door. Typical Diggums, he breaks into the most secure facility under the planet, then tries to sell an alchemy vat to one of my squeals.'

Artemis sat up. 'Alchemy? You have alchemy vats?'

'Stop drooling, Mud Boy. They're experimental. The ancient warlocks used to be able to turn lead into gold, according to the Book, but the secret was lost. Even Opal Koboi hasn't managed it yet.'

'Oh,' said Artemis, disappointed.

'Believe it or not, I almost miss that criminal. He had a way of insulting a person ...' Root glanced towards the heavens. 'I wonder if he's up there now, looking down on us.'

'In a manner of speaking,' said Holly guiltily. 'Actually, Commander, Mulch Diggums is in Los Angeles.'

CHAPTER II: MULCH ADO ABOUT NOTHING

LOS ANGELES, USA

 MULCH Diggums was, in fact, outside the apartment of an Oscar-winning actress. Of course, she didn't know he was there. And, naturally, he was up to no good. Once a thief, always a thief.

Not that Mulch needed the money. He'd done very well out of the Artemis Fowl Affair. Well enough to take out a lease on a penthouse apartment in Beverly Hills. He'd stocked the apartment with a Pioneer entertainment system, a full DVD library and enough beef jerky to last a lifetime. Time for a decade of rest and relaxation.

But life is not like that. It refuses to curl up and sit quietly in a corner. The habits of several centuries would not go away. Halfway through the James Bond Collection, Mulch realized that he missed the bad old days. Soon the penthouse suite's reclusive occupant was taking midnight strolls. These strolls generally ended up inside other people's homes.

Initially Mulch just visited, savouring the thrill of defeating sophisticated Mud Man security systems. Then he began to take trophies. Small things – a crystal goblet, an ashtray, or a cat if he was peckish. But soon Mulch Diggums began to crave the old notoriety and his pilferings grew larger. Gold bars, goose egg diamonds, or pit bull terriers if he was really famished.

The Oscar thing began quite by accident. He nabbed one as a curiosity on a midweek break to New York. Best original screenplay. The following morning he was front page news coast to coast. You'd think he'd ripped off a medical convoy instead of a gilded statuette. Mulch, of course, was delighted. He'd found his new nocturnal pastime.

In the next fortnight, Mulch filched best soundtrack and best special effects Academy Awards. The tabloids went crazy. They even gave him a nickname: the Grouch, after another well-known Oscar. When Mulch read that one, his toes wriggled for joy. And dwarf toes wriggling are quite a sight. They are as nimble as fingers, double-jointed and the less said about the smell the better. Mulch's mission became clear. He had to assemble an entire set.

Over the next six months, the Grouch struck all across the United States. He even made a trip to Italy to collect a best foreign-language film award. He had a special cabinet made, with tinted glass that could be blacked out at the touch of a button. Mulch Diggums felt alive again.

Of course, every Oscar winner on the planet trebled their security, which was just the way Mulch liked it. There was no challenge in breaking into a shack on the beach. High rise and high-tech. That's what the public wanted. So that's what the Grouch gave them. The papers ate it up. He was a hero. During the daylight hours, when he couldn't venture outside, Mulch busied himself writing the screenplay of his own exploits.

Tonight was a big night. The last statuette. He was going for a best actress award. And not just any old best actress. Tonight's target was the tempestuous Jamaican beauty, Maggie V. This year's winner for her portrayal of Precious, a tempestuous Jamaican beauty. Maggie V had stated publicly that if the Grouch tried anything in her apartment, he would get a lot more than he had bargained for. How could Mulch resist a challenge like that?

The building itself was easy to locate, a ten-storey block of glass and steel just off Sunset Boulevard, a midnight stroll south of Mulch's own home. So one cloudy night, the intrepid dwarf packed his tools, preparing to burglarize his way into the history books.

Maggie V was on the top floor. There was no question of going up the stairs, lift or shaft. It would have to be an outside job.

꒦ ꒦ ꒦ ꒦ ꒦

In preparation for the climb, Mulch had not had anything to drink in two days. Dwarf pores are not just for sweating, they can take in moisture too. Very handy when you are trapped in a cave-in for days on end. Even if you can't get your mouth to a drink, every centimetre of skin can leech water from the surrounding earth. When a dwarf was thirsty, as Mulch was now, his pores opened to the size of pinholes and began to suck like crazy. This could be extremely useful if, say, you had to climb up the side of a tall building.

Mulch took off his shoes and gloves, donned a stolen LEP helmet and began to climb.

CHUTE E93

Holly could feel the commander's glare crisping the hairs on the back of her neck. She tried to ignore it, concentrating on not dashing the Atlantean ambassador's shuttle against the walls of the Arctic chute.

'So, all this time, you knew Mulch Diggums was alive?'

Holly nudged the starboard thruster to avoid a missile of half-melted rock. 'Not for sure. Foaly just had this theory.'

The commander wrung an imaginary neck. 'Foaly! Why am I not surprised?'

Artemis smirked from his seat in the passenger area.

'Now, you two, we need to work together as a team.'

'So tell me about Foaly's theory, Captain,' ordered Root, belting himself into the co-pilot's seat.

Holly activated a static wash on the shuttle's external cameras. Positive and negative charges dislodged the sheets of dust from the lenses.

'Foaly thought Mulch's death a bit suspicious, given that he was the best tunnel fairy in the business.'

'So why didn't he come to me?'

'It was just a hunch. With respect, you know what you're like with hunches, Commander.'

Root nodded grudgingly. It was true, he didn't have time for hunches. It was hard evidence, or get out of my office until you've got some.

'The centaur did a bit of investigating in his own time. The first thing he realized was that the gold recovered was a bit light. I negotiated for the return of half the ransom and, by Foaly's reckoning, the cart was about two dozen bars short.'

The commander lit one of his trademark fungus cigars. He had to admit it sounded promising: gold missing, Mulch Diggums within a hundred miles. Two and two make four.

'As you know, it's standard procedure to spray any LEP property with solinium-based tracker, including the ransom gold. So, Foaly runs a scan for solinium, and he picks up hot spots all over Los Angeles. Particularly at the

190

Crowley Hotel in Beverly Hills. When he hacks into the building computer, he finds the penthouse resident is listed as one Lance Digger.'

Root's pointy ears quivered. 'Digger?'

'Exactly,' said Holly, nodding. 'A bit more than coincidence. Foaly came to me at that point, and I advised him to get some satellite photos before taking the file to you. Except …'

'Except Mister *Digger* is proving very elusive. Am I right?'

'Dead on.'

Root's colouring went from rose to tomato. 'Mulch, that rascal. How did he do it?'

Holly shrugged. 'We're guessing he transferred his iris-cam to some local wildlife, maybe a rabbit. Then collapsed the tunnel.'

'So the life signs we were reading belonged to some rabbit.'

'Exactly. In theory.'

'I'll kill him,' exclaimed Root, pounding the control panel. 'Can't this bucket go any faster?'

Los Angeles

Mulch scaled the building without much difficulty. There were external closed-circuit cameras, but the helmet's ion filter showed exactly where these cameras were pointed. It was a simple matter to crawl along the blind spots.

Within an hour, the dwarf was suckered outside Maggie V's apartment on the tenth floor. The windows were triple glazed with a bulletproof coating. Movie stars. Paranoid, every one of them.

Naturally, there was an alarm point sitting on top of the pane and a motion sensor crouching on a wall like a frozen cricket. Only to be expected.

Mulch melted a hole in the glass with a bottle of dwarf rock polish, used to clean up diamonds in the mines. Humans actually cut diamonds to shine them. Imagine. Half the stone down the drain.

Next, the Grouch used the helmet's ion filter to sweep the room for the motion sensor's range. The red ion-stream revealed that the sensor was focused on the floor. No matter. Mulch intended going along the wall.

Pores still crying out for water, the dwarf crept along the partition, making maximum use of a stainless-steel shelving system that almost completely surrounded the main sitting room.

The next step was to find the actual Oscar. It could be hidden anywhere, including under Maggie V's pillow, but this room was as good a place to start as any. You never knew, he might get lucky.

Mulch activated the helmet's X-ray filter, scanning the walls for a safe. Nothing. He tried the floor; humans were getting smarter these days. There, under a fake zebra rug, a metal cuboid. Easy.

The Grouch approached the motion sensor from above, very gently twisting the neck until the gadget was surveying the ceiling. The floor was now safe.

Mulch dropped to the rug, testing the surface with his tactile toes. No pressure pads sewn into the rug's lining. He rolled back the fake skin, revealing a hatch in the wooden floor. The joins were barely visible to the naked eye. But Mulch was an expert and his eyes weren't naked, they were aided by LEP zoom lenses.

He wormed a nail into the crack, flipping the hatch. The safe itself was a bit of a disappointment. Not even lead-lined; he could see right into the mechanism with the X-ray filter. A simple combination lock. Only three digits.

Mulch turned the filter off. What was the point in breaking a see-through lock? Instead he put his ear to the door, jiggling the dial. In fifteen seconds the door was open at his feet.

The Oscar's gold plating winked at him. Mulch made a big mistake at that moment. He relaxed. In the Grouch's mind he was already back in his own apartment, swigging from a two-litre bottle of ice-cold water. And relaxed thieves are destined for prison.

Mulch neglected to check the statuette for traps, plucking it straight from the safe. If he had checked he would have realized that there was a wire attached magnetically to the base. When the Oscar was moved, a circuit was broken allowing all hell to break loose.

Chute E93

Holly set the auto-pilot to hover at three thousand metres below the surface. She slapped herself on the chest, releasing the harness, and joined the others in the rear of the shuttle.

'Two problems. Firstly, if we go any lower, we'll be picked up on the scanners, presuming they're still operating.'

'Why am I not looking forward to number two?' asked Butler.

'Secondly, this part of the chute was retired when we pulled out of the Arctic.'

'Which means?'

'Which means the supply tunnels were collapsed. We have no way into the chute system without supply tunnels.'

'No problem,' declared Root. 'We blast the wall.'

Holly sighed. 'With what, Commander? This is a diplomatic craft. We don't have any cannons.'

Butler plucked two concussor eggs from a pouch on his Moonbelt. 'Will these do? Foaly thought they might come in handy.'

Artemis groaned. If he didn't know better, he'd swear the manservant was enjoying this.

Los Angeles

'Uh oh,' breathed Mulch.

In a matter of moments, things had gone from rosy to extremely dangerous. Once the security circuit was broken, a side door slid open admitting two very large German shepherds. The ultimate watchdogs. They were followed by their handler, a huge man covered in protective clothing. It looked as though he were dressed in doormats. Obviously the dogs were unstable.

'Nice doggies,' said Mulch, slowly unbuttoning his bum-flap.

Chute E93

Holly nudged the flight controls, inching the shuttle closer to the chute wall.

'That's as near as we get,' she said into her helmet mike. 'Any closer and the thermals could flip us against the rock face.'

'Thermals?' growled Root. 'You never said anything about thermals before I climbed out here.'

The commander was spread-eagled on the port wing, a concussor egg jammed down each boot.

'Sorry, Commander, someone has to fly this bird.'

Root muttered under his breath, dragging himself closer to the wing-tip. While the turbulence was nowhere as severe as it would have been on a moving aircraft, the buffeting thermals were quite enough to shake the commander like dice in a cup. All that kept him going was the thought of his fingers tightening around Mulch Diggums's throat.

'Another metre,' he gasped into the mike. At least they had communications, the shuttle had its own local intercom. 'One more metre and I can make it.'

'No go, Commander. That's your lot.'

Root risked a peek into the abyss. The chute stretched on forever, winding down to the orange magma glow at the Earth's core. This was madness. Crazy. There must be another way. At this point, the commander would even be willing to risk an over-ground flight.

Then Julius Root had a vision. It could have been the sulphur fumes, stress or even lack of food. But the commander could have sworn Mulch Diggums's features appeared before him, etched into the rock face. The face was sucking on a cigar and smirking.

His determination returned in a surge. Bested by a criminal. Not likely.

Root clambered to his feet, drying sweaty palms on his

jumpsuit. The thermals plucked at his limbs like mischievous ghosts.

'Ready to put some distance between us and this soon-to-be hole?' he shouted into the mike.

'Bet on it, Commander,' responded Holly. 'Soon as we have you back in the hold, we're out of here.'

'OK. Standby.'

Root fired the piton dart from his belt. The titanium head sank easily into the rock. The commander knew that tiny charges inside the dart would blow out two flanges securing it inside the face. Five metres. Not a great distance to swing on a piton cord. But it wasn't the swing really. It was the bone-crushing drop and the lack of handholds on the chute wall.

Come on, Julius, sniggered the Mulch edifice. Let's see what you look like splattered against a wall.

'You shut your mouth, convict,' roared the commander. And he jumped, swinging into the void.

The rock face rushed out to meet him, knocking the breath from his lungs. Root ground his back teeth against the pain. He hoped nothing was broken, because after the Russian trip, he didn't even have enough magic left to make a daisy bloom, never mind heal a fractured rib.

The shuttle's forward lights picked out the laser burns where the LEP tunnel dwarfs had sealed the supply chute. That weld line would be the weak spot. Root slotted the concussor eggs along two indents.

'I'm coming for you, Diggums,' he muttered, crushing the capsule detonators embedded in each one. Thirty seconds now.

Root aimed a second piton dart at the shuttle wing. An easy shot, he made this kind of thing in his sleep in the sim-range. Unfortunately, the simulators didn't have thermals fouling things up at the last moment.

Just as the commander fired his dart, the edge of a particularly strong whirlpool of gas caught the shuttle's rear, spinning it forty degrees anti-clockwise. The dart missed by a metre. It spun into the abyss, trailing the commander's lifeline behind it. Root had two options: he could rewind the cord using his belt winch, or he could jettison the piton and try again with his spare. Julius unhooked the cord; it would be faster to try again. A good plan, had he not already used his spare to get them out from under the ice. The commander remembered this half a second after he'd cut loose his last piton.

'D'Arvit,' he swore, patting his belt for a dart which he knew wouldn't be there.

'Trouble, Commander?' asked Holly, her voice strained from wrestling with the controls.

'No pitons left, and the charges are set.'

There followed a brief silence. Very brief. No time for lengthy think-tanks. Root glanced at his moonomenter. Twenty-five seconds and counting.

∴ ⟋ ▽ |,| ⌐ ∴

When Holly's voice came over the headset, it was not bursting with enthusiasm or confidence.

'Er ... Commander. You wearing any metal?'

'Yes,' replied Root, puzzled. 'My breastplate, buckle, insignia, blaster. Why?'

Holly nudged the shuttle a shade closer. Any nearer was suicide.

'Put it like this. How fond are you of your ribs?'

'Why?'

'I think I know how to get you out of there.'

'How?'

'I could tell you, but you're not going to like it.'

'Tell me, Captain. That's a direct order.'

Holly told him. He didn't like it.

Los Angeles

Dwarf gas. Not the most tasteful of subjects; even dwarfs don't like to talk about it. Many a dwarf wife is known to scold her husband for venting gas at home and not leaving it in the tunnels. The fact is that, genetically, dwarfs are prone to gas attacks, especially if they've been eating clay in the mine. A dwarf can take in several kilos of dirt a second through his unhinged jaws. That's a lot of clay, with a lot of air in it. All this waste has to go somewhere. So it goes south. To put it politely, the tunnels are self-sealing.

Mulch hadn't eaten clay in months, but he still had a few bubbles of gas at his disposal when he needed them.

The dogs were poised to attack. Slobber hung in ribbons from their gaping jaws. He would be torn to pieces. Mulch concentrated. The familiar bubbling began in his stomach, pulling it out of shape. It felt as though a couple of gnome garbage wrestlers were going a few rounds in there. The dwarf gritted his teeth, this was going to be a big one.

The handler blew a football whistle. The dogs lunged forward like torpedoes with teeth. Mulch let go with a stream of gas, blowing a hole in the rug and propelling himself to the ceiling, where his thirsty pores anchored him. Safe. For the moment.

The German shepherds were particularly surprised. In their time they had chewed their way through most creatures in the food chain. This was something new. And not altogether pleasant. You have to remember that a dog's nose is far more sensitive than a human one.

The handler blew his whistle a few more times, but any control he might have had disappeared the moment Mulch flew through the air on a jet of recycled wind. As soon as the dogs' nasal passages cleared, they began to leap, teeth gnashing at the apex.

Mulch swallowed. Dogs are smarter than the average goblin. It was only a matter of time before they thought to scale the furniture and make a jump from there.

❧ ┃ ❧

Mulch made for the window, but the handler was there before him, blocking the hole with his padded body. Mulch noticed him fumbling with a weapon at his belt. This was getting serious. Dwarfs are many things, but bulletproof is not one of them.

To make matters worse, Maggie V appeared at the bedroom door, brandishing a chrome baseball bat. This was not the Maggie V the public was used to. Her face was covered with a green mask, and there appeared to be a tea bag taped under each eye.

'Now we have you, Mister Grouch,' she gloated. 'And suction pads aren't going to save you.'

Mulch realized that his career as the Grouch was over. Whether he escaped or not, the LAPD would be visiting every dwarf in the city come sunrise.

Mulch only had one card left to play. The gift of tongues. Every fairy has a natural grasp of languages, as all tongues are based on Gnommish, if you trace them back far enough. Including American Dog.

'*Arf*,' grunted Mulch. '*Arf, rrruff rruff.*'

The dogs froze. One attempted to freeze in mid-leap, landing on his partner. They chewed each other's tails for a moment, then remembered that there was a creature on the ceiling barking at them. His accent was terrible, something mid-European. But it was Dog nevertheless.

'*Aroof?*' enquired dog number one. 'Whaddya sayin'?'

Mulch pointed at the handler. '*Woof arfy arrooof!* That

human has a big bone inside his shirt,' he grunted. (Obviously, that's been translated.)

The German shepherds pounced on their handler, Mulch scampered through the hole in the window, and Maggie V howled so much that her mask cracked and her tea bags fell off. And even though the Grouch knew that this particular chapter in his career was closed, the weight of Maggie V's Academy Award inside his shirt gave him no little satisfaction.

CHUTE E93

Twenty seconds left before the concussors blew, and the commander was still flattened against the chute wall. They had no wing sets, and no time to get one outside even if they had. If they couldn't pull Root out of there right now, then he'd be blown off the wall and into the abyss. And magic didn't work on melted slop. There was only one option. Holly would have to use the gripper clamps.

All shuttles are equipped with secondary landing gear. If the docking nodes fail, then four magnetic gripper clamps could be blasted from recessed grooves. These clamps will latch on to the metal underside of the landing-bay dock, reeling the shuttle into the airlock. The grippers also came in handy in unfamiliar environments, where the magnets would seek out trace elements and latch on like sucker slugs.

'OK, Julius,' said Holly. 'Don't move a muscle.'

Root paled. Julius. Holly had called him Julius. That was not good.

Ten seconds.

Holly flicked down a small view screen. 'Release forward port docking clamp.'

A grating hum signalled the clamp's release.

The commander's image appeared in the view screen. Even from here he looked worried. Holly centred a cross hair on his chest.

'Captain Short. Are you absolutely sure about this?'

Holly ignored her superior. 'Range fifteen metres. Magnets only.'

'Holly, maybe I could jump. I could make it. I'm sure I could make it.'

Five seconds …

'Fire port clamp.'

Six tiny charges ignited around the clamp's base, sending the metal disc rocketing from its socket, trailed by a length of retractable polymer cable.

Root opened his mouth to swear, then the clamp crashed into his chest, driving every gasp of air from his body. Several somethings cracked.

'Reel it in,' spat Holly into the computer mike, simultaneously peeling across the chute. The commander was dragged behind like an extreme surfer.

Zero seconds. The concussors blew, sending two thousand kilograms of rubble careering into the void. A drop in an ocean of magma.

A minute later, the commander was strapped on a gurney in the Atlantean ambassador's sick bay. It hurt to breathe, but that wasn't going to stop him talking.

'Captain Short!' he rasped. 'What the hell were you thinking? I could have been killed.'

Butler ripped open Root's tunic to survey the damage. 'You could have been. Five more seconds and you were pulp. It's thanks to Holly that you are still alive.'

Holly set the auto-pilot to hover and grabbed a medi-pac from the first-aid box. She crumpled it between her fingers to activate the crystals. Another of Foaly's inventions. Ice packs infused with healing crystals. No substitute for magic, but better than a hug and a kiss.

'Where does it hurt?'

Root coughed. A bloody string splattered his uniform. 'The general bodily area. Coupla ribs gone.'

Holly chewed her lip. She was no doctor and healing was by no means an automatic business. Things could go wrong. Holly knew a vice-captain once who had broken a leg and passed out. He woke up with one foot pointing backwards. Not that Holly hadn't performed some tricky operations before. When Artemis wanted his mother's depression cured, she was in a different time zone. Holly had sent out a strong positive signal, with enough sparks in it to hang around for a few days. A sort of general pick-me-up. Anyone who even visited Fowl Manor for the following week should have gone away whistling.

'Holly,' groaned Root.

'O-OK,' she stammered. 'OK.'

She laid her hands on Root's chest, sending the magic scurrying down her fingers. 'Heal,' she breathed.

The commander's eyes rolled back in his head. The magic was shutting him down for recuperation. Holly laid a medi-pac on the unconscious LEP officer's chest.

'Hold that,' she instructed Artemis. 'Ten minutes only. Otherwise there'll be tissue damage.'

Artemis applied pressure to the pack. His fingers were quickly submerged in a pool of blood. Suddenly the desire to pass a smart remark utterly deserted him. First physical exercise, then actual bodily harm. And now this. These past few days were turning out to be quite educational. He'd almost prefer to be back in St Bartleby's.

Holly returned quickly to the cockpit, panning the external cameras towards the supply tunnel.

Butler squeezed into the co-pilot's chair. 'Well,' he asked. 'What've we got?'

Holly grinned. And for a second her expression reminded the manservant of Artemis Fowl. 'We've got a big hole.'

'Good. Then let's go visit an old friend.'

Holly's thumbs hovered over the thrusters. 'Yes,' she said. 'Let's.'

The Atlantean shuttle disappeared into the supply tunnel faster than a carrot down Foaly's gullet. And for those who don't know, that's pretty fast.

THE CROWLEY HOTEL, BEVERLY HILLS, LOS ANGELES

Mulch made it back to his hotel undetected. Of course, this time he didn't have to scale the walls. It would have been more of a challenge than Maggie V's building. The walls here were brick, very porous. His fingers would have leeched the moisture from the stone and lost their suction.

No, this time Mulch used the main foyer. And why wouldn't he? As far as the doorman was concerned, he was Lance Digger, reclusive millionaire. Short, maybe. But short and rich.

'Evening, Art,' said Mulch, saluting the doorman on his way to the lift.

Art peered over the marble-topped desk.

'Ah, Mister Digger, it's you,' he said, slightly puzzled. 'I thought I heard you passing below my sightline only moments ago.'

'Nope,' said Mulch, grinning. 'First time tonight.'

'Hmm. The night wind perhaps.'

'Maybe. You'd think they'd block up the holes in this building. All the rent I'm paying.'

'You would indeed,' agreed Art. Always agree with the tenants, company policy.

Inside the mirrored lift, Mulch used a telescopic pointer to push P for penthouse. For the first few months, he had jumped to reach the button, but that was undignified behaviour for a millionaire. And besides, he was certain that Art could hear the thumping from the security desk.

The mirrored box rose silently, flickering past the floors towards the penthouse. Mulch resisted the urge to take the Academy Award out of his bag. Someone could board the lift. He contented himself with a long drink from a bottle of Irish spring water, the closest to fairy pure it was possible to get. As soon as he had stowed the Oscar he would run a cold bath and give his pores a drink. Otherwise he could wake up in the morning glued to the bed.

Mulch's door was key-coded. A fourteen-number sequence. Nothing like a bit of paranoia to keep you out of prison. Even though the LEP believed that he was dead, Mulch could never quite shake the feeling that one day Julius Root would figure it all out and come looking for him.

The apartment's decor was quite unusual, for a human

dwelling. A lot of clay, crumbling rock and water features. More like the inside of a cave than an exclusive Beverly Hills residence.

The northern wall appeared to be a single slab of black marble. Appeared to be. Closer inspection revealed a forty-inch flat-screen television, a DVD slot and a tinted glass pane. Mulch hefted a remote control bigger than his leg, popping the hidden cabinet with another complicated key code. Inside were three rows of Oscars. Mulch placed Maggie V's on a waiting velvet pad.

He wiped an imaginary tear from the corner of his eye. 'I'd like to thank the Academy,' giggled the dwarf.

'Very touching,' said a voice behind him.

Mulch slammed the cabinet door shut, cracking the glass pane.

There was a human youth beside the rockery. In his apartment! The boy's appearance was strange, even by Mud Man standards. He was abnormally pale, raven-haired, slender and dressed in a school uniform that looked as though it had been dragged across two continents.

The hairs on Mulch's chin stiffened. This boy was trouble. Dwarf hair is never wrong.

'Your alarm was amusing,' continued the boy. 'It took me several seconds to bypass it.'

Mulch knew he was in trouble then. Human police don't break into people's apartments.

'Who are you, hu … boy?'

'I think the question here is, who are you? Are you reclusive millionaire Lance Digger? Are you the notorious Grouch? Or perhaps, as Foaly suspects, you are escaped convict Mulch Diggums?'

Mulch ran, the last vestiges of gas providing him with an extra burst of speed. He had no idea who this Mud Boy was, but if Foaly sent him, then he was a bounty hunter of one kind or another.

The dwarf raced across the sunken lounge, making for his escape route. It was the reason he'd chosen this building. In the early nineteen hundreds a wide-bore chimney had run the length of the multi-storey building. When a central-heating system had been installed in the fifties, the building contractor had simply packed the chute with dirt, topping it off with a seal of concrete. Mulch had smelled the vein of soil the second his estate agent had opened the front door. It had been a simple matter to uncover the old fireplace and chip away the concrete. *Voilà*. Instant tunnel.

Mulch unbuttoned his bum-flap on the run. The strange youth made no attempt to follow him. Why would he? There was nowhere to go.

The dwarf spared a second for a parting shot. 'You'll never take me alive, human. Tell Foaly not to send a Mud Man to do a fairy's job.'

Oh dear, thought Artemis, rubbing his brow. Hollywood had a lot to answer for.

Mulch tore a basket of dried flowers from the fireplace and dived right in. He unhinged his jaw and was quickly submerged in the century-old clay. It was not really to his taste. The minerals and nutrients had long since dried up. Instead, the soil was infused with a hundred years of burnt refuse and tobacco ash. But it was clay nevertheless, and this was what dwarfs were born to do. Mulch felt his anxiety melt away. There wasn't a creature alive that could catch him now. This was his domain.

The dwarf descended rapidly, chewing his way through the storeys. More than one wall collapsed on his way past. Mulch had a feeling that he wouldn't be getting his deposit back, even if he had been around to collect it.

In a little over a minute, Mulch had reached the basement car park. He rehinged, gave his rear-end a shake to dislodge any bubbles of gas, then tumbled through the grate. His specially adapted four-wheel drive was waiting for him. Fuelled up, blacked out and ready to go.

'Suckers,' gloated the dwarf, fishing the keys from a chain around his neck.

Then Captain Holly Short materialized not a metre away. 'Suckers?' she said, powering up her buzz baton.

Mulch considered his options. The basement floor was asphalt. Asphalt was death to dwarfs, sealed up their insides like glue. There appeared to be a man mountain blocking the basement ramp. Mulch had seen that one before in Fowl Manor. That meant the human upstairs must be the infamous Artemis Fowl. Captain Short was dead ahead looking none too merciful. Only one way to go. Back into the flue. Up a couple of storeys, and hide out in another apartment.

Holly grinned. 'Go on, Mulch. I dare you.'

And Mulch did, he turned, launching himself back into the chimney, expecting a sharp shock in the rear-end. He was not disappointed. How could Holly miss a target like that?

CHUTE E116, BELOW LOS ANGELES

The Los Angeles shuttle port was sixteen miles south of the city, hidden beneath the holographic projection of a sand dune. Root was waiting for them in the shuttle. He had recovered just enough to crack a grin.

'Well, well,' he grunted, hauling himself off the gurney, a fresh medi-pac strapped across his ribs. 'If it isn't my favourite reprobate, back from the dead.'

Mulch helped himself to a jar of squid paté from the Atlantean ambassador's personal cooler.

'Why is it, Julius, that you never pay me a social visit? After all, I did save your career back in Ireland. If it hadn't been for me, you never would have known about Fowl's copy of the Book.'

When Root was fuming, as he was now, you could have toasted marshmallows on his cheeks.

'We had a deal, convict. You broke it. And now I'm bringing you in.'

Mulch scooped dollops of paté from the jar with his stubby fingers.

'Could use a little beetle juice,' he commented.

'Enjoy it while you can, Diggums. Because your next meal is going to be pushed through a slot in a door.'

The dwarf settled back in a padded chair. 'Comfortable.'

'I thought so,' agreed Artemis. 'Some form of liquid suspension. Expensive, I shouldn't wonder.'

'Sure beats prison shuttles,' agreed Mulch. 'I remember this one time they caught me selling a Van Gogh to a Texan. I was transported in a shuttle the size of a mouse hole. They had a troll in the next cubicle. Stank something awful.'

Holly grinned. 'That's what the troll said.'

Root knew he was being goaded, but he blew his top anyway. 'Listen to me, convict. I have not travelled all this way to listen to your war stories. So shut your trap before I shut it for you.'

Mulch was unimpressed by the outburst. 'Just out of interest, Julius, why have you travelled all this way? The great Commander Root commandeering an ambassador's shuttle just to apprehend little old me? I don't think so.

So, what's going on? And what's with the Mud Men?' He nodded at Butler. 'Especially that one.'

The manservant grinned. 'Remember me, little man? Seems to me I owe you something.'

Mulch swallowed. He had crossed swords with Butler before. It hadn't ended well for the human. Mulch had vented a bowel full of dwarf gas directly at the manservant. Very embarrassing for a bodyguard of his status, not to mention painful.

For the first time Root chortled, even though it stretched his ribs. 'OK, Mulch. You're right. Something is going on. Something important.'

'I thought so. And, as usual, you need me to do your dirty work.' Mulch rubbed his rump. 'Well, assaulting me isn't going to help. You didn't have to buzz me so hard, Captain. That's going to leave a mark.'

Holly cupped a hand around one pointed ear. 'Hey, Mulch, if you listen really hard you can just about make out the sound of nobody giving a hoot. From what I saw, you were living pretty well on LEP gold.'

'That apartment cost me a fortune, you know. The deposit alone was four years of your salary. Did you see the view? Used to belong to some movie director.'

Holly raised an eyebrow. 'Glad to see the money was put to good use. Heaven forbid you should squander it.'

Mulch shrugged. 'Hey, I'm a thief. What did you expect – I'd start a shelter?'

'No, Mulch, funnily enough I didn't expect that for one second.'

Artemis cleared his throat. 'This reunion is all very touching. But while you're exchanging witticisms, my father is freezing in the Arctic.'

The dwarf zipped up his suit. 'His father? You want me to rescue Artemis Fowl's father? In the Arctic?' There was real fear in his voice. Dwarfs hated ice almost as much as fire.

Root shook his head. 'I wish it were that simple, and in a few minutes so will you.'

Mulch's beard hairs curled in apprehension. And as his grandmother always said, trust the hair, Mulch, trust the hair.

CHAPTER 12: THE BOYS ARE BACK

 FOALY was thinking. Always thinking. His mind popped off ideas like corn in a microwave. But he couldn't do anything with them. He couldn't even call up Julius and pester him with his hair-brained schemes. Fowl's laptop seemed to be the centaur's only weapon. It was like trying to fight a troll with a toothpick.

Not that the human computer was without some merit, in an ancient-history kind of way. The e-mail had already proved useful. Provided there was anybody alive to answer it. There was also a small camera mounted on the lid, for video-conferencing. Something the Mud People had only come up with recently. Until then, humans had communicated purely through text or sound waves. Foaly tutted, barbarians. But this camera was pretty high quality, with several filter options. If the centaur didn't know better, he'd swear someone had been leaking fairy technology.

Foaly swivelled the laptop with his hoof, pointing the camera towards the screens on the wall. Come on, Cudgeon, he thought. Smile for the birdie.

He didn't have long to wait. Within minutes, a com screen flickered into life and Cudgeon appeared, waving a white flag.

'Nice touch,' commented Foaly sarcastically.

'I thought so,' said the elf, waving the pennant theatrically. 'I'm going to need this later.'

Cudgeon pressed a button on the remote control. 'Why don't I show you what's going on outside?'

The windows cleared to reveal several squads of technicians feverishly trying to break the booth's defences. Most were aiming computer sensors at the booth's various interfaces, but some were doing it the old-fashioned way. Whacking the sensors with big hammers. None were having any luck.

Foaly swallowed. He was a rat in a trap. 'Why don't you fill me in on your plan, Briar? Isn't that what the power-crazed villain usually does?'

Cudgeon settled back into his swivel chair. 'Certainly, Foaly. Because this isn't one of your precious human movies. There will be no hero rushing in at the last moment. Short and Root are already dead. As are their human partners. No reprieve, no rescue. Just certain death.'

Foaly knew he should be feeling sadness, but hatred was all he could find.

'Just when things are at their most desperate, I shall instruct Opal to return weapons control to the LEP. The B'wa Kell will be rendered unconscious, and you will be blamed for the entire affair, provided you survive, which I doubt.'

'When the B'wa Kell recover, they will name you.'

Cudgeon wagged a finger. 'Only a handful know I am involved, and I shall take care of them personally. They have already been summoned to Koboi Labs. I shall join them shortly. The DNA cannons are being calibrated to reject goblin strands. When the time comes I shall activate them, and the entire squadron will be out for the count.'

'And then Opal Koboi becomes your empress, I suppose?'

'Of course,' said Cudgeon aloud. But then he manipulated the remote's keyboard, making certain they were on a secure channel.

'Empress?' he breathed. 'Really, Foaly. Do you think I'd go to all this trouble to share power? Oh no. As soon as this charade is over Miss Koboi will have a tragic accident. Perhaps several tragic accidents.'

Foaly bristled. 'At the risk of sounding clichéd, Briar, you'll never get away with this.'

⋮ ˹ △ ⊼ ⋮

Cudgeon's finger hovered over the terminate button. 'Well if I don't,' he said pleasantly, 'you won't be alive to gloat this time.' And he was gone, leaving the centaur to sweat it out in the booth. Or so Cudgeon thought.

Foaly reached below the desk to the laptop. 'And cut,' he murmured, pausing the camera. 'Take five, people, that's a wrap.'

CHUTE E116

Holly clamped the shuttle to the wall of a disused chute.

'We got about thirty minutes. Internal sensors say there's a flare coming up here in half an hour, and no shuttle is built to withstand that kind of heat.'

They gathered in the pressurized lounge to put together a plan.

'We need to break into Koboi Labs and regain control of the LEP weaponry,' said the commander.

Mulch was out of his chair and heading for the door. 'No way, Julius. That place has been upgraded since I was there. I heard they've got DNA-coded cannons.'

Root grabbed the dwarf by the scruff of his neck. 'One, don't call me Julius. And two, you're acting like you have a choice, convict.'

Mulch glared at him. 'I do have a choice, Julius. I can

218

just serve out my sentence in a nice little cell. Putting me in the line of fire is a violation of my civil rights.'

Root's facial tones alternated from pastel pink to turnip purple. 'Civil rights!' he spluttered. 'You're talking to me about civil rights! Isn't that just typical?'

Then, strangely, he calmed down. In fact, he seemed almost happy. Those who were close to the commander knew that when *he* was happy, somebody else was about to be extremely sad.

'What?' asked Mulch suspiciously.

Root lit one of his noxious fungus cigars. 'Oh, nothing. Just that you're right, that's all.'

The dwarf squinted. 'I'm right? You're saying, in front of witnesses, that I'm right.'

'Certainly you are. Putting you in the line of fire would violate every right in the book. So, instead of cutting you the fantastic deal that I was about to offer, I'm going to add a couple of centuries to your sentence and throw you in maximum security.' Root paused, blowing a cloud of smoke at Mulch's face. 'In Howler's Peak.'

Mulch paled beneath the mud caking his cheeks. 'Howler's Peak? But that's a ...'

'A goblin prison,' completed the commander. 'I know. But for an obvious escape risk such as yourself, I don't think I'd have any trouble convincing the board to make an exception.'

Mulch dropped into the padded gyro chair. This wasn't

good. The last time he'd been in a cell with goblins, it hadn't been any fun. And that had been in Police Plaza. He wouldn't last a week in general population.

'So what was this deal?'

Artemis smiled, fascinated: Commander Root was smarter than he looked. Then again, it would be almost impossible not to be.

'Oh, now you're interested?'

'I might be. No promises, mind.'

'OK, here it is. One-time offer. Don't even bother bargaining. You get us into Koboi Labs and I give you a two-day head start when this is over.'

Mulch swallowed. That was a good offer. They must be in a whole lot of trouble.

POLICE PLAZA

Things were hotting up at Police Plaza. The monsters were at the door. Literally. Captain Kelp was running between stations, trying to reassure his men.

'Don't worry, people, they can't get through those doors with Softnoses. Nothing less than some kind of missile —'

At that moment, a tremendous force buckled the main doors, like a child blowing up a paper bag. They held. Barely.

Cudgeon came rushing out of the tactical room, his commander's acorns glinting on his breast. With his reinstatement by the Council, he had made history by becoming the only commander in the LEP to have been appointed twice.

'What was that?'

Trouble brought up a front view on the monitors. A goblin stood with a large tube on his shoulder.

'Bazooka of some kind. I think it's one of the old wide-bore Softnose cannons.'

Cudgeon smacked his own forehead. 'Don't tell me. They were all supposed to have been destroyed. A curse on that centaur! How did he manage to sneak all that hardware out from under my nose?'

'Don't be too hard on yourself,' said Trouble. 'He fooled all of us.'

'How much more of that can we stand?'

Trouble shrugged. 'Not much. A couple more hits. Maybe they only had one missile.'

Famous last words. The doorway shook a second time; large chunks of masonry tumbled from the marble pillars.

Trouble picked himself off the ground, magic zipping a gash on his forehead. 'Paramedics, check for casualties. Have we got those weapons charged yet?'

Grub hobbled over, hampered by the weight of two electric rifles. 'Ready to go, Captain. Thirty-two weapons. Twenty pulses each.'

'OK. Best marks-fairies only. Not one shot fired until I give the word.'

Grub nodded, his face grim and pale.

'Good, Corporal, now move it out.'

When his brother was out of earshot, Trouble spoke quietly to Commander Cudgeon. 'I don't know what to tell you, Commander. They blew the Atlantis tunnel, so there's no help coming from there. We can't get a pentagram around them to stop time. We're completely surrounded, outnumbered and outgunned. If the B'wa Kell breaches the blast doors, it will be over in seconds. We have to get into that Operations' booth. Any progress?'

Cudgeon shook his head. 'The techies are working on it. We have sensors pointed at every centimetre of the surface. If we hit on the access code, it will be blind luck.'

Trouble rubbed the tiredness from his eyes. 'I need time. There must be a way to stall them.'

Cudgeon drew a white flag from inside his tunic. 'There is a way …'

'Commander! You can't go out there. It's suicide.'

'Perhaps,' admitted the commander. 'But if I don't go, we could all be dead in a matter of minutes. At least this way, we'll have a few minutes to work on the Operations' booth.'

Trouble considered it. There was no other way. 'What have you got to bargain with?'

'The prisoners in Howler's Peak. Maybe we could negotiate some kind of controlled release.'

'The Council will never go for that.'

Cudgeon drew himself up to his full height. 'This is not a time for politics, Captain. This is a time for action.'

Trouble was, quite frankly, amazed. This was not the same Briar Cudgeon he knew. Someone had given this fairy a spine transplant.

Now the newly appointed commander was going to earn that acorn cluster on his lapel. Trouble felt an emotion well up in his chest. One that he'd never before associated with Briar Cudgeon. It was respect.

'Open the front door a crack,' ordered the commander in steely tones. Foaly would be just loving this on camera. 'I'm going out to talk to these reptiles.'

Trouble relayed the command. If they ever got out of this, he would see to it that Commander Cudgeon was awarded a posthumous Golden Acorn. At the very least.

Uncharted chute, below Koboi Laboratories

The Atlantean shuttle sped down a vast chute, sticking tightly to the walls. Close enough to scrape paint from the hull.

Artemis poked his head through from the passenger bay.

'Is this really necessary, Captain?' he asked, as they avoided death by a centimetre for the umpteenth time. 'Or is it just more fly-boy grandstanding?'

Holly winked. 'Do I look like a fly boy to you, Fowl?'

Artemis had to admit that she didn't. Captain Short was extremely pretty in a dangerous sort of way. Black-widow pretty. Artemis was expecting puberty to hit in approximately eight months, and he suspected that at that point he would look at Holly in a different light. It was probably just as well that she was eighty years old.

'I'm hugging the surface to search for this alleged crack that Mulch insists is along here,' Holly explained.

Artemis nodded. The dwarf's theory. Just incredible enough to be true. He returned to the aft bay for Mulch's version of a briefing.

The dwarf had drawn a crude diagram on a backlit wall panel. In fairness, there were more artistic chimpanzees. And less pungent ones. Mulch was using a carrot as a pointer — or, more accurately, several carrots. Dwarfs liked carrots.

'This is Koboi Labs,' he mumbled around a mouthful of vegetable.

'That?' exclaimed Root.

'I realize, Julius, that it is not an accurate schematic.'

The commander exploded from his chair. If you didn't know better, you'd swear there was dwarf gas involved. 'An accurate schematic? It's a rectangle, for heaven's sake!'

Mulch was unperturbed. 'That's not important. This is the important bit.'

'That wobbly line?'

'It's a fissure,' protested the dwarf. 'Anybody can see that.'

'Anybody in kindergarten, maybe. So it's a fissure, so what?'

'This is the clever bit. Y'see, that fissure is not usually there.'

Root began strangling the air again. Something he was doing more and more lately. But Artemis was suddenly interested.

'When does the fissure appear?'

But Mulch wasn't just going to give a straight answer. 'Us dwarfs. We know something about rocks. Been digging around 'em for ages.' Root's fingers began beating a tattoo on his buzz baton. 'What fairies don't realize is that rocks are alive. They breathe.'

Artemis nodded. 'Of course. Heat expansion.'

Mulch bit the carrot triumphantly. 'Exactly. And, of course, the opposite. They contract when they cool down.' Even Root was listening now. 'Koboi Labs is built on solid mantle. Three miles of rock. No way in, short of sonix warheads. And I think Opal Koboi might notice them.'

'And that helps us how?'

'A crack opens up in that rock when it cools down. I

225

worked on the foundations when they were building this place. Gets you right in under the labs. Still a way to go, but at least you're in.'

The commander was sceptical. 'So how come Opal Koboi hasn't noticed this gaping fissure?'

'Oh, I wouldn't say it was gaping.'

'How big?'

Mulch shrugged. 'Dunno. Maybe five metres. At its widest point.'

'That's still a pretty big fissure to be sitting there all day.'

'Only it's not there all day,' interrupted Artemis. 'Is it, Mulch?'

'All day? I wish. I'd say, at a guess, this is only an approximation mind ...'

Root was losing his cool. Being one step behind all the time didn't agree with him.

'Tell me, convict, before I add another scorch mark to your behind!'

Mulch was injured. 'Stop shouting, Julius, you're curling my beard.'

Root opened the cooler, letting the icy tendrils play over his face.

'OK, Mulch. How long?'

'Three minutes max. Last time I did it with a set of wings, wearing a pressure suit. Nearly got crushed and fried.'

'Fried?'

'Let me guess,' said Artemis. 'The fissure only opens when the rock has contracted sufficiently. If this fissure is on a chute wall, then the coolest time would be moments before the next flare.'

Mulch winked. 'Smart, Mud Boy. If the rocks don't get you, the magma will.'

Holly's voice crackled over the com speakers. 'I've got a visual on something. Could be a shadow, or it could just be a crack in the chute wall.'

Mulch did a little dance, looking very pleased with himself. Now, Julius, you can say it. I was right again! You owe me, Julius, you owe me.'

The commander rubbed the bridge of his nose. If he made it through this alive, he was never leaving the station again.

KOBOI LABORATORIES

Koboi Labs was surrounded by a ring of B'wa Kell goblins. Armed to the teeth, tongues hanging out for blood. Cudgeon was hustled past roughly, prodded by a dozen barrels. The DNA cannons hung inoperative in their towers, for the moment. The second Cudgeon felt the B'wa Kell had outlived its usefulness, then the guns would be reactivated.

The commander was taken to the inner sanctum, and forced to his knees before Opal and the B'wa Kell generals. Once the soldiers had been dismissed, Cudgeon was back on his feet and in command.

'Everything proceeds according to plan,' he announced, crossing to stroke Opal's cheek. 'In an hour Haven will be ours.'

General Scalene was not convinced. 'It would be ours a lot faster if we had some Koboi blasters.'

Cudgeon sighed patiently. 'We've been through this, General. The disruption signal knocks out all neutrino weapons. If you get blasters, so will the LEP.'

Scalene shuffled into a corner, licking his eyeballs.

Of course, that was not the only reason for denying the goblins neutrino weapons. Cudgeon had no intention of arming a group he intended to betray. As soon as the B'wa Kell had disposed of the Council, Opal would return power to the LEP.

'How are things proceeding?'

Opal swivelled in her Hoverboy, legs curled beneath her. 'Deliciously. The main doors fell moments after you left to … negotiate.'

Cudgeon grinned. 'Good thing I left. I might have been injured.'

'Captain Kelp has pulled his remaining forces into the Operations' room, ringing the booth. The Council is in there too.'

'Perfect,' said Cudgeon.

Another B'wa Kell general, Sputa, banged the conference table. 'No, Cudgeon. Far from perfect. Our brothers are wasting away in Howler's Peak.'

'Patience, General Sputa,' said Cudgeon soothingly, actually laying a hand on the goblin's shoulder. 'As soon as Police Plaza falls, we can open the cells in Howler's Peak without resistance.'

Internally Cudgeon fumed. These idiot creatures. How he detested them. Clothed in robes fashioned from their own cast-off skin. Repulsive. Cudgeon longed to reactivate the DNA cannons and stop their jabbering for a few sweet hours.

He caught Opal's eye. She knew what he was thinking. Her tiny teeth showed in anticipation. What a delightfully vicious creature. Which was, of course, why she had to be disposed of. Opal Koboi could never be happy as second in command.

He dropped her a wink.

'Soon,' he mouthed silently. 'Soon.'

CHAPTER 13: INTO THE BREACH

BELOW KOBOI LABORATORIES

 AN LEP shuttle is shaped like a teardrop, bottom heavy with thrusters and a nose that could cut through steel. Of course our heroes weren't in an LEP shuttle, they were in the ambassador's luxury cruiser. Comfort was definitely favoured over speed. It had a nose like a gnome's behind. Bulky and expensive-looking, with a grill you could use to barbecue buffalo.

'So, you're saying this fissure is going to open up for a couple of minutes and I have to fly through. And that's the entire plan?' said Holly.

'It's the best we've got,' said Root glumly.

'Well, at least we'll be in padded seats when we get squashed. This thing handles like a three-legged rhinoceros.'

'How was I to know?' grumbled Root. 'This was supposed to be a routine run. This shuttle has an excellent stereo.'

Butler raised his hand. 'Listen. What's that sound?'

They listened. The noise came from below them, like a giant clearing its throat.

Holly consulted the keel cams.

'Flare,' she announced. 'Big sucker. It'll be roasting our tail feathers any minute.'

The rock face before them cracked and groaned in constant expansion and retraction. Fissures heaved like grinning mouths lined with black teeth.

'That's it. Let's go,' urged Mulch. 'That fissure is going to seal up faster than a stink worm's —'

'Not enough room yet,' snapped Holly. 'This is a shuttle, not one fat dwarf riding stolen wings.'

Mulch was too scared to be insulted. 'Just move it. It'll widen as we go.'

Generally Holly would have waited for Root to give the green light. But this was her area. No one was going to argue with Captain Holly Short at the controls of a shuttle.

The chasm shuddered open another metre.

Holly gritted her teeth. 'Hold on to your ears,' she said, ramming the thrusters to maximum.

The craft's occupants clutched their armrests, and more than one of them closed their eyes. But not Artemis.

He couldn't. There was something morbidly fascinating about flying into an uncharted tunnel at a reckless speed, with only a kleptomaniac dwarf's word for what lay at the other end.

Holly concentrated on her instruments. Hull cameras and sensors fed information to various screens and speakers. Sonar was going crazy, beeping so fast it was almost a continuous whine. Fixed halogen headlights fed frightening images to the monitors, and laser radar drew a green 3D line picture on a dark screen. Then, of course, there was the quartz windscreen. But with sheets of rock dust and larger debris, the naked eye was next to useless.

'Temperature increasing,' she muttered, glancing at the rear-view monitor. An orange magma column blasted past the fissure mouth, spilling over into the tunnel.

They were in a desperate race. The fissure was closing behind them and expanding before the craft's prow. The noise was terrific. Thunder in a bubble.

Mulch covered his ears. 'Next time, I'll take Howler's Peak.'

'Quiet, convict,' growled Root. 'This was all your idea.'

Their arguing was interrupted by a tremendous grating, sending sparks dancing across the windscreen.

'Sorry,' apologized Captain Short. 'There goes our communications array.'

She flipped the craft sideways, scraping between two shifting plates. The magma's heat coated the rock face, dragging the plates together. A jagged edge clipped the shuttle's rear as the plates crashed behind them. A giant's handclap. Butler held his Sig Sauer. It was a comfort thing.

Then they were through, spiralling into a cavern towards three enormous titanium rods.

'There,' gasped Mulch. 'The foundation rods.'

Holly rolled her eyes. 'You don't say,' she groaned, firing the docking clamps.

Mulch had drawn another diagram. This one looked like a bendy snake.

'We're being led by an idiot with a crayon,' said Root, with deceptive calmness.

'I got you this far, didn't I, Julius?' said Mulch, pouting.

Holly was finishing the last bottle of mineral water. A good third of it went over her head.

'Don't you dare start sulking, dwarf,' she said. 'As far as I can see, we're stuck in the centre of the Earth, with no way out and no communications.'

Mulch backed up a step. 'I can see you're a bit tense after the flight. Let's all calm down now, shall we?'

Nobody looked very calm. Even Artemis seemed slightly shaken by the ordeal. Butler still hadn't let go of the Sig Sauer.

'That's the hard bit over. We're in the foundations now. The only way is up.'

'Oh really, convict?' said Root. 'And how do you suggest we go up exactly?'

Mulch plucked a carrot from the cooler, waving it at his diagram. 'This here is …'

'A snake?'

'No, Julius. It's one of the foundation rods.'

'The solid titanium foundation rods, sunk in impregnable bedrock?'

'The very ones. Except one isn't exactly solid.'

Artemis nodded. 'I thought so. You cut corners on this work, didn't you, Mulch?'

Mulch was unrepentant. 'You know what building regulations are like. Solid titanium pillars? Do you have any idea how expensive that is? Threw our estimate right off. So me 'n' cousin Nord decided to forget the titanium packing.'

'But you had to fill that column with something,' interrupted the commander. 'Koboi would have run scans.'

Mulch nodded guiltily.

'We hooked up the sewage pipes to it for a couple of days. The sonographs came up clean.'

Holly felt her throat clench. 'Sewage. You mean …'

'No. Not any more. That was a hundred years ago, it's just clay now. Very good clay as it happens.'

Root's face could have boiled a large cauldron of water.

‣ ||| ▽ ♪ ‣

'You expect us to climb through twenty metres of ... manure?'

The dwarf shrugged. 'Hey, do I care? Stay here forever if you want, I'm going up the pipe.'

Artemis did not like this sudden turn of events. Running, jumping, injury. OK. But sewage? 'This is your plan?' he managed to mutter.

'What's the matter, Mud Boy,' smirked Mulch. 'Afraid of getting your hands dirty?'

It was only a figure of speech, Artemis knew. But true nevertheless. He glanced at his slender fingers. Yesterday morning they were pianist's fingers with manicured nails. Today they could have belonged to a builder.

Holly clapped Artemis on the shoulder. 'OK,' she declared. 'Let's do it. As soon as we save the Lower Elements, we can get back to rescuing your father.'

Holly noticed a change in Artemis's face. Almost as if his features weren't sure how to arrange themselves. She paused, realizing what she had said. For her, the remark had been a casual encouragement, the kind of thing an officer said every day. But it seemed as though Artemis was not accustomed to being a member of a team.

'Don't think I'm getting chummy or anything. It's just that when I give my word, I stick to it.'

Artemis decided not to respond. He'd already been punched once today.

*

They descended from the shuttle on a folding stairway.

Artemis stepped on to the surface, picking his way through the jagged stones and construction debris abandoned by Mulch and his cousin a century earlier. The cavern was lit by the star-like twinkle of rock phosphorescence.

'This place is a geological marvel,' he exclaimed. 'The pressure at this depth should be crushing us, but it isn't.' He knelt to examine a fungus sprouting from a rusting paint tin. 'There's even life.'

Mulch wrenched the remains of a hammer from between two rocks.

'So that's where this got to. We overdid it a bit on the explosives, blasting the shaft for these columns. Some of our waste must have ... fallen down here.'

Holly was appalled. Pollution is an abomination to the People.

'You've broken so many laws here, Mulch, I don't even have the fingers to count them. When you get that two-day head start, you better move fast, because I'm going to be the one chasing you.'

'Here we are,' said Mulch, ignoring the threat. When you'd heard as many as he had, they just rolled right off.

There was a hole bored into one of the columns. Mulch rubbed the edges fondly.

'Diamond laser cutter. Little nuclear battery. That baby could cut through anything.'

'I remember that cutter too,' said Root. 'You nearly decapitated me with it once.'

Mulch sighed. 'Happy days, eh, Julius?'

Root's reply was a swift kick in the behind. 'Less talk, more eating dirt, convict.'

Holly placed her hand into the hole. 'Air currents. The pressure field from the city must have equalized this cave over the years. That's why we're not flat as manta rays right now.'

'I see,' said Butler and Root simultaneously. Another lie for the list.

Mulch undid his bum-flap.

'I'll tunnel up to the top and wait for you there. Clear as much of the debris as you can. I'll spread the recycled mud around, to avoid closing up the shaft.'

Artemis groaned. The idea of crawling through Mulch's *recyclings* was almost intolerable. Only the thought of his father kept him going.

Mulch stepped into the shaft. 'Stand back,' he warned, unhinging his jaw.

Butler moved quickly – he was not about to get nailed by dwarf gas again.

Mulch disappeared up to his waist in the titanium column. In moments he had disappeared entirely. The pipe began to shudder with strange, unappetizing sounds. Chunks of clay clattered against the metal walls. A constant stream of condensed air and debris spiralled from the hole.

'Amazing,' breathed Artemis. 'What I could do with ten like him. Fort Knox would be a pushover.'

'Don't even think about it,' warned Root. He turned to Butler. 'What have we got?'

The manservant drew his pistol. 'One Sig Sauer handgun with twelve rounds in the magazine. That's it. I'll take the gun, as I'm the only one who can lift it. You two pick up whatever you can on the run.'

'And what about me?' asked Artemis, even though he knew what was coming.

Butler looked his master straight in the eye. 'I want you to stay here. This is a military operation. All you can do is get yourself killed.'

'But ...'

'My job is to protect you, Artemis, and this is quite possibly the safest spot on the planet.'

Artemis didn't argue. In truth, these facts had already occurred to him. Sometimes being a genius was a burden.

'Very well, Butler. I shall remain here. Unless ...'

Butler's eyes narrowed. 'Unless what?'

Artemis gave a dangerous smile. 'Unless I have an idea.'

POLICE PLAZA

In Police Plaza the situation was desperate. Captain Kelp had pulled the remaining forces into a circle behind overturned workstations. The goblins were taking pot shots through the doorway, and none of the warlocks had a drop of magic left in them. Anyone who got injured from now on, stayed injured.

The Council was huddled behind a wall of troops. All except Wing Commander Vinyáya, who had demanded to be given one of the electric rifles. She hadn't missed yet.

The techs were crouched behind their desks, trying every code combination in the book to gain access to the Operations' booth. Trouble didn't hold out much hope on that front. If Foaly locked a door then it stayed locked.

Meanwhile, inside the booth, all the centaur could do was pound his fists in frustration. It was a sign of Cudgeon's cruelty that he allowed Foaly to view the battle beyond the blast windows.

It seemed hopeless. Even if Julius and Holly had received his message, it was too late now to do anything. Foaly's lips and throat were dry. Everything had deserted him. His computer, his intellect, his glib sarcasm. Everything.

BELOW KOBOI LABORATORIES

Something wet slapped Butler in the head.

'What was that?' he hissed at Holly, who was bringing up the rear.

'Don't ask,' croaked Captain Short. Even through her helmet filters the smell was foul.

The contents of the column had had a century to ferment, and smelled as toxic as the day it went in. Probably worse. At least, thought the bodyguard, I don't have to eat this stuff.

Root was on point, his helmet lights cutting swathes through the darkness. The pillar was on a forty-degree angle, with regular grooves that were intended to anchor the titanium block filling.

Mulch had done a sterling job of breaking down the pipe's contents. But the recycling had to go somewhere. Mulch, in fairness to him, chewed every mouthful thoroughly to avoid too many lumps.

The raiding party struggled on grimly, trying not to think about what they were actually doing. By the time they caught up with the dwarf, he was clinging to a ridge, face constricted in pain.

'What is it, Mulch?' asked Root, concern accidentally slipping into his tones.

'Geddup,' Mulch groaned. 'Geddup rih now.'

Root's eyes widened with something approaching panic. 'Up!' he hissed. 'Everybody up!'

They scrambled into the tight wedge of space above the dwarf. Not a second too soon. Mulch relaxed, releasing a burst of dwarf gas that could have inflated a circus tent. He rehinged his jaw.

'That's better,' he sighed. 'Lotta air in that soil. Now would you mind getting that beam out of my face. You know how I feel about light.'

The commander obliged, switching to infra-red.

'OK, now we're up here, how do we get out? You didn't bring your cutter, I seem to remember.'

The dwarf grinned. 'No problem. A good thief always plans on a return visit. See here.' Mulch was pointing to an area of titanium that seemed exactly like the rest of the pipe. 'I patched this up last time. It's just flexi-bond.'

Root had to smile. 'You are a cunning reprobate. How did we ever catch you?'

'Luck,' replied the dwarf, elbowing a section of the pipe. A large circle popped out, revealing the hundred-year-old hole. 'Welcome to Koboi Labs.'

They clambered into a dimly lit corridor. Loaded hover trolleys were stacked four deep around the walls. Strip lighting operated with minimum illumination overhead.

'I know this place,' noted Root. 'I've been here before on inspection for the special-weapons permits. We're two corridors across from the computer centre. We have a real chance of making it.'

'What about these DNA stun cannons?' enquired Butler.

'Tricky,' admitted the commander. 'If the cannon's on-board doesn't recognize you, you're dead. They can be programmed to reject entire species.'

'Tricky,' agreed the manservant.

'I'm betting they're not active,' continued Root. 'First, if this place is crawling with goblins, they hardly came in through the front door. And second, if Foaly is being blamed for this little uprising, Koboi will want to pretend they had no weapons, just like the LEP.'

'Strategy?' asked Butler.

'Not much,' admitted the commander. 'Once we turn the corner, we're on camera. So down the corridor as fast as you can, hit anything that gets in your way. If it has a weapon, confiscate it. Mulch, you stay here and widen the tunnel, we may need to get out fast. Ready?'

Holly extended a hand. 'Gentlemen, it's been a pleasure.'

The commander and manservant laid their hands on hers. 'Likewise.'

They headed down the corridor. Two hundred goblins versus our three virtually unarmed heroes. It was going to be close.

Inner Sanctum, Koboi Laboratories

'Intruders,' squealed Opal Koboi delightedly. 'Inside the building.'

Cudgeon crossed to the surveillance plasma screen.

'I do believe it's Julius. Amazing. Obviously your hit team was exaggerating, General Sputa.'

Sputa licked his eyeballs furiously. Lieutenant Nyle would be losing his skin before shedding season.

Cudgeon whispered into Opal's ear. 'Can we activate the DNA cannons?'

The pixie shook her head. 'Not immediately. They've been reprogrammed to reject goblin DNA. It would take a few minutes.'

Cudgeon turned to the four goblin generals. 'Have an armoured squad come up behind and another one from the flank. We can trap them at the door. There will be no way out.'

Cudgeon stared raptly at the plasma screen. 'This is even better than I'd planned. Now, my old friend, Julius, it's my turn to humiliate you.'

Artemis was meditating. This was a time for concentration. He sat cross-legged on a rock, visualizing the various rescue strategies that could be utilized when they returned to the Arctic. If the Mafiya managed to set up the drop before Artemis could reach them, then there was only one plan that could work. And it was a high-risk plan. Artemis searched deeper inside his brain. There must be another way.

He was disturbed by an orchestral noise emanating from the titanium column. It sounded like a sustained note on a bassoon. Dwarf gas, he reasoned. The column had decent acoustics.

What he needed was a brainwave. One crystal thought that would slice through this mire he had become embroiled in, and save the day.

After eight minutes, he was interrupted again. Not gas this time. A cry for help. Mulch was in trouble, and in pain.

Artemis was about to suggest that Butler deal with it when he realized that his bodyguard wasn't there. Off on his mission to save the Lower Elements. It was up to him.

He poked his head into the column. It was black as the inside of an old boot, and twice as pungent. Artemis decided that an LEP helmet was his first requirement. He quickly retrieved a spare from the shuttle and, after a moment's experimentation, activated the lights and seals.

'Mulch? Are you up there?'

No reply. Could this be a trap? Was it possible that he, Artemis Fowl, was about to fall for the oldest ruse in the book? Entirely possible, he decided. But in spite of that, he couldn't really afford to take chances with that hairy little creature's life. Somewhere since Los Angeles, and against his better judgement, he had bonded with Mister Diggums. Artemis shuddered. It was happening more and more since his mother's return to sanity.

Artemis climbed into the tube, beginning his journey to the disc of light above. The smell was horrendous. His shoes were ruined, and no amount of dry-cleaning could redeem the St Bartleby's blazer. Mulch had better be in a lot of pain.

When he reached the entrance, he found Mulch writhing on the floor, face contorted in genuine agony.

'What is it?' he asked, peeling off the helmet and kneeling by the dwarf's side.

'Blockage in my gut,' grunted the dwarf, beads of sweat sliding down his beard hairs. 'Something hard. Can't break it down.'

'What can I do?' Artemis asked, though he dreaded the possible replies.

'My left boot. Take it off.'

'Your boot? Did you say boot?'

'Yes,' howled the dwarf, pain stiffening his entire torso. 'Get it off!'

Artemis couldn't stifle a relieved sigh. He'd been fearing much worse. He hefted the dwarf's leg into his lap and pulled at the climbing boot.

'Nice boots,' he commented.

'Rodeo Drive,' gasped Mulch. 'Now, if you wouldn't mind.'

'Sorry.'

The boot slid off, revealing a not-quite-so-designer sock, complete with toe holes and darn patches.

'Little toe,' said Mulch, eyes closed with pain.

'Little toe what?'

'Squeeze the joint. Hard.'

Squeeze the joint. Must be a reflexology thing. Every part of the body corresponds to an area of the foot. The body's keyboard, so to speak. Practised in the Orient for centuries.

'Very well. If you insist.'

Artemis placed his finger and thumb around Mulch's hairy toe. It could have been his imagination, but it seemed that the hairs parted to allow him access.

'Squeeze,' gasped the dwarf. 'Why aren't you squeezing?'

Artemis wasn't squeezing because his eyes were crossed, looking at the laser barrel in the middle of his forehead.

Lieutenant Nyle, who was holding the weapon, couldn't believe his luck. He'd single-handedly captured two intruders, plus he'd discovered their bolt hole. Who said hanging back to avoid the fighting didn't have advantages? This was turning out to be an exceptional revolution for him. He'd be colonel before shedding his third skin.

'On your feet,' he ordered, panting blue flames. Even through the translator it sounded reptilian.

Artemis stood slowly, lifting Mulch's leg with him. The dwarf's bum-flap flopped open.

'What's wrong with him anyway?' asked Nyle, bending in for a closer look.

'Something he ate,' said Artemis, and squeezed the joint.

The resulting explosion knocked the goblin off his feet, sending him tumbling down the corridor. There was something you didn't see every day.

Mulch hopped to his feet.

'Thanks, kid. I thought I was a goner there. Must've been something hard. Granite maybe, or diamond.'

Artemis nodded. Not ready for words.

'Those goblins are dumb. Did you see the look on his face?'

Artemis shook his head. Still not ready.

'Do you want to go look?'

The tactless humour snapped Artemis out of his daze. 'That goblin. I doubt he was on his own.'

Mulch buttoned up his bum-flap. 'Nope. A whole squadron of 'em just went past. This guy must have been trying to avoid the action. Typical goblin.'

Artemis rubbed his temples. There must be something he could do to help his friends. He had the highest tested IQ in Europe, for heaven's sake.

'Mulch, I have an important question for you.'

'I suppose I owe you one, for saving my hide.'

Artemis draped an arm around the dwarf's shoulder. 'I know how you got into Koboi Labs. But you couldn't go back that way, the flare would get you. So, how did you get out?'

Mulch grinned. 'Simple. I activated the alarm, then left in the LEP uniform I came in.'

Artemis scowled. 'No use, there must be another way. There has to be.'

The DNA cannons were obviously out of commission. Root was just starting to feel optimistic when he heard the thunder of approaching boots.

'D'Arvit. Rumbled. You two keep going. I'll hold them here as long as I can.'

'No, Commander,' said Butler. 'With respect, we only have one weapon, and I can hit a lot more with it than you. I'll take them coming around the corner. You try to get the door open.'

Holly opened her mouth to argue. But who was going to argue with a man that size?

'OK. Good luck. If you're wounded, lie as still as you can until I get back. Four minutes, remember.'

Butler nodded. 'I remember.'

'And, Butler?'

'Yes, Captain?'

'That little misunderstanding last year. When you and Artemis kidnapped me.'

Butler gazed at the ceiling. He would have stared at his shoes, but Holly was in the way. 'Yes, that. I've been meaning to talk to ...'

'Just forget it. After this, all square.'

'Holly, move it out,' ordered Root. 'Butler, don't let them get too close.'

Butler wrapped his fingers around the gun's moulded grip. He looked like an armed bear. 'They better not. For their sake.'

Artemis climbed up on a hover trolley, tapping one of the overhead conduits that ran the length of the corridor.

'This pipe appears to run along the entire ceiling structure. What is it, a ventilation system?'

Mulch snorted. 'I wish. It's the plasma supply for the DNA cannons.'

'So why didn't you come in this way?'

'Oh, a little matter of there being enough charge in every drop of plasma to fry a troll.'

Artemis placed his palm against the metal. 'What if the cannons weren't operational?'

'Once the cannons are deactivated, the plasma is just so much radioactive slop.'

'Radioactive?'

Mulch tugged at his beard thoughtfully. 'Actually, Julius reckons the cannons *have* been turned off.'

'Any way to be certain?'

'We could open this unopenable panel.' Mulch ran his fingers along the curved surface. 'Ahh, see here. A micro-keyhole. To service the cannons. Even plasma needs recharging.' He pointed to a tiny hole in the metal. It could have been a speck of dirt. 'Now, observe a master at work.'

The dwarf fed one of his chin hairs into the hole. When the tip reappeared, Mulch plucked the hair out by the root. The hair died as soon as Mulch plucked it, stiffening in rigor mortis and retaining the precise shape of the lock's interior.

Mulch held his breath, twisting the makeshift key. The hatch dropped open.

'That, my boy, is talent.'

Inside the pipe, an orange jelly pulsed gently. Occasional sparks roiled in its depths. The plasma was too dense even to spill from the hatch, and hung on to its cylindrical shape.

Mulch squinted through the wobbling gel. 'Deactivated all right. If that stuff were live, our faces would be getting a nice tan about now.'

'What about those sparks?'

'Residual charge. They'd give you a bit of a tingle, but nothing serious.'

Artemis nodded. 'Right,' he said, strapping on the helmet.

Mulch blanched. 'You are not serious, Mud Whelp? Do you have any idea what will happen if those cannons are activated?'

'I'm trying not to think about it.'

'It's probably just as well.' The dwarf shook his head, bewildered. 'OK. You've got thirty metres to go, and no more than ten minutes of air in that helmet. Keep the filters closed. The air may get a bit stale after a while, but it's better than sucking plasma. And here, take this.' He plucked the stiffened hair from the keyhole.

'What for?'

'I presume you will want to get out again at the other end. Or hadn't you thought of that, genius boy?'

Artemis swallowed. He hadn't. There was more to this heroism thing than rushing in blindly.

'Just feed it in gently. Remember, it's hair not metal.'

'Feed it in gently. Got it.'

'And don't use any lights. Halogen could reactivate the plasma.'

Artemis felt his head beginning to spin.

'And make sure you get foamed as soon as you can. The anti-rad canisters are blue. They're everywhere in this facility.'

'Blue canisters. Anything else, Mister Diggums?'

'Well, there are the plasma snakes …'

Artemis's knees almost collapsed. 'You're not serious?'

'No,' Mulch conceded. 'I'm not. Now, your reach is about half a metre. So calculate for sixty pulls and then get out of there.'

'Slightly under half a metre I'd say. Perhaps sixty-three pulls.' He placed the dwarf hair inside his breast pocket.

Mulch shrugged. 'Whatever, kid. It's your skin. Now in you go.'

The dwarf interlaced his fingers and Artemis stepped

into the makeshift stirrup. He was considering changing his mind when Mister Diggums heaved him into the pipe. The orange gel sucked him in, enveloping his body in a second.

The plasma coiled around him like a living being, popping bubbles of air trapped in his clothing. A residual spark brushed his leg, sending sharp pain spasming through his body. A bit of a tingle?

Artemis gazed out through the orange gel. Mulch was there giving him the thumbs up. Grinning like a loon. Artemis decided that if he made it through this, then he would have to place the dwarf on the payroll.

He began to crawl blindly. One pull, two pulls …

Sixty-three seemed a long way off.

Butler cocked the Sig Sauer. The footsteps were ear-splitting now, bouncing off the metal walls. Shadows stretched around the corner, ahead of their owners. The manservant took approximate aim.

A head appeared. Froglike. Licking its own eyeballs. Butler pulled the trigger. The slug punched a melon-sized hole in the wall above the goblin's head. The head was hurriedly withdrawn. Of course, Butler had missed on purpose. Scared was always better than dead. But it couldn't last forever. Twelve more shots to be precise.

The goblins grew braver, sneaking out further and further. Eventually, Butler knew he would be forced to shoot one.

The manservant decided that it was time to go close-quarters. He rose from his hunkers, making slightly less noise than a panther, and hurtled down the corridor towards the enemy.

There were only two men on the planet better educated in the various martial arts than Butler, and he was related to one of them. The other lived on an island in the South China Seas and spent his days meditating and beating up palm trees. You really had to feel sorry for those goblins.

The B'wa Kell had two guards on the sanctum door. Both armed to the teeth and both as thick as several short planks. In spite of repeated warnings, they were both falling asleep inside their helmets when the elves came running around the corner.

'Look,' mumbled one. 'Elves.'

'Huh?' said the other, the denser of the two.

'Don't matter,' said number one. 'LEP don't got no guns.'

Number two gave his eyeballs a lick. 'Yeah, but they sure are irritable.'

And that was when Holly's boot impacted with his chest, slamming him into the wall.

'Hey,' complained number one, bringing up his own gun. 'Not fair.'

Root didn't bother with fancy spinning kicks,

preferring instead to body-slam the sentry against the titanium door.

'There,' panted Holly. 'Two down. That wasn't so hard.'

A premature statement as it happened. Because that was when the rest of the two-hundred-strong B'wa Kell squadron thundered down the perpendicular corridor.

'That wasn't so hard,' mimicked the commander, curling his fingers into fists.

Artemis's concentration was failing him. There seemed to be more sparks now, and each shock disrupted his focus. He had lost count twice. He was at fifty-four now. Or fifty-six. The difference was life or death.

He trawled ahead, reaching out one arm and then the other, swimming through a turgid sea of gel. Vision was next to useless. Everything was orange. And the only confirmation he had that any progress was being made was when his knee sank into a recess, where the plasma diverted into a cannon.

Artemis punched one last time through the gel, filling his lungs with stale air – sixty-three. That was it. Soon the air purifiers in his helmet would be useless and he would be breathing carbon dioxide.

He placed his fingertips against the pipe's inner curve, searching for a keyhole. Again his eyes were no help. He couldn't even activate the helmet lamps for fear of igniting a river of plasma.

Nothing. No indent. He was going to die here alone. He would never be great. Artemis felt his brain going, spiralling off into a black tunnel. Concentrate, he told himself. Focus. There was a spark approaching. A silver star in the sunset. It coiled lazily along the tube, lighting each section it passed.

There! A hole. *The* hole. Revealed for a moment by the passing spark. Artemis reached into his pocket like a drunken swimmer, pulling out the dwarf hair. Would it work? There was no reason this access port should have a different locking mechanism.

Artemis slid the hair into the keyhole. Gently. He squinted through the gel. Was it going in? He thought so. Perhaps sixty per cent sure. It would have to be enough.

Artemis twisted. The flap dropped open. He imagined Mulch's grin. *That, my boy, is talent.*

It was quite possible that every enemy he had in the underworld was waiting outside that hatch, big nasty guns pointed at his head. At that point, Artemis didn't much care. He couldn't bear one more of his own oxygen-depleted breaths or one more excruciating shock to his body.

So, Artemis Fowl poked his helmet through the plasma's surface. He flipped the visor, savouring what could very well be his last breath. Lucky for him, the room's occupants were looking at the view screen.

Watching his friends fight for their lives. Not so lucky for his friends.

There are too many, thought Butler as he rounded the corner and saw almost an entire army of B'wa Kell slotting fresh batteries into their weapons.

The goblins, when they noticed Butler, began to think things like, O gods, it's a troll in clothes; or, why didn't I listen to Mummy and stay out of the gangs?

Then Butler was above them and on the way down. He landed like the proverbial tonne of bricks, except with considerably more precision. Three goblins were out cold before they knew they'd been hit. One shot himself in the foot and several others lay down pretending to be unconscious.

Artemis watched it all on the control room's plasma screen. Along with all the other occupants of the inner sanctum. It was entertainment to them. TV. The goblin generals chuckled and winced as Butler decimated their men. It was all immaterial. There were hundreds of goblins in the building and no way into this room.

Artemis had seconds to decide on a course of action. Seconds. And he had no idea how to use any of this technology. He scanned the walls below him for something he could use. Anything.

There. On a small picture-in-picture screen, away from the main console, was Foaly. Trapped in the Operations' booth. The centaur would have a plan. He had certainly had time to come up with one. Artemis knew that as soon as he emerged from the conduit he was a target. They would kill him without hesitation.

He dragged himself from within the tube, falling to Earth with a thick slap. His saturated clothes slowed his progress to the monitor bank. Heads were turning, he could see them out the corner of his eye. Figures came his way. He didn't know how many.

There was a reed mike below Foaly's image. Artemis pressed the button.

'Foaly!' he rasped, globs of gel splatting on to the console. 'Can you hear me?'

The centaur reacted instantly. 'Fowl? What happened to you?'

'Five seconds, Foaly. I need a plan or we're all dead.'

Foaly nodded curtly. 'I've got one ready. Put me on all screens.'

'What? How?'

'Press the conference button. Yellow. A circle with lines shooting out, like the sun. Do you see it?'

Artemis saw it. He pressed it. Then something pressed him. Very painfully.

General Scalene first noticed the creature flopping out of

the plasma pipe. What was it? A pixie? No. No, by all the gods. It was human.

'Look!' he cackled. 'A Mud Man.'

The others were oblivious, too interested in the spectacle on-screen.

But not Cudgeon. A human in the inner sanctum. How could this be? He seized Scalene by the shoulders. 'Kill him!'

All the generals were listening now. There was killing to be done. With no danger to themselves. They would do this the old-fashioned way: with claws and fireballs.

The human stumbled to one of the consoles and they surrounded him, tongues dangling excitedly. Sputa spun the human around to face his fate.

One by one, the generals conjured fireballs around their fists, closing in for the kill. But then something made them completely forget the injured human. Cudgeon's face had appeared on all the screens. And the B'wa Kell executive didn't like what it was saying:

'— Just when things are at their most desperate, I shall instruct Opal to return weapons control to the LEP. The B'wa Kell will be rendered unconscious, and you will be blamed for the entire affair, provided you survive, which I doubt —'

Sputa whirled on his ally. 'Cudgeon! What does this mean?'

The generals advanced, hissing and spitting. 'Treachery, Cudgeon! Treachery!'

Cudgeon was not unduly worried. 'OK,' he said. 'Treachery.'

It took Cudgeon a moment to figure out what had happened. It was Foaly. He must have recorded their conversation somehow. How tiresome. Still, you had to hand it to the centaur. He was resourceful.

Cudgeon quickly crossed to the main console, shutting off the broadcast. It wouldn't do for Opal to hear the rest of it. Particularly the part concerning her tragic accident. He really would have to cut out this grandstanding. Still, no matter. Everything was on track.

'Treachery!' hissed Scalene.

'OK,' admitted Cudgeon. 'Treachery.' And directly after that he said, 'Computer, activate DNA cannons. Authorization Cudgeon B. Alpha alpha two two.'

On her hoverchair, Opal spun with sheer joy, clapping her tiny hands in delight. Briar was sooo ugly, but he was sooo evil.

Throughout Koboi Labs, robot DNA cannons perked up in their cradles and ran swift self-diagnostics. Apart from a slight drain in the inner sanctum, everything was in order. And so, without further ado, they began to obey their program parameters and target anything with goblin DNA at a rate of ten blasts per second.

It was swift and, as with everything Koboi, efficient. In less than five seconds, the cannons settled back into their cradles. Mission accomplished: two hundred unconscious goblins throughout the facility.

'Phew,' said Holly, stepping over rows of snoring goblins. 'Close one.'

'Tell me about it,' agreed Root.

Cudgeon kicked Sputa's sleeping body.

'You see, you haven't accomplished anything, Artemis Fowl,' he said, drawing his Redboy.

'Your friends are out there. You're in here. And the goblins are unconscious, soon to be mind-wiped with some particularly unstable chemicals. Just as I planned.' He smiled at Opal hovering above them. 'Just as *we* planned.'

Opal returned the smile.

At another time, Artemis would have been forced to pass a snide comment. But the possibility of imminent death was occupying his thoughts for the moment.

'Now, I simply reprogram the cannons to target your friends, return power to the LEP cannons, and take over the world. And nobody can get in here to stop me.'

Of course, you should never say something like that, especially when you're an arch-villain. It's just asking for trouble.

Butler hurried down the corridor, catching up with the

others outside the inner sanctum. He could see Artemis's predicament through the door's quartz pane. In spite of all his efforts, Master Artemis had still managed to place himself in mortal danger. How was a bodyguard supposed to do his job when his charge insisted on jumping into bear pits, so to speak?

Butler felt the testosterone building in his system. One door was all that separated him from Artemis. One little door, designed to withstand fairies with ray guns. He took several steps backwards.

Holly could tell what he was thinking. 'Don't bother. That door is reinforced.'

The manservant didn't answer. He couldn't. The real Butler was submerged beneath layers of adrenalin and brute force.

With a roar, Butler charged the entrance, concentrating all of his considerable might in the triangular point of his shoulder. It was a blow that would have felled a medium-sized hippopotamus. And while this door was tested for plasma dispersion and moderate physical resistance, it was certainly not Butler-proof. The metal portal crumpled like tin foil.

Butler's momentum took him halfway across the inner sanctum's rubber tiling. Holly and Root followed, pausing only to grab some Softnose lasers from the unconscious goblins.

:|| ⌐ ☰ △　|.| ⌐ ☰ .⌐|:

Cudgeon moved fast, dragging Artemis upright. 'Don't move, any of you. Or I'll kill the Mud Boy.'

Butler kept right on going. His last rational thought had been to disable Cudgeon. Now this was his sole aim in life. He raced forward, arms outstretched.

Holly dived desperately, latching on to Butler's belt. He dragged her like a string of cans behind a wedding car.

'Butler, stop,' she grunted.

The bodyguard ignored her.

Holly hung on, digging in her heels. '*Stop!*' she repeated, this time layering her voice with the *mesmer*.

Butler seemed to wake up. He shook the cave man from his system.

'That's right, Mud Man,' said Cudgeon. 'Listen to Captain Short. Surely we can work something out here.'

'No deals, Briar,' said Root. 'It's all over, so just put the Mud Boy down.'

Cudgeon cocked the Redboy. 'I'll put him down all right.'

This was Butler's worst nightmare. His charge was in the hands of a psychopath with nothing to lose. And there was nothing he could do about it.

A phone rang.

'I think it's mine,' said Artemis automatically.

Another ring. Definitely his mobile phone. Amazing the thing worked at all really, considering what it had been through. Artemis ripped open the case.

'Yes?'

It was one of those frozen moments. Nobody knew what to expect.

Artemis tossed the handset at Opal Koboi. 'It's for you.'

The pixie swooped low to catch the tiny mobile phone. Cudgeon's chest heaved. His body knew what was happening even if his brain hadn't figured it out yet.

Opal placed the tiny speaker to her pointed ear.

'– Really, Foaly,' said Cudgeon's voice. 'Do you think I'd go to all this trouble to share power? Oh no. As soon as this charade is over, Miss Koboi will have a tragic accident. Perhaps several tragic accidents –'

All colour drained from Opal's face. 'You!' she screeched.

'It's a trick!' protested Cudgeon. 'They're trying to turn us against each other.'

But his eyes told the real story.

Pixies are feisty creatures, in spite of their size. They put up with so much and then explode. For Opal Koboi, it was explosion time. She manipulated the Hoverboy's controls, dropping in a steep dive.

Cudgeon didn't hesitate. He put two bursts into the chair, but the thick cushion protected its pilot.

Opal Koboi flew straight at her former partner. When the elf raised his arms to protect himself, Artemis slid to the floor. Briar Cudgeon was not so lucky. He became entangled in the Hoverboy's safety rail and was borne aloft by the wildcat pixie. They whirled around the chamber ricocheting off several walls before crashing straight through the open plasma panel in the cannon pipe.

Unfortunately for Cudgeon, the plasma was now active. He had activated it himself. But this irony did not occur to him as he was fried by a million radioactive tendrils.

Koboi was lucky. She was pitched from the hoverchair and lay moaning on the rubber tiles.

Butler was on the move before Cudgeon landed. He flipped Artemis over, checking his frame for wounds. A couple of scratches. Superficial. Nothing a shot of blue sparks wouldn't take care of.

Holly checked Opal Koboi's status.

'She conscious?' asked the commander.

Koboi's eyes flickered open. Holly shut them with a swift rabbit punch to the forehead. 'Nope,' she said innocently. 'Out cold.'

Root took one look at Cudgeon and realized there was no point checking for vitals. Maybe he was better off. The alternative would have been a couple of centuries in Howler's Peak.

Artemis noticed movement by the door. It was Mulch. He was grinning and waving. Waving goodbye, just in case Julius forgot about his two-day head start. The dwarf

264

pointed to a blue canister mounted on a wall bracket and he was gone.

'Butler,' rasped Artemis, with the absolute last ounce of his strength. 'Could someone spray me down? And then could we please go to Murmansk?'

Butler was mystified. 'Spray? What spray?'

Holly unhooked the anti-rad foam canister, flipping the safety catch. 'Allow me,' she said, grinning. 'It would be my pleasure.'

She directed a jet of foul-smelling foam at Artemis. In seconds, he resembled a half-melted snowman. Holly laughed. Who said there were no perks in law enforcement?

Operations' Booth

Once the cannon plasma had short-circuited Cudgeon's remote control, power came rushing back to the Operations' booth. Foaly lost no time in activating the subcutaneous sleepers planted below goblin offenders' skin. That put half of the B'wa Kell out of action straight away. Then he reprogrammed Police Plaza's own DNA cannons for non-lethal bursts. It was all over in seconds.

Captain Kelp's first thought was for his subordinates. 'Sound off,' he shouted, his voice slicing through the chaos. 'Did we lose anyone?'

The squadron leaders answered in sequence, confirming that there had been no fatalities.

'We were lucky,' remarked a warlock medic. 'There's not a drop of magic left in the building. Not even a medi-pac. The next officer to go down would have stayed down.'

Trouble turned his attention to the Ops' booth. He did not look amused.

Foaly depolarized the quartz window and opened a channel. 'Hey, guys. I wasn't behind this. It was Cudgeon. I just saved everyone. I sent a sound recording to a mobile phone; that wasn't easy. You should be giving me a medal.'

Trouble clenched his fist. 'Yeah, Foaly, come on out here and let me give you your medal.'

Foaly may not have had many social skills, but he knew thinly veiled threats when he heard them.

'Oh no. Not me. I'm staying right here until Commander Root gets back. He can explain everything.'

The centaur blacked out the window and busied himself running a bug sweep. He would isolate every last trace of Opal Koboi and flush it out of the system. Paranoid was he? Who was the paranoid one now, Holly? Who was the paranoid one now?

CHAPTER 14: FATHER'S DAY

MURMANSK

 THE Arctic seascape between Murmansk and Severomorsk had become a submarine graveyard for Russia's once mighty fleet. Easily a hundred nuclear submarines lay rusting in the coastline's various inlets and fjords, with only the odd danger sign or roving patrol to warn off curious passers-by. At night, you didn't have to look too hard to see the glow, or listen too hard to hear the hum.

One such submarine was the *Nikodim*. A twenty-year-old Typhoon class, with rusty pipes and a leaky reactor. Not a healthy combination. And it was here that the Mafiya kingpin, Britva, had instructed his lackeys to make the exchange for Artemis Fowl Senior.

Mikhael Vassikin and Kamar were none too happy with the situation. They had been bunked in the captain's quarters for two days already, and were convinced their lives were growing shorter by the minute.

Vassikin coughed. 'You hear that? My guts aren't right. It's the radiation, I'm telling you.'

'This whole thing is ridiculous,' snarled Kamar. 'The Fowl boy is thirteen. Thirteen! He's a baby. How can a child raise five million dollars? It's crazy.'

Vassikin sat up on his bunk. 'Maybe not. I've heard stories about this one. They say he has powers.'

Kamar snorted. 'Powers? Magic? Oh, go stuff your head in the reactor, you old woman.'

'No, I have a contact in Interpol. They have an active file on this boy. Thirteen years old and with an active file? I am thirty-seven, and still no Interpol file.' The Russian sounded disappointed.

'An active file. What's magic about that?'

'But my contact swears that this boy, Fowl, is sighted all over the world, on the same day. The same hour.'

Kamar was unimpressed. 'Your contact is a bigger coward than you are.'

'Believe what you want. But I'll be happy to get off this cursed boat alive. One way or the other.'

Kamar pulled a fur cap down over his ears. 'OK. Let's go. It's time.'

'Finally,' sighed Vassikin.

The two men collected the prisoner from the next cabin. They were not worried about an escape attempt.

Not with one leg missing and a hood secured over his head. Vassikin slung Fowl Senior over his shoulder and climbed the rungs to the conning tower.

Kamar used a radio to check in with the back-up. There were over a hundred criminals hiding among the petrified bushes and snowdrifts. Cigarette tips lit the night like fireflies.

'Put those cigarettes out, idiots,' he hissed over an open frequency. 'It's almost midnight. Fowl could be here any second. Remember, no one shoots until I give the order. Then everybody shoots.'

You could almost hear the hiss as a hundred cigarette butts were flicked into the snow. A hundred men. It was a costly operation. But a mere drop in the ocean compared to the twenty per cent promised them by Britva.

Wherever this boy Fowl came from, he would be trapped in a deadly crossfire. There was no way out for him or his father, while he and Vassikin were safe behind the steel conning tower.

Kamar grinned. Let's see how much magic you have then, *Irlanskii*.

Holly surveyed the scene through the hi-res night-sight filter in her helmet with the eyes of a seasoned Recon officer. Butler was stuck with plain old binoculars.

'How many cigarettes did you count?'

'More than eighty,' replied the captain. 'Could be up to

a hundred men. You walk in there and you'll be carried out.'

Root nodded in agreement. It was a tactical nightmare.

They were bivouacked on the opposite side of the fjord, high on a sloped hill. The Council had even approved wings, on account of Artemis's recent services.

Foaly had done a mail retrieval from Artemis's computer and found a message: Five million US. The *Nikodim*. Murmansk. Midnight on the fourteenth. It was short and to the point. What else was there to say? They had missed their opportunity to snatch Artemis Senior before he was moved to the drop point, and now the Mafiya were in control.

They gathered around while Butler sketched a diagram in the snow with a laser pointer.

'I would guess that the target is being held here, in the conning tower. To get there, you've got to walk all the way along the sub. They've got a hundred men hiding out around the perimeter. We have no air support, no satellite information and minimal weaponry.' Butler sighed. 'I'm sorry, Artemis. I just don't see it.'

Holly knelt to study the diagram. 'A time-stop would take days to set up. We can't shield either because of the radiation, and there's no way to get close enough to mesmerize.'

'What about LEP weaponry?' asked Artemis, though he knew the answer.

Root chewed an unlit cigar. 'We discussed this, Artemis. We have as much firepower as you like, but if we start blasting, your father will be their first target. Standard kidnapping rules.'

Artemis pulled an LEP field parka closer to his throat, staring at the rough diagram. 'And if we give them the money?'

Foaly had run them up five million in small bills on one of his old printers. He had even had a squad of sprites crumple it up a bit.

Butler shook his head. 'That's not the way these people do business. Alive, Mister Fowl is a potential enemy. He has to die.'

Artemis nodded slowly. There was absolutely no other way. He would have to implement the plan he had concocted in the Arctic shuttle port.

'Very well, everyone,' he said. 'I have a plan. But it's going to sound a bit extreme.'

Mikhael Vassikin's mobile phone rang, shattering the Arctic silence. Vassikin almost fell down the tower hatch.

'*Da?* What is it? I'm busy.'

'This is Fowl,' said a voice in flawless Russian, colder than Arctic pack ice. 'It's midnight. I'm here.'

Mikhael swung around, scanning the surroundings through his binoculars.

'Here? Where? I don't see anything.'

'Close enough.'

'How did you get this number?'

A chuckle rattled through the speakers. The sound set Vassikin's fillings on edge.

'I know someone. He has all the numbers.'

Mikhael took deep breaths, settling himself. 'Do you have the money?'

'Of course. Do you have the package?'

'Right here.'

Again the cold chuckle. 'All I see is a fat imbecile, a little rat and someone with a hood over his head. It could be anyone. I'm not paying five million for your cousin Yuri.'

Vassikin ducked below the lip of the tower. 'Fowl can see us!' he hissed at Kamar. 'Stay low.'

Kamar scuttled to the far side of the tower, opening a line to his men. 'He's here. Fowl is here. Search the area.'

Vassikin brought the phone back to his ear. 'So come down here and check. You'll see soon enough.'

'I can see fine from right here. Just take the hood off.'

Mikhael covered the phone. 'He wants me to take the hood off. What should I do?'

Kamar sighed. Now it was becoming plain who was the brains in this outfit. 'Take it off. What difference does it make? Either way they're both dead in five minutes.'

'OK, Fowl. I'm taking off the hood. The next face you see will be your father's.' The big Russian propped up the prisoner, high over the lip of the conning tower. He reached up with one hand and pulled off the rough sackcloth hood.

On the other end of the line, he heard a sharp intake of breath.

Through the filters of his borrowed LEP helmet, Artemis could see the conning tower as though it were a metre away. The hood came off, and he could not suppress a sharp gasp.

It was his father. Different certainly. But not beyond recognition. Artemis Fowl the First, without a shadow of a doubt.

'Well,' said a Russian voice in his ear. 'Is it him?'

Artemis struggled to stop his voice from shaking. 'Yes,' he said. 'It is him. Congratulations. You have an item of some value.'

In the conning tower, Vassikin gave his partner the thumbs up. 'It's him,' he hissed. 'We're in the money.'

Kamar didn't share his confidence. There would be no celebrating until the cash was in his hand.

Butler steadied the fairy Farshoot rifle on its stand. He had selected it from the LEP armoury. Fifteen hundred metres. Not an easy shot. But there was no wind, and Foaly had given him a scope that did the aiming for him. Artemis Fowl Senior's torso was centred in the crosshair.

He took a breath. 'Artemis. Are you sure? This is risky.'

Artemis did not reply, checking for the hundredth time that Holly was in position. Of course he wasn't sure. A million things could go wrong with this deception, but what choice did he have?

Artemis nodded. Just once.

Butler fired the shot.

The shot caught Artemis Senior in the shoulder. He spun around, slumping over the startled Vassikin.

The Russian howled in disgust, heaving the bleeding Irishman over the lip of the conning tower. Artemis Senior slid along the keel, crashing through the brittle ice plates clinging to the sub's hull.

'He shot him,' yelped the *khuligany*. 'That devil shot his own father.'

Kamar was stunned. 'Idiot!' he howled. 'You've just thrown our hostage overboard!' He peered into the black Arctic waters. Nothing remained of the *Irlanskii* but ripples.

'Go down and get him, if you wish,' said Vassikin sullenly.

'Was he dead?'

His partner shrugged. 'Maybe. He was bleeding bad. And if the bullet doesn't finish him, the water will. Anyway, it's not our fault.'

Kamar swore viciously. 'I don't think Britva will see it that way.'

'Britva,' breathed Vassikin. The only thing the *Menidzher* understood was money. 'O gods. We're dead.'

The mobile phone rattled on the deck. The speaker was vibrating. Fowl was still on the other end.

Mikhael picked up the mobile as though it were a grenade. 'Fowl? You there?'

'Yes,' came the reply.

'You crazy devil! What are you doing? Your father is as good as dead. I thought we had a deal!'

'We still do. A new one. You can still make some money tonight.'

Mikhael stopped panicking and started paying attention. Could there possibly be a way out of this nightmare?

'I'm listening.'

'The last thing I need is for my father to return and destroy what I have built up over the past two years.'

Mikhael nodded. This made perfect sense to him.

'So he had to die. I had to see it done myself, just to be sure. But I could still leave you a little something.'

Mikhael could barely breathe. 'A little something?'

'The ransom. All five million.'

'And why would you do that?'

'You get the money; I get safe passage home. Fair enough?'

'Seems fair to me.'

'Very well. Now look across the bay, above the fjord.'

Mikhael looked. There was a flare burning, right at the snow-covered hill's tip.

'There is a briefcase tied to that flare. The flare goes out in ten minutes. I'd get there before then if I were you. Otherwise the case could take years to find.'

Mikhael didn't bother to cut the connection. He just dropped the phone and ran. 'The money,' he shouted at Kamar. 'Up there. The flare.'

Kamar was after him in a heartbeat, shouting instructions into the radio. Someone had to reach that money. Who cared about a drowning *Irlanskii* when there were five million dollars to be claimed?

Root pointed at Holly the moment Artemis Senior had been shot. 'Go!' he ordered.

Captain Short activated her wings, launching herself right off the hilltop. Of course, what they were doing here was against all the regulations, but the Council was cutting Foaly a lot of slack having more or less convicted him of treason. The only conditions were that the centaur was in constant communication, and that every member of the party was fitted with remote incineration packs, so that they and all their fairy technology could be destroyed in the event of capture or injury.

Holly followed events on the submarine through her visor. She saw the charge impact on Artemis Senior's shoulder, knocking him against the larger Russian. Blood registered in her field of vision. It was still warm enough to be picked up by her thermal imager. Holly had to admit, it looked effective. Maybe Artemis's plan could actually work. Maybe the Russians would be fooled. After all, humans generally saw what they wanted to see.

Then things went horribly wrong.

'He's in the water!' shouted Holly into her helmet mike, opening the wing rig's throttle to the max. 'He's alive, but not for long unless we get him out.'

She skimmed silently over the glistening ice, arms crossed over her chest for speed. She was moving too fast for human vision to pin her down. She could be a bird, or a seal breaking the waves. The submarine loomed before her.

On board the *Nikodim*, the Russians were evacuating. Clambering down the tower ladder, feet slipping in their haste. And ashore, the same. Men breaking cover, crashing through the frosted undergrowth. The commander must have set the flare. Those Mud Men would be delirious to find their precious money, only to have it dissolve in seventy-two hours. That should just about give them time to deliver it to their boss. Odds on he wouldn't be happy with disappearing cash.

Holly skimmed the sub's keel, safe from radiation in her suit and helmet. At the last moment, she flipped upwards, shielded from the northern shore by the conning tower. She popped the throttle, hovering above the ice hole where the human had fallen in. The commander was talking into her ear, but Holly didn't reply. She had a job to do and no time for talk.

Fairies hate cold. They hate it. Some are so phobic about low temperatures that they won't even eat ice cream. The last thing Holly wanted to do right now was put so much as a toe into that sub-zero, radioactive water. But what choice did she have? 'D'Arvit,' she swore, and plunged into the water.

The micro-filaments in her suit deadened the cold, but they could not dispel it entirely. Holly knew that she had seconds before the temperature-drop slowed her reactions and sent her into shock.

Below her, the unconscious human was as pale as a ghost. Holly fumbled with her wing controls. A touch too much on the throttle could send her too deep. Not enough and she would fall short. And at these temperatures, you got one shot only.

Holly hit the throttle. The engine buzzed once, sending her ten fathoms down. Perfect. She grabbed Fowl Senior by the waist, quickly clipping him on to her Moonbelt. He hung there limply. He needed an infusion of magic, and the sooner the better.

Holly glanced upwards. It seemed as though the ice hole was already closing. Was there anything else that could go wrong? The commander was shouting in her ear, but she shut him out, concentrating on getting back to dry land.

Ice crystals spun themselves across the hole like spiders' webs. The ocean seemed determined to claim them.

I don't think so, thought Holly, pointing her helmeted head at the surface, and opening the throttle as far as it would go. They crashed through the ice, arced through the air and landed on the slatted surface of the sub's forward deck.

The human's face was the colour of the surrounding landscape. Holly crouched on his chest like a predatory creature, exposing the supposed wound to the night air. There was blood on the deck, but it was Artemis Junior's blood: they had pried the cap from a Hydrosion shell, and half filled it with blood taken from Artemis's arm. On impact, the Fizzer had knocked Artemis Senior off his feet, sending the crimson liquid spiralling through the air. Very convincing. Of course, being thrown into the freezing waters had not been part of the plan.

The shell had not penetrated his skin, but Mister Fowl was not safe yet. Holly's thermal imager showed that his heartbeat was dangerously slow and weak. She laid her hands on his chest. 'Heal,' she whispered. 'Heal.'

And the magic scurried down her fingers.

Artemis couldn't watch Holly's rescue attempt. Had he done the right thing? What if the Hydrosion shell penetrated? How could he ever face his mother again?

‡ⵐ ⌐ △ ⌐ ⵢ ‡

'Oh no,' said Butler.

Artemis was at his side in an instant. 'What is it?'

'Your father is in the water. One of the Russians threw him in.'

The boy groaned. That water was as deadly as any bullet. He'd been afraid that something like this would happen.

Root had also been following the rescue attempt. 'OK. She's over the water. Can you see him, Holly?'

No answer. Just static in his earphones.

'Status, Captain? Respond.'

Nothing.

'Holly?'

She's not talking because it's too late, thought Artemis. There's nothing she can do to save my father and it's all my fault.

Root's voice cut through his thoughts. 'The Russians are evacuating,' he said. 'Holly's at the sub now, over the hole in the ice. She's going in. Holly, what have you got? Come on, Holly. Talk to me.'

Nothing. For the longest time.

Then Holly erupted through the ice like a mechanized dolphin. She arced briefly through the Arctic night, crash-landing on the Typhoon's deck.

'She has your father,' said the commander.

Artemis slipped on the spare Recon helmet, willing Holly's voice to sound through the speakers. He magnified the picture in his visor until it seemed as though he could touch his father and watched Holly lean over his father's chest, pulses of magic shooting down her fingers.

After several moments, Holly looked up, straight into Artemis's eyes, as though she knew he was watching. 'I got him,' she gasped. 'One live Mud Man. He's not pretty, but he's breathing.'

Artemis sank to the ground, sobs of relief shaking his thin shoulders. He cried for a whole minute. Then he was himself again.

'Well done, Captain. Now let's get out of here before Foaly activates one of these incinerator packs by accident.'

In the bowels of the Earth, the centaur leaned back from his communications console.

'Don't tempt me,' he chuckled.

AN EPILOGUE OR TWO

TARA

Artemis was heading back to St Bartleby's. This was where he had to be when the Helsinki medical services identified his father from the suitably weathered passport Foaly had run up for him.

Holly had done her best for the injured man, healing his chest wound and even restoring sight to his blinded eye. But it was too late to reattach the leg, which they didn't have in any case. No, Artemis Senior needed prolonged medical attention, and it had to begin somewhere that could be rationally explained. So Holly had flown south-west to Helsinki, depositing the unconscious man at the doors of the University Hospital. One porter had spotted the flying patient, but he had been successfully mind-wiped.

When Artemis Senior regained consciousness the past two years would be a blur, and his last memory would be a happy one: bidding his family farewell at Dublin harbour. Thanks again to Foaly and his mind-wiping technology.

'Why don't I just move in with you?' the centaur had quipped when they returned to Police Plaza. 'Do your ironing while I'm at it.'

Artemis smiled. He had been doing that a lot lately. Even the parting with Holly had gone better than he could have expected, considering she'd seen him shoot his own father. Artemis shuddered. He anticipated many sleepless nights over that particular strategy.

The captain escorted them to Tara, slipping them out through a holographic hedge. There was even a holographic cow chewing the virtual leaves to throw humans off the fairy scent.

Artemis was back in his school uniform, which had been miraculously restored by the People's technology. He sniffed his lapel.

'This blazer smells unusual,' he commented. 'Not unpleasant, but unusual.'

'It's completely clean,' said Holly, smiling. 'Foaly had to put it through three cycles in the machine to purge ...'

'To purge the Mud People from it,' completed Artemis.

'Exactly.'

꒛ ꓲꓲ ꠹ ꠹ ꓲ, ꒛

There was a full moon overhead, bright and pocked like a golf ball. Holly could feel its magic singing to her.

'Foaly said, in the light of the help you've given us, he's pulling the surveillance on Fowl Manor.'

'That's good to know,' said Artemis.

'Is it the right decision?'

Artemis considered it. 'Yes. The People are safe from me.'

'Good. Because a large section of the Council wanted you mind-wiped. And with a chunk of memory this big, your IQ could take a bit of a dip.'

Butler extended a hand. 'Well, Captain. I don't suppose I'll see you again.'

Holly shook it. 'If you do, it'll be too late.' Captain Short turned towards the fairy fort. 'I had better go. It will be light soon. I don't want to be caught unshielded on a spy satellite. The last thing I need is my photo all over the Internet. Not when I've just been reinstated at Recon.'

Butler elbowed his employer gently.

'Oh, Holly ... Eh, Captain Short.' Eh? Artemis couldn't believe he'd actually said *eh*. It wasn't even a word.

'Yes, Mud B ... Yes, Artemis?'

Artemis looked Holly in the eye, just as Butler had instructed. This 'being civil' business was more difficult than one would think. 'I would like to ... I mean. What

I mean is ...'

Another elbow from Butler.

'Thank you. I owe you everything. Because of you I have my parents. And the way you flew that craft was nothing short of spectacular. And on the train ... Well, I could never have done what you ...'

A third elbow. This time to stop the babbling.

'Sorry. Well, you get the idea.'

Holly's elfin features wore a strange expression. Somewhere between embarrassment and – could it possibly be? – delight. She recovered quickly.

'Maybe I owe you something too, human,' she said, drawing her pistol. Butler almost reacted, but decided to give Holly the benefit of the doubt.

Captain Short plucked a gold coin from her belt, flicking it twenty metres into the moonlit sky. With one fluid movement, she brought her weapon up and loosed a single blast. The coin rose another twenty metres, then spun earthwards. Artemis somehow managed to snatch it from the air. The first cool moment of his young life.

'Nice shot,' he said. The previously solid disc now had a tiny hole in the centre.

Holly held out her hand, revealing the still-raw scar on her finger. 'If it wasn't for you, I would have missed altogether. No mech-digit can replicate that kind of accuracy. So, thank you too, I suppose.'

Artemis held out the coin.

'No,' said Holly. 'You keep it, to remind you.'

'To remind me?'

Holly stared at him frankly. 'To remind you that deep beneath the layers of deviousness, there is a spark of decency. Perhaps you could blow on that spark occasionally.'

Artemis closed his fingers around the coin. It was warm against his palm. 'Yes, perhaps.'

A small two-seater plane buzzed overhead. Artemis glanced skywards, and when he looked back Holly was gone. A slight heat haze hovered above the grass.

'Goodbye, Holly,' he said softly.

The Bentley started on the first turn of the key. In less than an hour they arrived at St Bartleby's main gate.

'Make sure your phone's switched on,' Butler said, holding the door. 'The Helsinki officials should be getting the results of their trace from Interpol soon. Your father's file has been reactivated in their mainframe thanks, once again, to Foaly.'

Artemis nodded, checking his phone was switched on. 'Try to locate Mother and Juliet before the news comes through. I don't want to be hunting through every spa in the south of France looking for them.'

'Yes, Artemis.'

'And check my accounts are well hidden. No need for Father to know exactly what I've been up to for the past

286

two years.'

Butler smiled. 'Yes, Artemis.'

Artemis took a few steps towards the school gates, then turned. 'And, Butler, one more thing. In the Arctic ...'

Artemis couldn't ask, but his bodyguard knew the answer anyway.

'Yes, Artemis,' he said gently. 'You did the right thing. It was the only way.'

Artemis nodded, standing by the gates until the Bentley had disappeared down the avenue. From this moment on, life would be different. With two parents in the manor, his schemes would have to be much more carefully planned. Yes, he owed it to the People to leave them alone for a while, but Mulch Diggums ... that was a different matter. So many secure facilities, so little time.

COUNSELLOR'S OFFICE, ST BARTLEBY'S SCHOOL FOR YOUNG GENTLEMEN

Not only was Doctor Po still employed at St Bartleby's, but he seemed fortified by his break from Artemis. His other patients were relatively straightforward cases of anger management, exam stress and chronic shyness. And that was just the teachers.

: △ Γ ▽ ‖ ⅄ ⊟ :

Artemis settled on to the couch, taking care not to accidentally press the power button on his mobile.

Doctor Po nodded at his computer. 'Principal Guiney forwarded me your e-mail. Charming.'

'I'm sorry about that,' muttered Artemis, surprised to find that he actually was sorry. Upsetting other people didn't usually upset him. 'I was in denial. So, I projected my anxieties on to you.'

Po half chuckled. 'Yes, very good. Just what it says in the book.'

'I know,' said Artemis. And he did know. Doctor F. Roy Dean Schlippe had contributed a chapter to that particular book.

Doctor Po laid down his pen, something he had never done before.

'You know, we still haven't resolved that last issue.'

'Which issue is that, Doctor?'

'The one we touched on at our last session. About respect?'

'Ah, that issue.'

Po steepled his fingers. 'I want you to pretend I'm as smart as you are, and give me an honest answer.'

Artemis thought of his father lying in a Helsinki hospital, of Captain Holly Short risking her life to help him and, of course, Butler, without whom he would never have made it out of Koboi Laboratories. He looked up, catching Doctor Po smiling at him.

'Well, young man, have you found anyone worthy of your respect?'

Artemis smiled back. 'Yes,' he said. 'I believe I have.'

THE END

A RARE INTERVIEW WITH THE CRIMINAL MASTERMIND ...

Name: Artemis Fowl

Most treasured possession: My dearest possession is my bodyguard, Butler. Without him I would have perished a dozen times over. Butler makes my more dubious enterprises possible by his enormous physical presence. In other words, he's big and he scares people.

You visited many locations around the world in your quest for the fairy book and the mission to rescue your father. Which was your favourite location and why? On my quests, I was totally obsessed. Scenery meant nothing to me. I regret not paying more attention now, of course. If I had to choose a favourite place, I would say Fowl Manor. A cliché, I know, but home is where the hidden reserves of gold are.

Deepest wish: Hmm ... a difficult question. I have so many ambitions. Obviously the main one is to restore the family fortune, so reduced by my father's attempt to expand his enterprise into Russia.

What do you do when not on your computer? I do tend to spend too much time on my computer. I occasionally stroll through Saint Stephen's Green Park in Dublin simply to observe human nature. If I am to exploit people, best to know what they are capable of.

Any ideas what your next adventure will be? I have had quite enough of adventures for one lifetime, thank you very much. I shall leave that sort of thing to Captain Holly Short and her comrades in the LEP. In future I plan to operate far from the explosive world of the Russian Mafiya. Computers, for example, are more my field. I have constructed a super-computer from some fairy technology that Butler managed to secure for me and am planning to demonstrate its capabilities to a certain American businessman with a reputation for ruthlessness - although I'm sure most of it is pure exaggeration. At any rate, I shall have Butler to protect me, so what could possibly go wrong ...?

To find out more about Artemis Fowl, click on to:

www.eoincolfer.com, www.puffin.co.uk or www.artemisfowl.co.uk

Bravo, Master Fowl . . .

you've made it this far . . .

now unlock the secrets of . . .

Artemis
Fowl
THE ETERNITY CODE

Don't miss the third thrilling instalment of *Artemis Fowl*.
Could fairy technology, a ruthless transatlantic villain
and an unbreakable code rule the world?

You know what you have to do.

ESTIMATED TIME OF ARRIVAL:
1 May 2003